The Procession

and

Other Stories

Theron Montgomery

Published by the UKA Press 2005

2 4 6 8 10 9 7 5 3 1

Cover Photo: *Memorial Illumination*, Antietam Battlefield, 2004.
Used by permission of the US National Parks Service.

First published in Great Britain in 2005 by the
UKA Press
PO Box 109
Portishead, Bristol. BS20 7ZJ

www.UKAuthors.com

A CIP catalogue record for this book is available from the British Library

ISBN 1-904781-26-8

This book was prepared for print by the
UKA Press
Cover design by Peter J. Merrigan

For Diana and the boys

Contents

Friends make pretense of following to the grave…
Robert Frost '*Home Burial*'

Our life was but a battle and a march…
Friedrich Von Schiller   *Wallensteins Tod*, III

The Lieutenant

As they tell it in the town – those still there and old enough to remember – the little 'Lieutenant' came all the way from England seven years after the war with a converted Spitfire to crop dust in Fermata Bend, Alabama. There are versions of the story from years of people getting together to talk. The story in common is that he came, not because he needed money – it seems he had money from somewhere – and not because he wanted to become an American, he didn't; or from a desire to see America or the Deep South. He did not. The reason he came was that Fermata Bend had no aerial regulations and he wanted to keep flying dangerously.

No one knew that at first. He was such an oddity, an unusual deliverance from the sky. Nor did they know what an isolated and childish stranger he would turn out to be, that the name 'Lieutenant' would become synonymous with him and the town's impression of the little man. For the young, especially the boys, the name became legendary, associated with manhood, glory, and being a hero.

He came to Fermata Bend on a June day, literally appearing out of the blue, unannounced, unanticipated, like a traveling salesman or a bum would; only in his case, from the *sky* with this dark, foreign, mean-looking aircraft: an olive green, oblong-winged plane with steel spray rods running under each wing. The warplane appeared from the direction of Legger Mound, the thick-wooded mound that no one owned, where Indians were buried and where there were worn, overgrown

9

mounds of Civil War breastworks; the warplane circling low over the cluster of one and two storey nineteenth century buildings, and descending on the long dirt road that cut though fields and toward town.

People stared as the plane taxied right into the quiet town square, blowing up dust, circling the median of the Confederate statue, the war memorial plaques and the World War One artillery pieces. The wind-storming plane slowly gyrated and the engine cut right in front of Miller's Hardware before the cars, trucks, and a couple of shying mules harnessed to wagons. The whirling propeller blades slowed to a stop and people stared as the pilot slid open the cockpit.

He looked like a human bug, somebody said, with his uniform, tight cap and goggles. He climbed down and off the plane, raising the goggles off his eyes; and peeling off his gloves, bowing, introduced himself to the group of gawking men on the tin covered porch of the hardware as 'Flight Lieutenant Barker': a soft voice, a serious face from a little man in leather headpiece and goggles, khaki jump suit and a sheer white scarf draped around his neck. It was like looking at a movie character or someone out of a costume party.

'Boy, you're lost,' came a simple impetuous utter invading the silence of the porch.

The little man ignored it, gave a parsimonic smile, pranced before them and spoke more at than to the gaping, rough men – their plain, weathered faces, in drab work clothes, work boots, broken and bent hats – with polite but laconic speech, and a unique English they had never heard.

'Like holding your breath 'til the end of a sentence and whining off the last word,' someone said.

Gloves in one hand, fists on his hips, the effect seemed more like a little dressed-up man daring the larger bullies to take him on, his imposing machine behind him in the dirt. They couldn't follow what he was saying very well; in fact, no one remembers what he said. But they got the gist of it: he inquired about, no, insisted they give him work.

This oddity finished his peculiar elocution and stood facing them with hazy eyes that didn't tell, didn't see, or seem to concern themselves with what anyone thought of him: his mouth frozen with an expectant smile, following what he had just said, as if insistence in itself would bring his sole reward.

The mules calmed down, the dust settled, the still group of men stood in the shade of the porch with this stranger standing his ground in the hot sun, arms akimbo. He waited, holding his courteous smile on no one in particular, appearing patient, polite, but expecting to receive from them what he wanted. They watched beads of sweat forming on his face.

'Who the hell does he think we are?' somebody muttered.

It seemed this bizarre and idiotic standoff would go on forever when stout Jupo Demus, who was always like someone out of the nineteenth century in Fermata Bend, too, in his dusty white coat, his plantation hat, and his trimmed, salt and pepper Vandyke, stepped off the porch and went forward, looking sidewise, with hand outstretched to meet the stranger in the dirt.

Only Jupo would do it. He was somebody in Fermata Bend, of old cotton and pecan family; and worse, he knew it. He drove the black Packard, had a family name and a thousand acres outside of town. Jupo gave the stranger a perfunctory nod, a handshake, and never looked at him twice, staring and smiling toward the plane, glancing back to the men, and asking vague questions. It was like he had seen something he wanted to devour, or more likely, it was just the idea of the plane, and a warplane at that; in actuality, a dissimulation of his: that he had not served in the military like his father or his grandfathers had before him, being too young for World War One and too old for World War Two; and now, the Korean Conflict, what the high school male graduates were going to, three boys having already come home in caskets, each to a somber town procession with a military honor guard, a folded flag and a

11

lingering taps played at an opened grave beside the old Confederate and Spanish American War tombstones in the Fermata Bend Cemetery.

Jupo had not lived up to Fermata Bend family tradition, what the older veterans of proper families had done and how Jupo had always wanted to think of himself – as he was brought up to idolize and emulate his soldier father and his soldier grandfathers, their stern portraits lined above the mantel of the fireplace at the old home place.

Glancing at the plane and then to the men on the porch with a slow smile and a wink, Jupo gave the stranger work without getting the little stranger's name or his price, nodding to the man without hearing him, taking the warplane in with a grin and an almost spellbound wonder.

Everyone knew with Jupo, hiring the stranger and the plane was a thing to show, something no one else could have. It was one of the things of land and indifference and what the Demuses thought of themselves, as with the old family home place (that as legend had it, Jupo's grandpa had swindled from a carpetbagger) that stood on a rise outside of town, overlooking the fields in view of Legger Mound and the surrounding countryside, its painted columns toward the railroad tracks that ran parallel to the paved county highway.

The two shook hands there in the dirt of the square before the mute and slighted onlookers. The pilot grinned with his luck; Jupo beamed. The men watched Jupo get into the black Packard, the pilot climb into his plane and start it – then grabbed their hats as the engine coughed and boomed, the blades whirled and the plane turned. The Packard led the way around the square and out of town and the pilot taxied his plane after it. The simple farmers watched them circle the square and leave. They shook their heads and scoffed.

'The rich act rich,' someone said.

At the Co-Op, Jon Stephens and his boys stopped what they were doing when the little 'Lieutenant' walked in.

'He pulled up in one of them Demus International trucks, O'Jupo driving,' Jon told it. 'They both come in, this little clown in his get up leading, his shoulders square 'cause he know Jupo behind him. I thought he was a circus character or a movie star, he was that pretty – with this damn scarf 'round his neck and a thin silver wristwatch flashing on his wrist. And he was sweating, ha, sweating like a laboring mule in that hot khaki get up and leather cap, goggles shining atop his head and all that – sweat running his uniform dark, sweat dripping off his fingers, his face, nose, and him trying to ignore it as if he could make us not notice. He was numb to reality. I figgered it quick, either they were the only clothes he had, or he *had* to wear them, know what I mean? Well, they fairly march up to the counter, this clown fighter pilot acting like he knows what he's about, and O'Jupo just behind him with this set closed smile and a look that knows he got something we don't; the whole time Jupo looking at me and then him, like a kid impressed with his new puppy.

'The little clown bids me good day, smiling with sweat flipping off his nose, and I know then and there he ain't from around here. He offers me a quick hand (the one without the watch) and it's limp, which is another bad sign. Jupo just stands behind him and keeps nodding to me. "Afternoon, Jupo," I say. The clown pipes up, says he wants a thousand gallons of liquid pesticide, may come back for more, he says, charming as you please, these hazel eyes, a quick smile, and he raining water the whole time. I wasn't in the mood, I didn't like his. I forgot my manners. "You don't say now," I said. "Boy, I thought the war was over. Ain't you hot? Or shall I get you a glass of water?" My boys, loading the shelves, look on and titter.

'He shoots me another short smile. "I'm on business," he pouts. And I want to hit him. "Yessir," I drawl it out as long as

I can. "But it goan take a week or more to bring it up from Mobile. Can you wait that long? *Sir?*"

'He shoots a querulous look at Jupo, then nods to me, detached and intent. "All right," he says. He says it funny, real crisp – "*All right*. You do that. Order it," he demands. "I'll be back in a week."

'Jupo nods, too, which means it's on his account. "You do that," the little man echoes, like the cameras are still rolling, the war's going on, and somebody's watching. He gives me this gamely nod and grin, turns around and slowly marches (or slushes, depending on how you want to look at it) out with Big Jupo behind him in his dirty white suit, who hasn't removed his hat, and who hasn't said a word all this time, which is not like Jupo. Jupo only gives us a quick look over his shoulder, nodding, and hurries to keep up with his new boy wonder – they go past the sacks of feed and seed, my shiny stacked buckets and plows – the boy walking like he leading an invisible parade. Soaked with sweat, he leads it all the way out the door with Jupo to the truck. Me and the boys watch them go, at the door we watch them climb in the truck and it obvious – O'Jupo is driving.'

Jupo Demus drove all day and the next. 'Meet *Lieutenant* Jonathan Barker,' he swaggered in and announced loudly to those at the hardware, the drug store, the barbershop and then the post office, 'formerly of the *RAF*,' he stressed, then added with emphasis, 'the *Royal* Air Force,' as though no one could know that and it was somehow superior and unique and a privilege let through Jupo, himself.

Entering and standing beside Jupo in his war outfit, the stranger acknowledged everyone with a tireless, zealous smile and a quick nod, flashing a silver wristwatch when his hand moved. People noticed how he smiled but avoided eyes, seemed somewhat smooth and indifferent, confident, and he had a quick, precise stride in his boots and an erect back –

overly erect, like a ramrod. A veteran at the barber shop noticed his abnormally wide and high boot heels. But no one said anything, at least not in public. They smiled and remembered their manners before Jupo, introduced themselves to the little stranger and spoke.

The little stranger held a small smile. He said 'ma'am' or 'sir,' to everyone and often glanced to Jupo. The little man gave quick smiles, laconic answers to questions about himself and his warplane, but offered no further conversation. Jupo grinned and nodded along with him until silence ensued and then Jupo nodded for them to leave. The stranger and Jupo turned for the door, the little stranger in his uniform, still held by the silent, staring onlookers, making a quick bow with his head before stepping out. In an instant imitation, Jupo did the same and everyone nodded back in imitation, too, watching them go out.

A farmer swore he saw a glint of silver above the little man's ear as he turned to go; and if so, that proved he had a mental injury.

'He ain't the real McCoy,' someone agreed.

The veterans scoffed. They said there wouldn't be an England left if the U.S. had not entered the war.

But everyone kept their manners, and in typical Fermata Bend fashion, never said what they were thinking, when a day later, Jupo bragged about the Lieutenant at the pecan farmer's meeting, and to anyone else who would listen. He had put the stranger in one of his abandoned sharecropper shacks below the Demus home place and the mean green warplane was parked before Jupo's big barn in full view of the highway, for everyone to see. Jupo told anyone who would listen – with Michael, his thin and silent teenage son with the club foot, standing there bareheaded and looking on – how he liked the fact that the Lieutenant had been a fighter pilot in the war and still acted like a military man.

Each time Jupo reminded the veterans that he, himself, had been too young for World War One and too old for World War Two. But he would have gone, yessir, he would have. He was a Demus. He paused, hesitated with quiet Michael watching, and added that Demuses had a long tradition of soldiers: his father's in the Spanish American War, both his grandfathers in the Confederacy, a great-grandfather in the Mexican War – all of their names at the base of the marble veteran's memorial on the town square, and as everyone knew, along with cousins, uncles, distant relatives, and the names of other old cotton and pecan families in Fermata Bend.

'Demuses are *always* fighters,' Jupo added, with a quick glance to and then away from his son. Those listening nodded out of politeness or respect to the memory of Jupo's father.

Besides, the Lieutenant was a man, Jupo said. He could hold his own.

'Brave and smart. Best damn mechanic I ever saw,' Jupo declared. 'He broke down my tractor engine and put it back together in a jiffy.' Jupo paused for emphasis and looked around. Those listening to him smiled and wondered. 'He's all right,' Jupo repeated to them. 'Quiet and sure of himself – he's all right.'

Someone would speak to Michael to break his silence and change the subject. Jupo would inevitably bring the Lieutenant up again.

'Well, I guess he's all right,' someone would say for Jupo.

'When is he leaving?' someone else would ask.

And they would watch Jupo's smile fall.

Jupo talked, the town rumored, and then in a week the Lieutenant went to work. However mysterious, odd in speech, dress and size he was; however quiet and aloof; whatever the reason he came to America and Fermata Bend – the fact was the boy could fly. He put on an aerial performance no one in Fermata Bend could have imagined. The dark green warplane did acrobatics, someone said.

16

'You never seen the likes of it,' people said.

'Oh, yes,' someone might add, whistle. 'It was a show, now, sure enough.'

People pulled their cars or trucks to the side of the road before the Demus Fields, got out and stood along the railroad tracks, shading their eyes to watch. They gathered on the town square before the Confederate statue three miles away, shading their eyes and gazing up, some with binoculars, while the plane did loops and rolls, circled high in the blue, disappeared into the blinding sun and then was back again in heart-stopping dives: dark form falling in the blue, engine screaming; the plane grew suddenly larger and swept low over the fields, white trails streaming from the wings as it swept over the verdant rows of young cotton. The trails would cut off, the plane would pull up, scaling the telephone wires, the treetops, or it would dip its wing and skirt the Demus' water tower like a deft, metallic bird, swaying back and forth before the rise of the thick-wooded Legger Mound, turn back up into the blue, climbing, disappearing into the blinding sun; before it dove again, sweeping over the fields, and streaming more spray – like a mirage: one moment it was there, loud and roaring; the next, it was gone with only a fading drone. Everyone had to look away or cover their eyes when the plane led them into the sun.

'It's a wonder,' someone said, whistling and shaking his head, 'a wonder what's in that boy's head.'

Farmers said that you couldn't crop dust like that. Too fast. And stupid. The veterans said he was using bombing or attack tactics, as in some serious game. The old people shook their heads. A young fool, they said.

'A looney is what he is,' someone declared.

For days, this lone, singular show of a foreigner appeared to be fighting an invisible foe, bombing before the local spectators and the silent, still fields and trees, beneath the infinite blue sky and bright sun. Some wondered why he came from so far to fly

17

like this, to this small, dull and telluric community of farmers: nothing but bland sun and flat, fertile land. This foreign oddity and this crop dusting war machine beat the traveling circus, the county fair or what the old timers remembered from barn storming days.

The plane was fun to watch. It looked like fierce play. It flew fast for no reason, did loops and rolls for no reason, ear splitting dives, hard and sharp climbs that just missed the telephone wires and trees as it pulled up and hid in the sun before bombing the fields again and again, day after day, releasing soft and settling mists.

Stout Jupo drove into town to grin broadly and wink.

'Quiet little fella,' Jupo remarked, and the farmers and veterans listened. 'Hard worker and got the cleanest table manners you ever saw.' Jupo said it matter-of-factly, stroking his Vandyke. The pilot had fought in the war, he was pretty sure: the Battle of Britain, Dunkirk and D-Day.

Jupo talked about the plane. It was double-walled construction. Had the biggest single engine he had ever seen.

'Rolls Royce,' Jupo announced with a nod.

There were brackets and welded plugs where the machine guns had been. The glass cockpit was a foot thick and there were bullet holes in the body that had been patched, welded over.

'He's the real thing,' Jupo declared, nodding for effect, his eyes searching the others. He wouldn't say how much he paid the man.

Among themselves, the veterans observed that his plane had to be a stripped, surplus fighter. How did he get it? How did he bring it over here? But now, the boy sure could fly. Everything the plane did had precision, control and daring speed. Their wives wanted to know what the English stranger looked like. Their girls wanted to know his name and whether he was good looking. Their boys imitated him on the playground at school, spreading their arms out like wings, chasing each other and issuing machine gun sounds from their mouths, inspired with the idea of such freedom.

Jupo Demus, in a clean white coat and his Vandyke trimmed, proudly brought the stranger with his teenage son and daughter to church.

Everyone saw Jupo take his hat off and that his gray, balding head was not so dark or shiny as his Vandyke. They saw the Lieutenant was a little, wiry man with a smooth face, wavy blonde, almost white hair; soft, shifting hazel eyes; and shy and uncomfortable in borrowed coat, shirt and slacks that were too large for him. The thin silver watch stood out on his wrist and he avoided eyes as he sat or stood beside Jupo.

After service, he quickly shook hands, but said little. As everyone went outside into the churchyard to congregate, he went to Jupo's Packard, and sat on the running board as if to guard his back, nervously popping lemon drops into his mouth from a brown paper bag, nodding and smiling quickly if he had to.

'Well,' someone commented, 'so much for his manners.'

While the adults talked in the yard, the boys and girls got a look at him, nudging one another and watching him: the boys at one end of the church yard under the trees; the girls on the church steps. It didn't matter what the adults thought. The little stranger was different. He was new. His silent, nervous reserve seemed esoteric and unique. The girls thought he was cute. The boys took his behavior as a sign of toughness, and they admired him, shooting furtive glances in his direction from beneath the trees in their stiff Sunday clothes.

There he was: Real. In flesh. Fighter pilot. A survivor of the war let to them, like their fathers, the men, and the men's talk – only this man flew the warplane with welded studs, as Jupo said, where the machine guns had been. They had watched the war machine fly and dive, again and again, in the sky. It had flown against the Germans. It still flew.

'Hey.' A boy dared to go close. Somehow 'mister' didn't seem appropriate. 'Were you really in the war?'

The other boys watched. The small, bareheaded stranger in his oversized, borrowed clothes looked up, his cheek bulging with lemon drops, made a slight grin with lemon-stained teeth.

'Yes,' he replied.

'Ever get shot down?' another boy called from the trees.

The smile broadened. 'Many times.'

'You kill any Germans?'

'Many, many times,' he replied.

A pause. 'You ever wounded?'

'Many, many, many times.'

A longer pause. 'Well, say, why are you *here*?'

'I can fly here,' he said.

In the pause that followed, he rose from the running board and stuffed the paper bag of lemon drops into his coat pocket. The boys followed him from a distance, whispering among themselves as he went to the WPA rock wall that bordered the street, seated himself, produced a cigarette from a small case (silver, they noted, too, as they thought was the lighter) and lit it. His thin wristwatch flashed once or twice in the morning sun and they watched the quiet stranger's reserved face as he smoked. They listened to thin Michael Demus, Jupo's son, who dragged his club foot in the special shoe.

'He don't talk much, but my Pa says that only means he's seen a lot,' Michael said.

'I didn't see any scars,' someone said.

'He let me sit in the plane,' Michael continued, searching the others.

They let Michael talk, his quiet monotone growing more and more matter-of-fact; watching the small, distant stranger who seemed somehow as stolid as the wall he sat on, calmly smoking. They watched, even as Jupo's daughter, Katrina, parted from the chattering girls on the church steps and came across the churchyard to the wall. She had the thin, forming body of a woman in a simple cotton print dress, like Jupo always kept her in. Katrina stopped a few feet from the Lieutenant, a set smile on her face, her hands clasped behind her back.

'Poppa told me I was to look after you,' she said. She grinned, began gently rocking on her heels and swinging her long, simple black braids.

'He might even take me up with him. He might teach me to fly,' Michael said.

A boy turned and looked at Michael. 'You can't *fly*,' he said.

Michael hushed at that and the boys watched the Lieutenant as he nodded to Katrina's constant, soft questions, her steady look on him. He smoked and looked away but Katrina would not leave him alone. She held her smile; her blank, eager look, and kept offering conversation until the stranger had to look at her. Then he laughed. The relaxed and briefly vulnerable look on his face was not the way the boys wanted to see him, nor was it a violation of their impression of him – it was just that he, somehow, was supposed to stay constant, distant, in the way he looked and acted. The silent and impervious manner on the wall was not supposed to waver.

A boy sneered and scoffed. 'What does she think she's doing?' he said morosely.

One of them commented that he had heard the Lieutenant shot down seven German planes. Two shot from under him, another said.

'Who said?' someone echoed.

Michael, looking on, would not confirm or deny it. It did not matter. They wanted to hear it. Someone said that he was lucky to be alive. They nodded and watched the pilot while he watched Katrina. He had not wavered. He was in control, independent. They watched him light another cigarette and cough slightly, though the steady gaze of his eyes, now, did not leave Katrina and she had stopped rocking on her heels.

The air went quiet when there was no more crop-dusting to do. The warplane remained parked before Jupo's barn for another day and then it was gone. It came back in two weeks, circling the square from the direction of Legger Mound and landing in the long, even pasture behind the Demus home place. It left the next day. It began coming back every week or two, staying a weekend or longer, the clean green war aircraft could be seen parked before Jupo's barn. By then, everyone knew it was Katrina. Or that it was he could fly here unlike he could fly in Mobile. Or both.

Katrina was young, beautiful and a lady, like her deceased mother, and was beginning to learn it. In the absence of a wife and ignorant of women, Jupo had kept her in simple dresses and no make up; though true to being an old-time gentleman from Fermata Bend, he had made her an idler as he had been reared to treat ladies, no less his deceased wife. Slender, with her mother's face and large, black, banal eyes, Katrina smiled a lot and often waited to be spoken to, knowing she was somebody's daughter. Jupo discouraged the local boys from approaching her, because as everyone knew, Jupo, who had married late in life after he found the right woman from another town, did not think anyone was good enough for his daughter. That Katrina was not bright, and was not expected to finish high school, did not matter. She was obedient to Jupo and attractive. A black maid ran the kitchen and cleaned the home place while Jupo waited on Katrina, drove her to town or high school in the Packard, to piano lessons and even to visits, teas or birthday parties of other respectable families.

But now, there were new events. Everyone knew when Jupo took Katrina to buy new clothes at Sue's Clothing. He took her to the drug store to buy lipstick, perfume and rouge. The ladies whispered about Katrina's 'romance.' The men joked and winked at the hardware. Katrina no longer wore her hair in braids, but long, full, gathered behind her like Tarzan's Jane in the old movies shown down the road at Citronelle; and she was suddenly taller and trimmer in new shoes. She was more eager and courteous in public. 'How are you? How are you?' she echoed, along with effusive 'Thank you's, offering little else but just the same smile to further discussion.

'And how's the *Lieutenant*?' people asked Katrina about town. Jupo stepped back and smiled. Neither Katrina's grin nor her eyes blinked. 'Oh, why, he's nice,' she drawled.

As the months went by, Jupo was seen with Katrina and the little stranger in his Packard. The couple was seen riding horseback on mornings over frosted fields. They were seen on picnics at Fermata Bend Springs. Jupo drove them to high school football games on Friday afternoons and the couple sat together holding hands on the bleachers, apart from everyone: Katrina beaming in a new overcoat and dark, heavy lipstick; the little stranger in uniform and a leather flight jacket.

Jupo was pleased that the little man was courting his daughter ('Who's courting whom?' someone said later). People knew it was Mobile now, where, as Jupo told them, he thought the Lieutenant did professional flying and mechanical work.

'It's a good match,' Jupo declared to everyone. He would smack his hands and grin. Jupo liked the little stranger because was a gentleman. He had manners. English manners were just like Southern manners. A man knew how to act, how to treat a lady, eat at the table, and how to treat a guest. 'It's a good match,' Jupo would repeat and he swore the Lieutenant had good blood, like the Demuses had good blood – going back five generations on the same land in Fermata Bend ('Hmm, that before or *after* the carpetbaggers?' someone quipped when Jupo left). 'We've got some English in us, too, you know,' Jupo would look about and nod.'

'The fact he's English don't mean shit,' someone muttered after Jupo was gone. 'He's just different is all.'

In May, Michael Demus forced the little man in his skivvies out of the sharecropper shack one night, brandishing one of his grandfather's service revolvers in each hand. He hobbled after the Lieutenant in his special shoe and his Sunday suit into the moon-blanched fields, ordered the Lieutenant to turn around and there he made a fervent declaration to the memory of his mother and how he was ready to kill or be killed for his family's honor. He finished and threw one of the revolvers at the Lieutenant's feet but the little man would not pick it up.

Michael then challenged the stranger's name, his country, his manhood, forgot his manners and insulted the stranger in every way he could think of, even spitting on him and calling him things perverted. When that did not bring results, Michael, in a righteous rage, decided to shoot him anyway, but then could not pull the trigger.

Weeping and humiliated, he threw down the other revolver and left, and the next morning, out of spite or anger, or shame, he confessed to Jupo what he knew. Jupo heard him out and said nothing, waited until the next weekend and caught Katrina and the little man nude in one of the old slave quarters used for a shed, just as Katrina had found a switch and was instructing the little man, as a stern schoolmarm would to a dunce child, on how to sit so she could mount him.

Jupo forced them to dress and get into his Packard at gunpoint, with tears in his eyes, and not by threatening the Lieutenant, but by slapping Katrina before the little man's eyes, and maybe with shame or fear, too, or even indignation and the memory of his dead wife, Jupo drove them over the state line into Mississippi to a Justice of the Peace. Jupo Demus could not tolerate disgrace.

The news hit town fast. It was stunning. All the ladies of proper families were shocked. A Demus? Married without

24

a formal engagement? It was beyond belief. Jupo was quiet, he wouldn't talk, but he ran a full-page announcement in the Fermata Bend Bugler and then brought the couple before the entire church congregation to have the marriage blessed.

On that Sunday, the little man with the warplane walked as if wooden, in stolid stupor and reticence, his face white as a sheet while he went through the motions in a coat and tie, with Jupo and Michael behind him: going before the altar, kneeling with his radiant, bland-smiling wife in her Sunday dress, before the minister and all the eyes of the packed church.

Afterwards, the women gave a party with presents for Katrina at a neighbor's farmhouse. Katrina, in a new white dress with lace that Jupo had ordered from Birmingham, couldn't stop smiling, or meeting everyone's gaze while her men looked on, the silent Lieutenant seated between Jupo and Michael.

The couple flew away to Mobile to live, but came back six days later; because, as everyone knew, especially the women, Katrina would become homesick – all she had ever known was Jupo and Fermata Bend – and some suspected, too, the Lieutenant still wanted to fly without restraint. Rumor had it in Mobile the Lieutenant only paced the floor of their apartment smoking cigarettes and saying little while he had to be with his wife; and that Katrina cried herself to sleep each night, going into a sweating fever with dreams of cruise ships leaving harbors to sink, mansions crumbling, and an old, white-bearded man waving goodbye. Within three days, Katrina went into violent fits, refused to eat and refused to sleep with her little husband until he agreed to take her home.

The Lieutenant and Katrina flew back to Fermata Bend. They settled in at the home place and lived there for over a year. The little man and Katrina went to church every Sunday with the Demuses and sat in the family pew.

The Lieutenant crop-dusted the Demus Fields and surrounding farms; sometimes he made trips to Mobile, but those stopped. He took on odd jobs and mechanical work at Morton's filling station and he flew alone every day, weather permitting, whether there was work or not. The plane would be high in the sky, screaming and droning, whirling and tumbling, falling and rising, over and over, like a metal bird in free flight. It looked like ecstasy, it looked like practice, it went on and on and on – but it went nowhere.

The boys at Fermata Bend Elementary School, when asked what they wanted to be when they grew up, all clamored that they wanted to be pilots. The girls said they wanted to be wives, mothers or nurses of pilots. The women in town thought the little man and Katrina made a cute couple. The men and veterans shook their heads over the thought that the weirdo was here among them to stay.

Jupo gave the new couple a dowry of fifty acres directly across the highway from the Demus Fields and the home place. He supervised the field hands in the construction of a new house, a small rock house with a shed and a dirt runway. The couple moved in the fall after their first anniversary, after crop dusting season, after harvest, and Jupo invited all Fermata Bend to the house warming.

People of Fermata Bend came in their Sunday clothes and saw the little man at the closest they would ever see him. He was in a dark blazer and tie, still quiet and small. Guests observed that Katrina, in a new yellow tunic dress, did most of the talking for the two of them and gave quick, apologetic smiles when she goaded the little man about his serving the punch, the sandwiches or the cashews; how he stood around and did nothing.

Within a few months after the house warming, the flying noise above Fermata Bend stopped. The warplane was parked by the shed and the new rock house. The Lieutenant was sometimes outside washing it, working on it. It was learned through the Demus' maid that within a few weeks of Katrina becoming pregnant she had gone into the fever again. This time she saw black cats, spider webs and crashing bats in her sleep and was too scared for the Lieutenant to fly. Katrina whined, begged, and nagged the little man, went into violent fits for weeks until she extracted a promise from him not to fly until after the child was born. The Lieutenant then wept, himself, groveled and begged her to recant – but Katrina remained firm. The child demanded it, she told him.

The town saw the Lieutenant driving Katrina around in their new Ford. He was by her side in town, out of uniform, in plain clothes and jacket; Katrina larger in a flower-print maternity dress. The little man was servile and attentive to his wife, nodding and speaking quietly to others when he had to. At the grocery, people watched Katrina goad him with plaintive whines, not waiting for his answers. She gave peremptory orders, read the shopping list, quick to smile at others, her cheeks fatter and glowing.

'Nature's call done caught him,' someone said later. 'Ha, yeah,' someone agreed. 'He's run right into what he was running away from.'

Three months before the baby was born, the warplane was gone. Katrina and the Demuses did not come to town. The first, polite response of people was that it was work, after all, perhaps in Mobile. Good manners required that no one ask outright. Had anyone heard the plane leave?

After the plane was absent for a month, the talk began to fly: he had jumped the coop; there had been an argument about living in Fermata Bend; the little foreigner had married thinking there would be money in it for him; there was another wife in England, or Mobile. So it went. Katrina and the Demuses became reclusive: silent, hard faced, and impervious. They kept to themselves, avoiding others and they would not talk.

Then one evening, people heard the plane come in from the direction of Legger Mound. In the morning, it was back in the runway, parked by the shed at an off-angle, dirty and mud-splattered, the paint chipped, the glass on the cockpit flimsy. It sat like that all day and in the afternoon, Jupo drove across the Demus Fields and slowly crossed the highway in a ton truck full of field hands, got out of the truck with his pump shotgun and blasted the tires of the warplane flat. He ordered the field hands into the woods where they felled a large oak, trimmed the limbs off and, with the truck, dragged it to the plane. Jupo produced a heavy chain from the back of the truck and directed the field hands to run it through the landing gear and spike the ends of the chain into the tree trunk.

'Barker!' Jupo bellowed at the rock house he had built for Katrina and the Lieutenant. But no one came out. Jupo stood and glared. He ordered the hands onto the truck and drove off, the truck tires lifting dust.

The warplane remained still, dirty and shackled. Jupo hired a biplane duster out of Waynesboro that summer, whose flying was ordinary and safe. The baby came, a girl, in the fall of '54. The Lieutenant was now a father; Katrina, a mother. Katrina stayed at home and the Lieutenant worked odd mechanical jobs, and in town, people gossiped. They stared at him, nudged one another, then smiled when he appeared on the square driving a Demus truck, walking about the stores, or in line at the post office: a little man in oversized, drab overalls and work boots, his slight frame and small shoulders not made for heavy work. He nodded, avoided people, spoke little. Whenever the subject of the Lieutenant was brought up to Jupo, he pressed his lips together and looked away.

'Why, I think I could whip him blindfolded and with one hand,' a farmer would declare at the hardware, in Jupo's absence, of course, before farmers and veterans who had gathered together, seated in the rockers or leaning on the counter, drinking soda pop or chewing tobacco, talking weather or planting, politics or history, or telling tales as men in Fermata Bend would do.

'For all them Demuses think, he ain't nothing much,' someone would drawl, spit. Slow snickers. A guffaw.

'That little stranger – he's so good, he's not one of us.'

'Take those wings away and he ain't much now is he?' Soft laughter.

'Flyboy,' someone would add and laugh low, 'got caught with his fly open.'

At the afternoon baptism, the child was christened Jimma Demus Barker. Jupo swelled in his new beige suit and tears welled in his eyes while he held his hat in his hands and looked on his grandchild, his gray and balding head not as dark or shiny as his Vandyke.

The Lieutenant and Michael stood beside him in new beige suits Jupo had ordered for them, too; not in fear, or even distance from what was before them in Katrina's arms at the baptismal font, but in a shifting and boyish awkwardness at what to do – which was nothing but to look on and be there while Katrina in her new, flowing and blue wrap dress, her cheeks still plump from pregnancy, smiled like her father, in a simple self-absorption and purpose, clutching the child in its gown and blanket, all aglow in the middle of her men. She handed the child forward to the preacher at the baptismal font and before everyone in the church, mostly women, who had come to watch.

The preacher gave a benevolent smile, as did, almost spontaneously, all the women in the church – mothers and mothers to be – their men either deceased, at work, or not claimed yet. Then everyone smiled in polite awe as the preacher prayed, touched the child's forehead with water and repeated her name.

A piercing cry uttered from the small and insistent creature in the blanket. Jupo and Katrina's smiles grew even larger. Michael's mouth closed, small and solemn. And the Lieutenant stared.

In April, people noticed as they drove by on the highway that the warplane was clean and the glass shone. The field hands that lived in the shacks beyond the runway began lining up on the fence in the evenings to smoke, talk, and hum to themselves with that ingrained placidity and defeated mentality of knowing one's place for so long that one did not even think or dare to question – on the other side of the fence – and watch Mister Jupo's son-in-law (the 'white man's white man,' they called him, for being from England): solitary, quiet, alone and looking even smaller in the runway beyond the fence, in the slow, quotidian and arduous restitution of his Spitfire.

In denim overalls now, and tee shirt, his long and unkempt hair fell in his face while they watched him evening after evening until it grew too dark, watched him wash the windows until the glass shone, scrub and hose off the dirt and grime. They watched him polish and mend: a lone man's slow, diligent labor, section by section of the warplane.

The field hands began to lean on the fence, talking and smoking everyday before dark and supper, and watching him with feigned indifference, slyly, with repressed eagerness; watching him with occasional exclamations under their breaths, guffaws or long, slow chuckles.

'He doing a whole lotta work for a man to go nowhere.'

'Ain't goan be no energy left for his woman tonight!'

'Hey, don't you know he ain't had none? Why you think he out there trying to fly?'

'Naw. That ain't it. He scared! He scared she wanting another one.'

And they watched every evening, every dusk, acting nonchalant, casual, but with quiet curiosity and respect – not that they understood what he was doing or why with his machine, that they could know or ever know, but at the white man's (the 'white man's white man') lone, daily, and self-driven labor.

Every evening after a hard day's work, they were there to watch, bemused, befuddled, a little awed – and with envy reborn from abnegation with whites – at this strange white and his strange machine, and stranger to them yet, his dogged, self-absorbed and assiduous devotion to it: a little white man, face set with determination, not of revenge or conspiracy, but with a look more like need – someone who could not leave the warplane alone, had to touch the machine, maintenance it, be with it – and not like love, but more like helplessness or desire.

The upstart was that he directed all this 'affection,' as the field hands called it, on a warplane that couldn't, didn't move, on flat tires that Jupo had shot out, alone in the overgrown dirt runway, like a dead, shackled steel bird that needed paint, chained and staked to the stripped tree trunk Jupo had made them do on his orders. Yet, they watched (wanted to watch, in a silent hope, too) the little 'caught' white man who married Boss' daughter, but didn't know 'he done married Boss.'

They watched him work with contained and impervious faces, wondering among themselves how the Boss could not know, and how much he would allow, and what he would do. And like many things, what they knew did not get outside their circle because something was about to happen between white folks.

They watched him work on the flaps and the engine from a ladder, and gradually polish the propellers and pivot the plane by its tail so it faced the highway. They watched him clean out the cockpit and check the flaps again. Over the weeks, their casual, quiet lounging on the fence grew into a hush, a rigid vigil of the evenings, their eyes riveted on the man transforming the tethered plane, interpolated with low exclamations when the little man brought new batteries and slowly, meticulously took the old ones out and installed the new ones. He changed the spark plugs, drained the oil and the radiator, and added new oil and radiator fluid. He greased the engine. He jacked up the wheel legs, straining the plane against the chain, removed the tires one at a time, replaced the inner tubes, patched and inflated the tires, and put them back on the warplane.

'He fool, sure enough.' someone said.

They watched him slowly fill the warplane's tanks with fuel, carrying two five gallon cans back and forth from the larger drums in the shed, and an evening in June, they watched him bring the warplane back to life after several moments in which the little man just sat in the cockpit in silence, staring ahead as if in seizure or prayer.

The engine coughed black smoke out the side exhaust pipes; the blades slowly turned, stopped. The engine coughed two more times, the blades stopped. Then the engine coughed, caught a rhythm, the blades slowly turned and spun into a blur, sending wind and dust into the falling dark.

The field hands caught their hats, bowed their heads and squinted their eyes; but in spite of themselves, grinned and laughed, danced and clapped. The little white man stood up in the opened cockpit and turned to them, the propeller wind blowing his hair to one side. He grinned and waved. The field hands' cheers were drowned in the wind and noise of the plane, but they waved back. The engine roared, the blades whirled a storm, the wings slightly rocked for fifteen or twenty full minutes...and the warplane went nowhere.

But Jupo knew. He was too conscious of being a gentleman, or too proud, too white, and too aware of his place in Fermata Bend to confront his son-in-law again in front of blacks, or in public, certainly not at church, or Sunday dinner at the home place before every member of the family; or to walk into a man's house, not so much because of his daughter, or even the respect of his daughter (he had that regardless), but some inherent principle that said a man did not demean another man in front of a woman, much less his wife, no matter whose daughter she was or what she may or may not have told her father in the first place.

Jupo drove in to Joe Morton's Rabbit Oil filling station in his big black Packard one morning and, smiling, told Joe Morton he had engine trouble and would like to see his son-in-law.

In the dim and contiguous rear of the small, cinder-blocked garage, with the hood of the Packard raised, out of the light and sight of anyone and the street, but not completely out of the hearing of one Joe Morton, came the sharp, metallic ring of a tool hitting the concrete floor and a thick 'whump' of what Joe later realized was the tall stack of new tires beside the back wall hitting the wall together, like someone had been flung or shoved against them, and then with Jupo's voice there was no question – coming hard, low and guttural: 'Do you think I'm blind, boy? You think I'm blind?'

What came after was a long, effusive tirade or sermon, depending on how one heard it, after which, came a pause, undoubtedly for air, and a quiet, plaintive reply: 'I'm just looking after my plane.'

'Sure now,' Jupo declared, his tone mocking, 'looking after your *plane*. It got you here, didn't it? It the only damn thing you can do well – except for maybe falling for a girl and then shunning your obligations and this family when you do. Oh, I been watching. Sure now, look after your wings – until you go buy rubber inner tubes and batteries. Then maybe you better kill the idea. Them days is over, son. You ain't leaving again. You should have thought everything out before you shacked up with a Demus. The only rubbers you're goan need, boy, are the ones you're collecting in the septic tank.'

Then, according to Joe Morton, came a long, bitter, bellowing laugh that echoed from the garage, that Joe Morton later realized contained all Jupo's fear of shame and disgrace, and all the hard anger that checked it.

Jupo could be heard, loudly now, talking and laughing at the same time. 'You think I don't know? Mike and me – we got us a telescope! We ordered it special through Sears Roebuck in Mobile two months ago. Ha. Set it up in the kitchen just to watch your house. What you do inside is your business, boy, but what you do outside is ours. We might say,' Jupo taunted, 'we Demuses got *vested* interest.'

Then as Joe Morton explained, the Packard's hood slammed, you could hear the car door open and shut, the engine start.

'Old Widow Beck drove up for gas in her Henry J, and I ran forward from the office to tend to her at the pumps as Jupo backed the Packard out of the garage and abruptly braked to doff his hat and smile out the Packard window to the Widow before he drove off. The Lieutenant...he come walking out, in his dirty maintenance overalls, wiping his hands fast on a rag, looking up the road after Jupo while I told the Widow good day and gassed up her Henry J, cleaned the windshield and checked her oil and tires – me acting like I don't know nothing but what I'm doing. The Lieutenant just stands there, bareheaded, staring hard up the road, and wiping his hands over and over, though they didn't need wiping to begin with; he hadn't done nothing to Jupo's car.

'It was the plane, you see. Jupo knew that. It weren't that he couldn't leave, if he had a mind to. Any man can run away from a woman. But it was the plane, for a reason I don't think anybody ever knew; and therefore, maybe that's why we never understood him. Maybe it was power, you know, though I think he was powerless, was a stuck-up fool, a stuck-up dreamer – and the plane was his dream, the magic that gave him a way he wanted to see himself. That, and that suit and scarf he liked to wear and that ever glinting wristwatch that he had to have polished everyday. I've wondered. Here I am years later, the same, alive and pumping gas. There he was – wanting to fly...and ruined.

'But it weren't the woman, nossir, not alone. A man can leave a woman. He could have slipped out at night, drove, or hitch hiked. Or hell, he could have caught the train at the cross switch, taken the Blue Goose that ran every Tuesday night through Citronelle and Mobile. It was the plane. There was something about him and that plane that weren't normal.

'He was polite enough. Courteous, is the word. He knew his manners and knew how you're supposed to treat a stranger and a lady – though he weren't good much after. That, and the fact he was married to a Demus, is why we tolerated him.

'And he was a good worker for a spell – not for long, mind you – he couldn't do the same thing over and over. He couldn't work on cars for more than a week. If it hadn't been for the different jobs he picked up, he would have quit working for me out of mounting boredom.

'You could see it coming in his eyes and the way he slowed down in his work. He was only good for a little while – but never any job for long. He sure couldn't just sit here, chew the fat with people stopping by and pump their gas. No, he would get edgy; that man couldn't stay still.'

Jupo's telescope was set up on a tri-pod in the kitchen: new, shiny metal and glass, beside the old wood kitchen table, before the large window, and aimed across the fields, railroad tracks and highway toward Katrina's.

What was learned about the telescope came through the maid who cooked for them or the teenage boys who delivered cords of firewood and came into the kitchen to wait for their money, among others. People in town talked and imagined the two men carefully watching the rock house and runway through the telescope in a contained but consistent and driven anxiety, participating in a private, coveted, even childish stealth; and of course, assuming they were in the hidden cloister of their act, their thoughts, and in their family house, never admitting or telling anyone, but doing it out of fear for the image of themselves and the belief in a reputation of their family name in Fermata Bend.

The stories grew. People imagined Jupo and Michael taking turns night and day, taking shifts from work, keeping vigilant watch; another version was of them taking shifts at breakfast and dinner – sunup and sundown – one sounding an alarm when the little man was spotted. People could imagine, too, Jupo shoving thin Michael aside to peer through the telescope, making loud declarations as he did so.

Months later, on a gray fall dawn, the field hands were awakened in their shacks by someone calling the Lieutenant's name. They looked out of their windows at the lone figure of Michael Demus doing a slow, circular dance, dragging his club foot in its shoe outside of one of the Demus trucks with its doors open, in the dew-covered runway by the wet, chain-tethered plane. Michael, the quiet, shy Demus, thin as a stick, who always worked in nervous silence in the shadow of his father, who couldn't brag or talk like Jupo – who never seemed to like girls, court one for long, or find one who was good enough for him – had a bottle of moonshine in one hand and a flame torch in the other. Despite the chill, his shirt was unbuttoned to his undershirt and a wide, diabolic laugh was frozen on his face as he whirled around, staggered, calling the Lieutenant again and again, hanging the name out like a long, primitive wall.

The chain lay parted from the wheels of the plane, the ends smothering on the ground. What the field hands saw was the little man come, first walking then running, out of the rock house in nothing but his Liberty overalls and untied work boots, his hair mussed from sleep, his face angry. He clambered over the fence, stopped and stood before Michael, blinking.

Michael swayed, gave a leering grin, struggled for balance,

and offered him the bottle, saying something inaudible, but like a pronouncement, like a declaration, maybe a boast. The little Lieutenant didn't seem to see him. He took the bottle and dropped it, staring at the plane, running to the chain and picking the ends up. Michael followed, holding out his arms, pointing, smiling with the flame torch, making a speech.

'I'm letting you go,' he said, 'I'm letting you go.'

But the Lieutenant didn't seem to hear. He dropped the chain ends and walked past Michael, out into the dew-touched, dead ragweed-encroached runway; gazing at the still, gray, foggy peace, toward the gray highway, the wet railroad tracks and the Demus Fields, heavy with cotton. Some of the field hands were outside and on the fence now, dressing, shivering and bleary eyed, and trying to affect indifference as they looked on, but not wanting to miss any of this.

Michael began yelling at the Lieutenant's back. He threw the flame torch down. The Lieutenant just stood there, gazing off. Then the field hands saw what apparently the Lieutenant was looking for: a plume of spurred dust rising in the distance of the dirt road across the Demus Fields, trailing a black spot: Jupo's black Packard coming pell-mell from the home place.

Katrina came running out of the house, her face covered in pale blue cream and pinched in a scold, unheedful of her appearance in a white nightgown, the ends of her hair tied in tissue papers, and the child forgotten for the moment. She halted at the fence, gripped the top rail, and uttered a 'No' like a demand, but too loud, too sudden, to mask her fear. She shook her head, hair, tissue papers, and uttered it again.

But the little Lieutenant, standing there and looking off, didn't hear her – or didn't choose to. He seemed deaf, oblivious to anything else. Katrina, Michael and the field hands stared, rooted and immobile, in that momentary hesitation of waiting for what someone else is going to do.

The little man turned for the plane and Katrina's mouth yelled 'No' again, only there wasn't any sound as he quickly climbed onto the wing and into the cockpit, the brown plume beyond the highway now a long cloud across the fields, Jupo's speeding Packard visible. Everyone stared as the plane coughed, died, coughed again, the propeller blades turned; the engine boomed to life, barking exhaust, making wind.

The field hands on the fence bowed their heads, the tails of Michael's loose shirt rose behind him, and the hem of Katrina's nightgown slanted up to her bare, white thighs. Katrina began mouthing 'No' over and over again as if she expected to be heard. The field hands could see the little man's set face. But he didn't look at anyone, or wave, or even close the cockpit.

He taxied the plane forward, leaving the trunk of the tree, the chains, gaining speed down the ragweed-encroached runway towards the oncoming black car: the two vehicles charging at each other with the highway between them. Jupo braked hard at the fence gate before the railroad tracks; the plane lifted, cleared the fence, swept over highway, railroad tracks and car in what seemed like a dreamlike suspension, its landing gear folding up under the wings as it turned up into the grey air, its thundering roar fading like a sigh.

Jupo jumped out of the Packard, bareheaded, gray and balding, in opened bathrobe and ragged long johns, and began firing away at the plane with his shotgun, unmindful of his appearance or who saw him, or that the plane was quite out of range and climbing with a distant drone. Katrina came running down the runway, the field hands behind her and Michael limping, no one considering, much less Katrina, how she was barefoot with a creamed face, only a thin nightgown on and tissue papers unraveling in her hair. Everyone stopped and stared up from the fence before the highway, across from the gate and the car and the fused, manic face and Vandyke of Jupo, who frantically reloaded and shot. They watched the warplane circle, dip a little and bank into a wide turn.

'He rusty,' a field hand said. The plane turned back, coming fast and low toward the car, its drone growing into a scream.

'He goan kill us!' someone said.

'Shit, man! Why don't he just fly off?' someone yelled.

Jupo stood his ground at the oncoming plane, firing until he and everyone dropped to the ground. The plane shot over them in a blasting scream, turned up over the pine trees beyond the runway and rock house, faded back into a drone and diminished into the sky. Everyone stood up, followed him with their eyes.

The warplane banked, wings wavering then steadying, seeming to follow the line of the gray horizon above the serrated tops of the pines. They watched it dive; come in from the north, perpendicular to the cotton fields and the dirt road.

'C'mon, you useless imp!' Jupo yelled.

He reloaded and began firing as the warplane came at him fast and low, as though delivering a bomb or a torpedo. Everyone dropped to the ground as it screamed over Jupo, the Packard and toward Legger Mound. Everyone stood up and turned to see the warplane's wing slice the stilts out from under the water tower, the tower collapse, breaking and bursting water; and the plane recoil, bouncing hard into the heavy cotton field, sliding and spinning, its wings and violent propeller rutting up stalks, cotton and earth, and instantaneously explode in a roaring, rising orb of flame that curled up into a thick, black line of smoke against the sky.

Jupo cursed and cursed and brandished his shotgun. Katrina began to scream and Michael began to howl in hysterical laughter. The field hands climbed the fence, hollering and running while they pointed and scattered across the highway and up onto the railroad tracks. A pickup truck pulled off the highway and a farmer got out. A school bus braked and the children inside pressed their wide-eyed faces against the window panes to see, their breaths fogging the glass.

Everyone stared.
Everyone waited and watched.

Emma Saw

When Emma looked up from the ladder and saw a red-headed man coming toward her from the barn in a blood-splattered tee shirt, what flashed to her mind was the memory of Howdy Doody on black and white TV – before she saw that the man's hands were bloody. Emma didn't know him. He walked, arms dangling limp at his sides as though their only connection to him was at the joints. But his arms came to life as he opened her gate and crossed the dirt road from the barn and paddocks, approaching her, where she was, until a moment ago, scraping rough paint off the side of the weathered house so that she and Bud could begin painting. *Where is the dog?* she thought, going rigid on the ladder and staring at the oncoming man's crude face. *Raoul* she remembered, then *Bud* she thought. Bud was in town getting toggle bolts for the tractor, she remembered, and clutched the scraper to her chest as the man in dirt-covered fatigue pants and work boots came on. He stopped before the ladder and looked up at her with vacant, yellow eyes. Then he made a slow grin at her with a glint in his teeth. His body was lean and strong. She stared down at him, feeling her heart pounding, and she noticed bloodied down feathers sticking onto his arms, shirt, and kinky red hair.

'Who are you?' She tried to make it sound terse. Her voice cracked, 'What are you doing here?'

'Lester,' he drawled softly after a moment. He made another grin, then offered his hands up as if it were Show and Tell. 'I been killing your pigeons.' He beamed at one hand, the other, then up at her. He held his smile of dull teeth and the instant memory of Raoul came to her: his hard, gray eyes. Everyone said he drove too fast. At sixteen, she slapped him when he tried to go too far and he became an animal. He pulled his belt, beat her black and blue, and held her down as he forced himself in her on the hood of his Jeep. 'You ain't got no place to hit me,' he had said afterwards.

Her paint scraper fell and hit the ground. The man didn't notice, his eyes steady on her, as if in a trance. Emma swallowed, imagined him creeping cat-like along the dust coated barn rafters and snatching the sleeping pigeons from the sills of the gable louvers above the stalls and heads of the horses. She imagined him grinning as he twisted their heads off.

The mouth closed, the man's hands lowered. 'My husband will be back in a minute,' she tried to say, and discovered she was crouching on the ladder, clutching a rung with both hands, her knees buckled onto a lower rung, and she could not take her eyes from the blankness of his stare. She gave a fleeting thought to the edge of the roof above the ladder.

He seemed to come to, slowly raised an arm toward Bud's green cornfield behind her, toward the line of oaks that concealed the highway and consumed most of the tin roof of an old church in the distance.

'I'll go now,' he said abruptly, his grin spreading slowly. 'Heh.' His eyes went over her; she felt them slide down to her mid-section and down her jean legs as she clung helpless before his look. She forced her eyes away, praying for Bud, the sound of his truck, anything. She didn't want to look, but she did, taking in again the man and his bloodied tee shirt, his grin and impenetrable eyes.

His grin closed. 'So long,' he sing-songed. 'So long.' He made a small wave and turned away. She held her breath and watched him go, following him with her eyes down the dirt road that divided the pasture and cornfield, toward the gate and the highway beyond the trees. She watched him begin an easy run. His slow, diminishing motion became almost mesmerizing. Then he was gone. He had ducked or turned – she wasn't sure – dissolved in the green immensity of field and trees.

She lowered herself one step, two, then scrambled down the ladder, shooting glances toward the cornfield as she pulled off her work gloves and ran into the house, to the gun rack in the hallway, spilling shotgun shells from the cabinet as she loaded the pump and marched outside into the yard to no one and nothing but the recollection of Raoul's fierce face and snarl. Her father's face with tired eyes and large cheeks occluded Raoul's. 'If you love me, Emma,' he had pleaded, 'don't go out with that boy.'

Scanning the fields in the morning sun, Emma cradled the shotgun in the crock of her arm and then walked across the road to the barn, pulling the double doors open and entering to the sound of her own breathing. She made herself pause, catch her breath, and go slowly down the row of stall doors, feeling reassured at the sight of the near-term pregnant mare munching hay. She patted the mare's neck in the familiar smell of hay and dirt. The yearling colt's curious nose came over its door, and in the end stall the gelding greeted her with its large eyes. She let herself relax and run a hand down the gelding's nose. The cooing of pigeons descended from the wood rafters above the loft and she jumped, startled. When she saw the mound of bloody feathered humps with limp wings before the feed-room door, she almost dropped the shotgun. The severed heads, with glazed or half-closed eyes, were stuck in a semicircle in the dirt, most with their beaks open, facing the pile of their own bodies. Emma trembled as she gaped at the scene. *Don't be ridiculous,* she fought down panic. Her father hunted, she had seen dead pigeons before, chickens, dove...deer and hogs. She was a country girl. *Where is Bud?* she thought. She would tell him when he got here, she told herself, but her hands shook as she gripped the shotgun.

She kept the gelding circling her on the lead line in the round pen when she heard Bud's pickup come down the dirt road and the dog come barking out of the woods. The truck's engine cut, its door opened and slammed, and she heard the swing of the gate and his playful talk to the dog. She popped the whip and the horse continued cantering, circling her, the long lead line to its halter in her hand. Bud appeared, resting his chin on folded forearms on top of the pen gate, his smile calm, his black, thin hair sticking out between his green cap and ears. He had missed his morning shave. She heard their chocolate Lab whining at his feet.

'Putting Big Boy in a sweat, aren't you?' he said over the hooves and the soft, floating dust.

Emma didn't answer, didn't take her eyes off the horse, popping the whip, continuing the canter under Bud's waiting look. Tootsie, the Lab, quieted down. 'Whoa,' she commanded after several minutes, letting the horse slow to a walk, its lathered sides heaving.

'Wondering when you were going to stop,' Bud said. 'Ain't you going to say something?' he said after a moment.

Bud stepped off the gate and opened it for her as she gathered the lead line and led the horse out. The dog rose from the ground and followed them to the side of the barn where Bud took the whip from her and turned on the hose. He let the dog drink as Emma unsnapped the lead line from the horse's halter and snapped on the chain from the grooming post.

'Thought you were working on the house,' Bud said. He stepped back as she dropped the coil of lead line and took the hose from him.

'I am,' she said. Tootsie nudged her hand with her nose and Emma ignored it.

Bud stood by as she hosed the horse down. He took the hose from her when she was through and turned the water off as she took the sweat scraper from a nail on the post and began going over the horse.

'Hey, Honey, is something wrong?'

'Nothing,' she said. 'Where have you been?'

'Oh,' and he began his nervous habit of jerking the brim of his cap up and down and looking off to the side, 'I was just chewing the fat with some of the boys at the hardware.'

Emma said nothing as she took the whip from him, picked up the coil of lead line, unsnapped the horse and led it into the barn. She looked back to see if he would follow. But Bud stopped in the barn doorway with the dog and waited while she slipped the halter off and shut the horse in its stall. Her hands shook as she hung the halter, the whip and the lead line in the tack room and they left the barn together.

'I ought to bush-hog the pecan pasture tomorrow,' Bud said as he opened the gate and they went through with the dog toward the house. She didn't reply. He looked away and kept readjusting his cap. They stopped at his truck and he handed her the mail from the seat and she led the way into the house shuffling through the envelopes.

In the house, the dog left outside, they stepped out of their boots in the closeness of the kitchen, the brick paver tile she had wanted for so long, and the cupboards and shelves she had stained and varnished herself to match the cherry molding. Bud removed his cap and washed his face and hands in the sink, drying himself on the dish towel while Emma fingered the ends of her hair just over her ear and remembered her wish for a burgundy wallpaper border. She poured both of them coffee and as they leaned on the opposite counters, facing each other in their jeans and tee shirts – she told him with controlled trembling, pausing, slowly settling her cup down and gripping the edge of the counter behind her; watching his face, trying not to repeat words. Bud's cup lowered as he listened. His lips pursed and his jaws grew taut.

45

'When?' he interrupted her as she began to describe what the man wore. She fought back her irritation, answered him and went back to the man's blood-covered shirt, his pants and boots, keeping control of her voice. Bud was not listening.

'Did he do anything to you?'

Emma shook her head, watching his face let out a breath and relax. She went on and told him about the pigeon heads but Bud's face did not change. Her voice faltered and she shut her eyes for an instant.

'Now, now,' Bud said. When he touched her, she felt an instant repulsion before relinquishing to his arms.

'Honey, are you okay? Are you okay?'

She nodded in his shoulder and hid her face in the darkness of his arm, for an instant seeing Raoul, then her father, who had listened with wearied patience at the dinner table to her talk about how nice he was. Her father had nodded and her mother had looked on, waiting on him to speak. 'Sure,' he had drawled. He had paused and that look had come over him as when she came through the door at night after a date: a weary, sad look. 'I know him,' her father had said. Her mother's eyes and hands would not stay still. 'If you love me, Emma,' he had almost begged, 'don't go out with that boy.' At the time, it seemed to Emma to have something to do with his driving so fast.

'Don't worry, Honey, we'll find him,' Bud stated. She felt his hard voice and the slow rising and falling of his chest. 'He don't need to be around here,' Bud said. 'That's for sure.'

Bud cocked his cap back on his head, crossed his socked feet and leaned on the wall as he called the sheriff on the kitchen wall phone, His mouth twisted as he repeated the story in a monotone, turning his head toward her. 'I want somebody to do something,' he demanded in a drawl. 'I want somebody to do something.'

'What? Okay,' he obeyed someone on the line. He looked at her and repeated questions as they came to him. The details.

46

There was no crime committed, except maybe trespassing. 'The pigeons,' she whispered, but Bud ignored her and kept echoing questions, his tone flat. The name was Lester, no last name. No knowledge of where he went. Emma gave the description again. Bud repeated it into the phone, his eyes on her but not seeing, his voice too loud. He spoke for the other voice: They would patrol the area and look out for any person fitting the name and description. If they found him, they'd question him, warn him, it was all they would do.

When Bud hung up the phone, he sighed and moved about the kitchen, avoiding her eyes and sliding his hands in and out of his pockets. 'Well,' he said, his face flushed. Emma felt suddenly alone. She leaned against the counter, watching him, clasping her elbows in her palms, while Bud paced the floor, hesitated, then stepped into his boots without tying the laces and walked out of the kitchen. She followed him into the hallway and he was lifting his deer rifle off the gun rack. He opened the breech and inserted cartridges from the cabinet drawer with slow, metallic clicks. 'Just in case,' he nodded, catching her eye. The intent on his face was the same one he went into the fields to drive his tractor or truck with.

'Bud,' she uttered. She heard her mother's voice. 'Don't you think you ought to take the shotgun? You could hit some-body in town with that rifle.'

'Oh. Oh, yeah.'

'There's work to do. I'll get back on the house. Why don't you go clean out the barn...and the mess,' she suggested.

Bud shrugged, nodded. 'Okay.' He seemed let down and awkward holding the rifle now. She watched him unload it, put it back on the rack and take the shotgun, shoving a handful of shells in his jeans pocket from the cabinet drawer. Emma watched him go, shutting the door behind him. She went back into the kitchen, looked at the phone and closed her eyes.

They had a quiet lunch in the kitchen. Afterwards, she continued scraping the house from the ladder, watching as Bud turned the horses out of the barn across the road. The gelding came out first, trotting with its nostrils flared and tail rising, and the mare came out, slow and heavy; the colt behind her, kicking. She watched Bud dump a wheelbarrow of manure and dirt far out into the pasture, then return the wheelbarrow to the barn and get into his pickup. He slowly drove by the grazing horses to check on the cattle, the shotgun in the rear window gun rack. Emma doggedly scraped the rough spots on the old boards and tried to make herself think of how the house would look primed, painted, clean and decent – the way she wanted it. She looked now and then to find Bud's truck in the pasture across from the cornfield, his figure standing among the cows at the salt lick. When she climbed down to move the ladder along the house, she found his figure leaning against the front of the truck, the shotgun braced against his leg, barrel pointed towards the corn.

She worked until she heard the school bus's distant winding brakes behind the house on the highway. By then, she had the ladder placed at the last weathered shutter of the front windows. Emma climbed down and carefully lowered the ladder to the ground. She pulled off her gloves, touched her hair, and made a smile for the boys as they came sauntering up the dirt road in their school clothes and haircuts, loosely holding their books. Steve, eleven, was brunette and looked like a thin Bud. Jonathan, nine, was blonde like her and her father. Like boys, they didn't care. Steve's shirt was hanging out the back as he walked. The alignment of Jonathan's belt was off and one of his shoes was becoming untied. Setting down her gloves and scraper on the porch, Emma held out her arms for hugs and asked about school. They mumbled vague answers.

*

Later, when the front door suddenly opened, Emma froze in the kitchen and then let out her breath at the sound of the door slamming, their voices, and the familiar confusion of feet in the foyer and family room. She heard the cabinet drawer open and close.

'We're having a favorite!' she raised her voice above the din. 'Chicken and dumplings.' Steve and Jonathan came into the kitchen grinning; Bud entered behind them, his cap cocked back on his head. 'So, go wash up!' she said, pointing toward the bathroom. She smiled, reached and squeezed Bud's arm. Bud looked at her and nodded with a wink as he followed the boys to the bathroom.

She poured milk as they came to the table clean, their hair combed. Bud had removed his cap and shaved. Emma remained standing until they seated themselves, became quiet and lowered their heads for her prayer.

'Did you bring the horses in? And feed?' she asked as they served themselves and began to eat.

Bud nodded.

'And the light,' she said. 'You leave the barn light on?'

Bud nodded. He kept eating. The boys talked and Emma served pie for dessert. When she sat down again, she looked at Bud and asked about the horses. His face relaxed, broke into a grin.

'Your mare, that baby – whew, she's heavy.' Bud whistled low. 'Your old girl's got to move slow now, don't she?'

'I know about that better than you,' Emma said.

Bud gave a quick nod.

The boys asked to be excused from the table. 'No TV until you finish your homework,' she reminded. As they left for their room, Emma got up with them to pour Bud and herself coffee.

'How are the cows?' she offered, sitting down.

He nodded. 'Fine.'

49

'You need to get more feed this week,' she reminded him. 'And you need to fix that leaking water trough in the pecan pasture.'

Bud nodded. 'I *need* to bush-hog the pecan pasture,' he thought out loud. They sipped coffee and Emma remembered that Tootsie had to be fed. That she must wash dishes, and check on the boys and their homework. She would have to wash clothes tomorrow.

'You sure had Big Boy in a sweat this morning,' Bud said slowly, taking her out of her thoughts. He shook his head, crossed his arms on the table and studied them. 'I guess I can understand – seeing as to what happened to you this morning.'

She instantly hated his face: his tone; his quiet demeanor. Bud glanced at her and his slight grin died. He looked away.

'How dare you,' she whispered.

'Sorry,' he mumbled. 'Didn't mean it.'

'That's just it. You don't mean *anything*.'

She stood up and began clearing the table, scraping the scraps onto one plate for the dog. At the counter, she stacked the dishes too hard and turned on the water to fill the sink. When she did look for him, he was gone. She heard the TV come on in the family room. She turned off the water and went to shut the boys' door, listening for the volume of the TV so that she could tell him to turn it down.

She didn't wake and coax him into making love as he liked for her to do. Instead, she lay under the sheets, limp on her back in bed, feeling him breathe on her neck before he turned his bare back to her. She listened to him softly snore, then stared at the night in the window beyond the foot of the bed and listened for the house, the dog, the boys' room. There was nothing but Bud's wheezing. She had an instant thought of a form moving in the dark corn – but rid herself of it, clutching the comforter to her and closing her eyes, still listening. Later in a dream, she went to the window of a white bedroom and stared down on

50

statue-like men. In the shadow of the yard beyond the figures stood a brawny, defiant man beside a fender-battered car: feet spread, arms akimbo, Raoul's sneer on its face. The car's engine was running. Her father was below on the porch: a stoic vigil under a lone porch light in a motionless rocker, a fatigued and creased face. As she looked down, she understood that with light she was safe. She began stroking the long flowing hair about her shoulders.

In the morning, in sweats and running shoes, Emma called to the boys and Bud to get up; she turned CNN on in the family room and the radio on the kitchen counter. The cacophony of news, weather, and old rock tunes accompanied the rising smell of brewing coffee while she banged the skillet on the stove and slapped the plates on the table.

'Noise, noise, noise,' Bud said. 'Can't we wake up quiet?' he muttered as he came to the table in his morning face and shadow, in sock feet and jeans. He wore his old high school football jersey and carried his boots. As he sat at the kitchen table and began pulling his boots on, Emma asked if he wanted coffee. He nodded. She asked how he wanted his eggs, even though she knew; she asked what he had to do today when she knew that, too. She waited to hear him repeat in a mumble that he had to buy feed, bush-hog the pecan orchard and spread lime in the pasture. The boys came to the table in their clean school clothes and Emma ran a hand through Jonathan's hair, buttoned a missed hole on Steve's shirt. They ate quickly and the boys kissed her as they grabbed their books and left for the school bus. Emma followed them out into the yard and the bright morning, calling Tootsie back and waving good-bye, while Bud came out onto the porch, in his cap now, holding a cup of coffee. He called out something cheerful as the boys grew smaller down the dirt road toward the highway.

Bud took his cup with him across the road to the shed where the car was parked under the galvanized roof with the tractor.

The dog followed Emma as she went to the barn and unlatched the double doors to the burning light in the tie beam overhead and the large calm eyes of the pregnant bay mare in the breezeway. Its stall door was open. The overlarge horse was tethered by its halter to an arch brace, its tail was tied to one back leg with a piece of hay rope. Behind the horse's hind legs was the stool from the tack room. The dog wagged its tail and entered the cool barn. Emma stared. A half circle of pigeon heads faced her in the dirt like a muted choir. She swallowed and managed to cry Bud's name, glancing about the barn and backing out of the doorway.

A Deputy Sheriff came this time in a brown car with a gold star on each front door, a blue light behind the front windshield. He got out, a tall black man in a brown and tan uniform and a pencil-thin mustache that made Emma think of a dark Errol Flynn. The dog went crazy barking. The deputy shut the car door and put on his Stetson. He looked at them and then at the dog.

'Shut that bitch up,' Bud said.

Emma grabbed Tootsie's collar and dragged her growling into the house. When she came back out, Bud and the deputy were talking.

'C'mon, I'll show you,' Bud said. He led the way through the gate to the barn, his cap pushed back on his head, the rage still in his voice. 'First my wife, now this,' he said, waving his hands in the air before the deputy. 'You need damages? The stud fee was two thousand alone. This is a Super Trey Bar mare,' he emphasized. 'She might miscarry or something.'

They stopped in the opened double doorway where the mare was as it had been found, tethered and calm. It shifted its weight from one back leg to the other. The deputy studied the horse, the stool, and the floor. He surveyed the inside of the barn. 'Somebody's sick,' he commented. He drew a pad and pen from his belt.

'Okay. Did anyone witness the person doing-this?'

Bud and Emma shook their heads. The deputy wrote something down.

'Didn't the dog bark?' The deputy looked up.

'No,' Bud said. 'Last night she would have been asleep on the back porch. It's possible....' He didn't finish. The deputy nodded and wrote.

'You suspect the same person you called about yesterday?'

'Yes,' Emma said.

Bud said yes. The pigeons were proof. The energy now was drained out of his voice. Emma watched Bud slowly reiterate the description and name they had called in yesterday.

After a few minutes, the deputy shook his head. 'I'm afraid there's not much to go on, sir. You have no real suspect and no real damage.'

'Rape,' Emma uttered. 'He *raped.* '

The men looked at her. Bud pulled the bill of his cap low over his eyes and caught his breath.

'Honey' he said, pausing, looking sheepish, 'you can't *rape* a horse.' Bud suppressed a laugh. The deputy checked a smile. They made her think of leering dogs. She said nothing more but watched the men talk – the one with the black face asking the other to sign the report, telling him to take precautions, lock up, call in any new information, and that they would patrol the area. 'Most of all,' the deputy said, 'don't confront this person by yourself.'

'Precautions,' Bud echoed and spit into the dirt road as the Deputy drove away.

'Don't leave me, Bud.'

Bud paused. 'But Emma, I...' She cut him short with her glare. Bud grimaced and looked away. He jerked the bill of his cap up and down. He looked at her, then toward the tractor shed. He let out a sigh.

After they brushed the mare, put her up and fed the horses, she watched as Bud dumped a shovelful of pigeon heads into the pasture. They went back through the gate together. At the house, Emma let Tootsie out and Bud got the shotgun down and loaded it. He marched around the front yard with it as if waiting for something to do. He finally leaned the shotgun on the porch against the house while Emma raised the ladder from the ground and propped it beside the last window and got her work gloves and scraper.

'I'm almost done, but you can help me if you want,' Emma said.

Bud shook his head. He made a seat on the front bumper of the pickup with Tootsie at his knee and gazed out at the cornfield in the lazy, growing sun while Emma moved the ladder, climbed, and began scraping the rough shutters. She looked to see Bud yawning or staring at the ground in silence, the dog sprawled in the grass and going to sleep.

'We need to go to the Co-Op and get feed,' Bud stated after awhile with an edge in his voice.

In the truck with him, the shotgun in the rear window rack, Emma couldn't think of anything to say. Bud was quiet. He seemed irritated and preoccupied with the wheel as he drove away from the house. She stole a glance at his eyes, his unshaven face, settled on the soft bulge around his waist and remembered when they were married, he was hard and lean, a marine back from Vietnam: a taut face, a shaved head and a uniform. After they were married, there were things he would not tell her and he had nightmares. 'He'll come around, Poppa. He'll come around,' she remembered telling her father on the phone. But Bud frightened her at nights, waking her with screams, bolting upright in the bed, sweating and shaking. So she began waking him after he went to sleep, to soothe him and make love, and began preparing big meals during the day like she used to have at home. 'You're feeding me too much,' Bud had said.

But the nightmares had ended.

She stole another sidelong glance at Bud's face as he drove down the dirt road and downshifted to a stop before the asphalt. She watched him yawn and interlock his hands into a long stretch before turning onto the highway.

'Bud, don't drive so fast,' Emma said, waiting for him to look at her. 'Don't drive so fast.'

I Hear You

Inside his dark barber shop off the town square, Joe sits in his barber chair under the glassy, dull stares of mounted deer heads and bass, and in the faint smell of Dixie Dust gone from the linoleum floor, watching his son and his son's two friends in the other barber seats as they sip bottled cokes in the pale castings of light from the TV on the opposite wall by the customers' chairs. Watching their silent, smooth faces engrossed on the screen and a Chuck Norris rerun, Joe wonders when last he was in that kind of rapture. He brought them here to escape the chatty commotion of women, another of Betty's bridge nights at the house. Before he could get away, he had to promise within earshot of her guests to get the boys home early and not let them watch sexy scenes.

Joe sighs and runs his hands over his stiff pant legs. He reluctantly put on the khaki slacks, the leather macadam belt and golf shirt Betty had bought for him last week, and went downstairs to meet her guests: all of them dressed-up and talking women with too much makeup. They gave him automatic smiles, seated at folding bridge tables with tablecloths, among tea cups and ashtrays, knowing they did not have to rise. Betty was pleased that he was not wearing jeans. She winked and put her arm through his and paraded him around.

Her divorced friend, Alice, who gives her a ride to work every day at the Shoe Mall, said hello. Alice wore a brooch at her neck in the form of a Dalmatian with matching polka dot bows in her too-black hair. Joe smiled and said something, too. Betty looked good in her white dress and permed wave, though it was still beyond him why she had become a frosted blonde. But that was women. Before he excused himself, Betty saw he was staring at her and she made her demure look with her eyes to the floor.

Joe doesn't like parties. He likes to go fishing and hunting. He likes to go home after a day at the barber shop, lean on the refrigerator, and watch his wife busy herself with dinner in the kitchen, wearing the blue Dutch apron he bought her for Christmas, while Steve watches TV or plays Nintendo in the dining room. When Joe asks her how her day went, Betty tells him in a whiny voice – moving from the stove, to the refrigerator, to the counter again – about the man in a white Stetson with socks that stunk to high heaven, say, who drove in from Fort Smith to buy three pairs of Florsheims; or that Alice isn't talking to Mary because Mary wore the same earrings and blouse to work that Alice did when she knew that Alice had bought hers first; or about Joan and her latest romance – Joan, whom they all talk to, but secretly hate because of her figure and the fact that she has a lot of male visitors and walks like a slut.

Joe listens, but waits for his question. 'How are things at the shop?' she says. He tells her then, getting a beer out of the fridge, waiting for her to stop and watch him, her head nodding as he tells her about the albino man's flax-like hair he cut, the talk at the shop on the fist fight at the Pit Stop Lounge, or the thirty pound catfish someone pulled out of Josie Lake. Joe leans on the fridge and slowly drinks his beer, knowing that she is watching him. He pauses between each swallow and tells her what.

Lately, though, Betty has had strange things brewing in her. Joe has decided the best way to deal with it is to avoid it. Like the other day, she started in on Steve's playing football in the fall. She was afraid he would get hurt. Her talk became a spiel;

she started to fidget and shake, to nag him about how Steve shouldn't run around with boys bigger than he is, and shouldn't go hunting and fishing all the time. Joe didn't answer. Betty got worked up: her small arms waved, her voice rose to a shrill, unlike anything he had ever seen. Joe took it until he had had enough.

'All right,' he said. When she wouldn't stop, 'All right,' he yelled. It seemed to clear the air. She stopped, blinked at him, and then looked down at the floor.

Joe gazes beyond his barber window at the slow, steady lines of headlights going through town, to and from the Interstate and Fort Smith. He has a fleeting image of herded lights going through a ghost town. He turns again from the window to the boys' rapt faces. He knows they have little to do. It's late summer, too hot to fish and too early to hunt. And they can't drive yet. He's their barber. He clipped their sides close like they wanted him to, leaving not-so-flat tops with tails they can comb. He razored lines along the sides of their heads to look like pro athletes on TV. Steve streaked his razored lines with blue and yellow watercolor the first time he went home with his new haircut. When Betty saw it she stared at him and got teary-eyed. 'Oh, now, let it go,' Joe said. 'It's just kid stuff. We were kids once.'

The boys suddenly cheer.

'Look at that car,' Clyde whistles from the other end chair. 'A Jaguar.'

The boys' faces stare into the yellow, amber, then blue shifting light of the TV. Each one, Steve, Clyde, and Jeff, is wearing stone-washed jeans, basketball shoes, and a T-shirt.

'Forget Jaguar,' answers Jeff, who's the heaviest and blonde. He leans back leisurely in his chair, his coke between his legs. 'Nissan's got one better. Their Z will do zero to sixty in six point two.'

'I want a Vette,' Steve says. Seated between his friends, he's thin, wiry and dark like Joe used to be. His face is like Betty's, though, with her brown eyes, her small nose and cheeks.

'Aw, you boys don't know,' Joe says. A shift in the light from the TV turns the boys' faces pale green as their eyes go to him and he makes a slow, deliberate stretch. 'A Camaro Super Sport with a three-ninety-six could do zero to sixty in six seconds flat,' Joe says. 'And no Jaguar or nothing could touch it.'

'A Super what?' Jeff echoes.

'An old car,' Steve tells him. 'A gas guzzler.'

'Bet it couldn't do no two hundred miles an hour,' Clyde counters.

'And where you going to go two hundred miles an hour?' Joe says.

'Race track,' Jeff answers. The boys grin.

Joe looks on. He smiles and shakes his head. He's removed, yet it's familiar. Before he met Betty, he and his buddies used to drag cars on the dirt river roads in Alabama, drink beer and brag. He was fresh out of high school and at barber school outside of Livingston when he met a preacher's daughter from Boligee. Five months later, she and her family moved to Antioch, Arkansas. Following a week of sleepless nights where he saw nothing but Betty's quiet and timid face, she called him one morning, collect and crying, begging him to come save her from her father. Throwing his clothes into the backseat of his Camaro before he left, Joe tried to explain it to his mother. His father was away at work or golf all day and only came home at night. 'I love her,' was the only way he could word it. He can remember his mother's mouth going slack, the light in her eyes falling; and then her quick reply, almost scoffing: 'It ain't *love* you feel for her.'

That was fourteen years ago. Joe moved from one rural town to another. He married the preacher's daughter. The preacher moved away. Now, Joe owns his own barber shop. He has a son, thirteen, a satellite dish, a Blazer 4x4, and an Evinrude bass boat. He can take afternoons off to hunt or fish, and every spring he takes Betty and Steve camping in the Ozarks.

But he found Betty crying in the hamper room Sunday night, three months ago, as he came in from emptying the trash. It was after *Sixty Minutes* and the *Fishing with Bill Dance Show*. As he came in, she turned her back to him. She was in shorts and an old Crimson Tide T-shirt of his, and her dark hair was tied up in a yellow bandana. When he turned her around, she avoided his eyes, butted her head into his chest, and clutched him hard. He felt a shudder in her body run through him.

'I'm scared of you,' she gasped. 'I'm scared shitless.'

Joe didn't know what to think. 'Why?' he said, and held her.

She cried, gathering his shirt into her fists as if in a seizure. It oddly reminded him of the way she used to climax years ago on the hood of his Camaro in the dark and the whisper of the pine trees, her softness the center of everything when he shut his eyes. Holding his wife in the hamper room, among dirty clothes baskets, folded linen, spilled detergent and mouse traps, Joe could see again her pale, thin legs pressed against the hood of the car. He tried to close his eyes and slide his hand down into her. But it was the wrong move. Her waistband was not loose. She thwarted him by pressing harder and remaining still. They had a house with a kid in it, and they didn't make love like that anymore.

She slipped away and ran to the bathroom, sniffing and wiping her eyes. That week Betty began wearing high heels every day and dyed her hair frosty blonde. It looked the color of artificial tails Joe could remember seeing in horse shows. And she began calling her friend, Alice, a lot on the telephone, who talked her into wearing pink eye shadow and taking a mail correspondence course from a Paramore Improvement Institute in Frostproof, Florida.

Joe began coming home from work to drink his beer alone. He and Steve watched TV with the upbeat voices of training tapes and an occasional marching song filtering through the closed bedroom door. Betty would come out tired and with a smile that was not for him.

'I want my dinner,' he told her. At that, her face would fall and her lips would purse and she would head into the kitchen. Later, she told him she and Alice were talking about taking up tennis. 'You *can't* play tennis,' Joe said.

She didn't play tennis, but in the weeks that followed, Betty painted her nails to match her eye shadow, and she made an 'A' in a course called 'Meeting People and Getting Ahead.' She also made a 'B' in an 'I Can Do It' course. She quit wearing sneakers and faded jeans, began ordering new clothes in L.L. Bean, Talbot's, and Eddie Bauer catalogues. She has had to get out and meet people, she says, to keep her confidence up – joining the PTA, the Methodist Women of the Church, the Antioch Bridge Club, the Antioch Book Club, the Antioch Flower Club, and even the old ladies' UDC. She came home to announce she'd been promoted from cashier to salesperson at the Shoe Mall. 'It's all in the attitude, honey,' Betty declared. 'It's all in the attitude.' She beamed and looked at him.

'Wonderful,' Joe said. But he felt neglected. He'd discovered vacation brochures from Jamaica, Lake Tahoe, and San Francisco by the telephone and she had begun smelling of something called Purple Passion. It was heavy and sweet.

Every morning while he's lying in bed, she poses for him now, before the bedroom dresser mirror, in chino or corded slacks with colored cloth belts, cotton blouses, mock turtlenecks, or silky fatigue shirts. 'How do I look, honey?'

she says. She wears lipstick with her eye shadow, all of her gold jewelry and high-heeled shoes. 'Don't you want to look at me?' She gives him a tentative smile and a quick wink from a colored eye showing powdered wrinkles.

'Sure,' he says, feeling sad. She reminds him of a hooker in an old movie he saw once, placed in New Orleans. He thinks of when they were both thinner, when they had longer hair: she had a tighter butt; he smoked Marlboros and drove a hot rod.

'Is that all you can say?' Betty says. Joe tells her she looks nice and makes a smile. He imagines men she meets at work giving her the eye.

Later, Steve doesn't say much, either. He gives a shrug from the kitchen table and goes back to his cereal before school.

'Don't the other women at work hate you?' Joe asks after a couple of weeks.

'Well, not Alice.'

'You're not going to keep wearing that to work, are you?' Joe says. 'A guy wants to buy some cheap shoes, not be waited on by a prima donna.'

Her face turns indirect and blank, the look he remembers she gave her father's stern pivotal stare at the dinner table when he was courting her. Joe can still picture the old man's arched eyebrows and hard eyes. He can hear the old man's harangue. Her father did the talking. He sliced the ham. He interrupted his wife and daughter.

'Well, yes,' Betty whines.

The day after Joe had the boys at the barber shop, he brings home flowers again, because he's been thinking bad about her all day. This time it's mums.

'Oh, honey,' Betty says. She's wearing her high heels in the kitchen, with new khaki gauchos and a maroon cotton blouse. Joe watches her bow her frosted head into the flowers and inhale. He is hoping for a kiss, but she takes the mums to the cabinet to find a vase, turns on the faucet, and begins paring the stems with a knife.

Joe watches and wonders who's seeing her at work. He can't tell her to quit her job. He's tired of coming home to dinners left on the stove while Betty is out – the house growing dusty in the corners – not being able to find a clean shirt, or having to hunt Steve down on the phone to tell him to get home to eat and do his homework. He told her last night after he came home from the barber shop, 'I'm getting tired of this crap. I want my wife home.' 'Oh, I'm sorry, honey,' she echoed, her tone and face unsettling, like something else was on her mind. And, sure enough, tonight she is going to some community project meeting about planting trees around the town square.

'How are things at the shop?' Betty says with her back to him, at the sink.

He sighs and begins to tell her, loosening his collar and getting a beer from the fridge: Jon Hand's wife up and left him with the kids, and Steve Mueller had a car wreck, and someone brought a dead deer to the shop, tied to the hood of his truck, having hit it head-on this morning in the fog on the highway; Norman at the other end chair has to quit to go into the army. They may have to double-up for a while; otherwise, business is pretty regular.

He's telling her this, leaning against the fridge, sipping his beer. Betty stops paring the stems in the sink and seems to stare at the wall in front of her.

'What is it?'

'Nothing,' she shakes her head. But she slowly lays the flowers in the sink, the knife on the counter, wipes her hands on a paper towel, turning to him with a ponderous look, as if she is trying to memorize something.

'I want to take Norman's place.' Her face is soft and hopeful.

'What?' Joe says. He thinks he misunderstood. 'But...you don't know how.'

'I can do it, honey,' she says. 'I can do it.'

'But why?' he stares at her.

Betty keeps her pink-shadowed eyes on him. 'I won't be confident until I prove myself in front of men,' she says, lowering her voice. And she stands there, her face hinging on his answer.

Joe wants to laugh; only he's afraid to. It's like the way she called him long distance, collect and crying, years ago; this voice, small and pleading, saying that if he loved her, to come save her from her father. 'I'm coming, baby,' he remembers bragging. 'I hear you, honey,' she sighed.

'It's going to mess things up,' Ed states when Joe tells the boys during a lull in Wednesday morning's business. Leaning on his elbows over the top of his barber chair, Ed peers at Joe over his half-glasses. He's graying at the temples and in need of a shave, as always. Charlie behind the third chair only shrugs. He's thin, young, and doesn't care.

'It'll only be until we find a replacement,' Joe promises. He fights down a tremor in the pit of his stomach. He wants to sound calm. He and Betty have been practicing comb-and-scissor trims for four nights in the shop, using Steve, the dog, and finally mops bought at Wal-Mart. Betty improved. She had had some experience cutting her father's hair. When he told her she could do trims and children Wednesday and Friday afternoons after she got off work, and all day Saturday, her flushed and sweaty face lit up at him and he felt like he had won her again. This morning he told her to take the Blazer and drop him off, so she could pick up Steve after school and come to the shop. He also told her to tone down the dress and makeup. He was relieved this morning when she only wore jeans and a blouse to drive him to work.

What Joe sees of himself in the wall mirror behind Ed has a trimmed pompadour, bags under its eyes, a pouch stomach, and needs sleep. He wants to laugh and tell Ed how his wife pitched a fit when he first told her no – unlike one he had ever seen before: falling, kicking and screaming, pummeling the floor with her fists – and that he was more scared than he would let anyone know.

Two farmers drift into the shop in their worn denim clothes and broken caps, dirty smiles, and boots muddy from the field. They give loud hellos and exclaim about what they've been doing in the soybeans, the thunderstorm two nights ago. The larger one stands with hands on hips before the magazine table and tells a lewd joke about a truck driver picking up a young college co-ed hitchhiker and teaching her something in the cab. The other farmer tells one about a nun losing her virginity. The men laugh. The farmers seat themselves in Joe and Ed's chairs. Joe and Ed remove their caps, snap bibs around their necks, and turn on the electric clippers while they keep talking and laughing: about where to shoot a goat and how to skin a muskrat.

The minute Betty enters the shop, the male customers turn in their chairs toward her and hush. Betty smiles at everyone. She cuts through the cigarette smoke and aftershave like a swathe, wearing a short-sleeved wintergreen jump suit with one button undone too low from the top, Joe thinks, and leather high heels; gold on her neck, wrists and ears, and pink lipstick to match her eye shadow and nails. Joe glares at her. He feels himself blush as she gives him a peck on the cheek. Ed and Charlie nod, become too polite, then become extra busy cutting hair. Beaming, Betty goes to the vacant barber chair, setting her purse on the counter and checking her hair in the wall mirror as she takes out her scissors and comb.

Joe's hand quivers as he goes back to leveling the top of a crew cut, and she has nothing to do but smile at everyone and unwrap a stick of gum to place in her mouth. Joe sees with relief that an elderly man with hair sprouting out of his ears comes forward, and he's even proud of her as she helps the man to be seated, speaking gently as she covers him with the bib and begins to trim his thin hair.

After she rings up the old man's money in the cash register at the counter, it's a little boy who comes in with another customer. Joe watches Betty place the worn board over her barber chair's arms for the kid and begins to relax. It's going all right, he tells himself. He tries to smile as he finishes another crew cut for an old farmer with tobacco-stained teeth ,and begins a close trim for another with horn-rimmed lenses and one good eye. All day, he's been sweeping hair up off the floor and re-checking the magazine table to make sure no one left a girlie mag.

The TV becomes the only noise in a shop of mute men. Betty goes and switches channels from *CMT* to *CNN Fashion News*, then to *The Oprah Winfrey Show*. As she trims another kid's hair, Joe notices a farmer enter the shop, stare at Betty, and leave, shaking his head.

Ed bumps him at the counter while he's washing his hands. 'It's either us or the Hardware,' Ed hisses. 'Men need a man's place. I've seen three back out the door since she came in here.' His face is accusing.

'They don't want to wait in line,' Joe remarks. But Ed doesn't look convinced. Joe smiles at him and fights down another tremor in his stomach.

With an hour until closing time, only the men barbers are cutting hair, with three customers waiting; and Betty is sitting in her barber chair with nothing to do but chew her gum, thumb through *Sports Afield*, and glance up at the TV. No one is talking much or telling jokes.

Joe looks up now and then over his customer's head and give Betty a wink, but she doesn't seem to see. Joe thinks how he'll tell her tonight that customers will come with time. He'll sit her down after they have dinner and give her a little talk; maybe make her go over the procedures again. And she'll watch him as he does. Then they'll have to talk about dress in a men's barber shop.

Joe's working with clippers and comb around an ear when a seedy-looking character enters, in cap, boots, an army T-shirt, and jeans. He stops in his tracks when he sees Betty and his mouth slants into a slow curve that turns Joe's stomach. The man's big, with narrow eyes that make one think of a rodent. He's got a three-day growth on his face. Joe isn't sure if he raises pigs somewhere.

'Hello,' Ed solicits. 'Have a seat. We'll be right with you.'

The man looks at Ed, momentarily distracted. 'I'll take the lady,' he says. He walks too slow, Joe thinks, to Betty, who just sits there with a full-toothed smile and then rises from her chair, holding her magazine. 'Hi,' she offers. Joe can't believe it.

'Hello, sweet thing,' the fellow coos. His eyes don't waver.

Joe stops cutting hair. Betty daintily spears the gum out of her mouth between her forefinger and thumb, drops it in the wastebasket, and puts on a receptive face as if she's at one of the bridge parties. She sets her magazine on the counter. The man seats himself in the barber chair and lets her remove his cap. He tilts his head back to look at her.

'I want it wet and hot,' he says, then laughs. Betty's smile ignores him. She sweeps the bib around his neck and takes a wet comb to his hair. The man submits to her combing and grins up at her. It'll be all right, it'll be all right, Joe tells himself as he goes back to his customer's ear.

'Take your time, sweet thing,' the man says, loud and for everyone to hear. 'Not so fast,' his voice comes slow and reigning.

Joe looks up and Betty is still smiling as she begins to comb and cut his limp, wet hair. After a minute or so, Joe sees the man shoot the other waiting men a wink. His hand slides off the armrest and touches her leg. Betty moves around him. He does the same thing with his other hand. Now Betty's smile goes

Theron Montgomery

empty: awkward, helpless, as though ignoring the man will make him go away.

Joe turns off his clippers and straightens up. 'Hey,' Joe says. All eyes turn to him. 'Take your paw off my wife.'

The man looks surprised. 'You talking to me? This your wife?'

Joe sets the clippers on the counter and faces him again. The man makes an insistent grin, his hair glistening wet and partially cut, looking like an unkempt kid with an oversized bib. His palms come out, suspended in the air, like *So what?* And Betty is backing away, as if on cue, clutching her scissors and comb in both hands, her look one Joe remembers from somewhere.

'Yeah. I'm talking to you.'

The man drops his hands, shrugs, fending nonchalance at everyone.

'It don't make a shit to me,' he counters. 'The old girl ain't worth much.'

Betty has backed to the corner of the counter and wall, her face closed and small. For a moment, Joe contemplates taking the grin off the ape's face.

'Get out,' Joe says. Their eyes make a challenge. The man doesn't move.

'Get out, buddy,' Ed says behind Joe. 'Get out, or I'll call the police.'

After he closes the shop, Joe drives the Chevy Blazer around the square, then toward home in silence. His wife keeps her head turned away from him in the front passenger's seat. Then in a quiet voice, without turning from her window, Betty asks if he wants hamburgers for dinner.

Joe replies, 'I want a beer,' and pulls the Blazer into the parking lot of Food Market.

When he cuts the engine, she turns to him, going into her parental tone, with quiet insistence telling him that she'll get it, she'll get it, to stay in the truck. He doesn't fight, but sits behind the wheel watching as Betty clicks on her high heels into the Food Market. Reflected in the large glass windows is a small face in a dirty Blazer with all the other muddy, old, and dull vehicles in the parking lot, the traffic on the road behind them going at a steady clip. Joe has a fleeting thought that this is as far as he will ever go.

When Betty comes back, wearing a bland face and carrying a grocery sack in her arms, Joe is slapping time on the dashboard to Hank Williams, Junior, on the radio, having made up his mind he and Steve are going to try for bass tomorrow at Dykes Lake. To hell with the heat. He leans over and opens Betty's door with a grin.

'Is this a party?' Betty remarks as she gets in and shuts the door, hugging the sack in her lap. Her face remains impervious and set, but she sighs as she reaches and turns down the volume.

'I stood up for my woman,' Joe declares. He reaches into her sack, tears a beer out of the carton, twists off the top and flips it out his window. He takes a long swallow and lets his breath out in a gasp.

'I stood up for my woman,' he says.

'Your hands were shaking,' she says, and she gets that far-away look, over the grocery sack, beyond the windshield and the parking lot.

Undaunted, Joe starts the Blazer. He squeals the tires out of the parking lot into the traffic with one hand on the wheel and the other on his beer. Betty keeps her composure in the lurch of the vehicle and even as they speed down the road.

'I was in love,' Joe announces. 'I was young and poor and lonely – do you hear me?' He shoots her a glance. 'Then you called...and I was driving to Arkansas.' Joe grins and takes a swallow of beer.

'Yes,' Betty replies. 'Yes, and here you are.'

Pierre's New Game

Since Carol has begun letting him visit Milly, Pierre dreams of Sted again. He sees him as a kid under the lights on Doc Roy, coming around the bend of the show ring in one of those George C. Wallace for President Horse Shows. Pierre sees the black, lathering horse high-stepping in the red clay; Sted sitting well, his soft blonde hair over his ears, and the royal blue coattails parted behind him over the saddle. Sted grins with large hazel eyes and a look that knows no tomorrow.

Pierre wakes in the mornings now with an old feeling that he has Tennessee Walkers, a boy, and a smiling wife. It lingers with the dresser, the mirror, the digital clock, then dissipates in the empty house when he goes down the hall and rinses his face over the kitchen sink like Laura used to do. He tries not to think. He makes coffee and toast, turns on Sted's old receiver and listens to National Public Radio. The TV is not soothing. At bad moments, Pierre remembers too well that Sted has been dead almost fifteen years, since a mortar training accident at Fort Bragg. 'It's your fault, you let him go,' Laura said after the funeral, dressed in black; her frail, rigid back to him in the kitchen among the food people had brought. 'He had to,' Pierre could only whisper. Laura gave him silence and let her hair go gray. For months she had to have tranquilizers. When he told her about Sted's girlfriend, Carol, running around at nights and getting arrested, Laura didn't want to discuss it. Her look remained narrow and she kept cleaning house and going outside to work in the garden. She went to church and prayed.

She kept Sted's room the way it was his last day on leave before Pierre drove him to the bus station to report to duty: an opened copy of September 1977 *Sports Illustrated* on the made bed, his bulletin board full of high school memorabilia, his closet of clothes; his book shelves of record albums, trophies and faded ribbons; his stereo system; framed photos: Sted and Carol, Sted on horseback, Sted in the church choir; his wall posters: a '77 Corvette, the Eagles, Lynnard Skinnard and Farrah Fawcett – their yellowed ends now curled up and dry.

It's warm as he drives his old model Jeep Wagoner around town and turns down Chickasaw Street. The small lots of one-level frame houses are crowded with old vehicles on the curbs in the quiet and growing light of Sunday morning. Pierre parks before Carol's house and checks his watch twice, feeling his heart pound. His suit feels stiff and so does the small felt Stetson. He's early again, but he didn't know what else to do. When Carol's screened door opens, Pierre feels caught. Milly, her daughter, comes out on the steps and picks up the morning paper, her face still flushed from sleep. She's in new tennis shoes and an orange warm up suit. When she sees him, she waves with the paper. Her face beams and she comes skipping down the front steps, her blonde ponytail bobbing. Pierre feels a knot rise in his chest and he is already smiling.

'Good morning,' he says as he gets out, remembering her gift on the seat. Each time he first sees her, he hopes for Sted in her smile, her light brown look, the turn of her head. It isn't there. She is just beautiful.

Milly nods her greetings at the curb before the Wagoner. She pats his arm and approves his suit. 'Did you go to church?'

Pierre shakes his head and hands her the wrapped cylinder. Milly gives him a knowing look, tucks the newspaper under her arm and tears the paper off the tin of tennis balls. 'Thanks,' she says.

'Is your mother ready?'

'No,' Milly shakes her head. 'But you can come in.' She waits for him. They go together to the house and up the steps. Milly opens the door. 'Mom?' she calls in. '*Ma-om*?'

'May I come in?' Pierre calls, removing his Stetson. They go in and Milly closes the door behind them. Inside is dim, the blinds are closed. Pierre smells stale beer and cigarettes, sees the simple chairs, rug, sofa, and TV. He stands by the door and rotates the brim of his hat through his fingers. Milly goes and sets the tin and the newspaper on the kitchen counter and disposes of the wrapping paper in the trash. She comes back around the counter, smiling, and Carol comes from one of the back rooms, wearing new Levis and a white blouse, shoving limp, dark hair out of her face. Her eyes have tunnels and her makeup looks hurried. 'Oh, hi,' she says.

'Good morning.' Pierre makes his voice cheerful, still rotates the brim of his hat through his fingers. 'Are we ready?'

Carol doesn't answer. He and Milly wait as she turns her back to them, goes behind the kitchen counter, opens a cabinet and rummages through it before taking her purse off the counter and slinging the strap over her shoulder.

'Okay,' she says, coming around the counter.

Pierre nods and pushes the door open.

Sitting across the table from them at Fred's Diner, his Stetson on the coat rack, Pierre has nothing to tell them but what he learned about Winslow Homer on NPR, a Civil War illustrator who abandoned the medium for painting; how he made direct and realistic American scenes against splendid senses of color – as in leaves, as in storms of sea. Carol and Milly watch him with patient, bland gazes. He then tells them what he remembers from the NPR interview this morning with the American ballet director, how the kids have to begin training when they're six and dedicate their lives to dance.

'Imagine spending all that time and then not making it,' Carol says.

'You could still dance,' Pierre offers.

The waitress brings the food and Carol doesn't answer. She looks tired. Pierre isn't sure she wants to be here. As if on cue, Milly begins to tell him about Steffi Graf and Martina Navritilova in the recent Virginia Slims Classic, the Serve and Volley, and the upcoming city tournament on Saturday, over her chicken and pasta. 'Low fat and high protein,' she tells him.

'I've got a new serve,' she says, grinning as she chews. 'A big swing that packs a wallop.'

Pierre carefully paces his bites of steak so as not to take his attention away. Carol stirs Sweet and Low in her iced tea while Milly tells him about the two matches she won this week on the high school tennis team. Milly covers the high points. Her coach, she says, wants her to Serve and Volley more. Pierre is grateful for Milly's excited eyes and face. He still doesn't understand half the terms. 'What's the difference between Steffi and Martina's games?' he asks. 'Oh, wow,' Milly exclaims and begins to tell him. Pierre glances at Carol, who's quiet, has barely touched her salad and sips her iced tea.

'You're not hungry?' Pierre asks.

Carol shakes her head.

'Are you going to the tournament?' he asks.

'Mom always goes,' Milly answers.

Carol sighs, looks at Milly and smiles.

Pierre tries a small smile, too.

When Pierre noticed Carol three cars ahead of him in line to the ATM, it had been four months since Laura had left him. Carol looked tired then, too; in a dented, sun-blanched Toyota, and wearing a work jacket and hair net from her shift at the mill. He watched her hang an arm out the driver's window, her look seeing nothing. He had heard she was divorced again. He studied her corroded dent, her slanted rear bumper, and her faded bumper sticker that read: *SHIT HAPPENS*. The feeling of waste engulfed him again. He was old. He no longer had a son or a wife, horses, or his job as an EMT and fireman. The years of feigning indifference at Carol, of not speaking, of seeing her turn her head whenever he saw her about town – was cruel and stupid. Pierre bit his lip, got out of his Wagoner, and riveting his eyes on her for fear she might get away, walked to her car. Her profile in the hair net was that of a small, old woman. Carol looked his way and recognized him coming on a double take. She touched her hair and glanced about. At the last moment, she looked away and shielded her face with her hand as he squatted at her door.

'What do you want?' she hissed. 'Go away.'

'Please – ,' said Pierre. It was in his tone. Like with horses, he realized later, when a tone means more than words. He must have repeated it. Carol lowered her hand and turned to him. The car in front went through the ATM. The pickup behind them began sounding its horn.

'Let me see her,' Pierre said. 'It's been long enough.'

She seemed to be holding her breath and studying him. Pierre recognized the old freckle on her nose. He saw a tired mouth and crows' feet around her eyes.

'All right, Mr. Goodwin,' Carol swallowed and nodded. 'All right.' It came like a sigh. 'But,' she added, 'don't you tell nothing.'

Milly finishes eating and asks to be excused.

'No dessert?' Pierre says, looking at her eyes.

Milly shakes her head, smiles. 'Thank you, no. Weight,' she says. She's trim and pretty. Pierre thinks she couldn't be prettier.

Carol lets Milly out of the booth and slides back in. Pierre watches Carol's face follow Milly to the Ladies Room.

'You okay?' Pierre says.

'I went out and partied too much last night,' Carol says. She props her purse on the table and rummages for her cigarettes and lighter.

74

'Where was Milly?'

'At home. Outside. Practicing her backhand against the side of the house.'

'At her age, do you think she should be left by herself?'

'Mind your own business, Pierre.'

He looks away, catches himself, then watches her light a cigarette and stare out the window by the booth.

'God,' she exhales smoke at the window, '*All* she cares about is tennis. It's all she talks about, all she does. She doesn't care about boys, make up, or even clothes.'

'We should be so lucky,' Pierre says.

Carol gives him a bland look. 'Yeah,' she admits. She shakes her head. 'I bought her a new racquet before she made the high school team, and we've had it restrung twice. Then there's shoes, shorts, the warm-up suit,' Carol shakes her head, 'now the coach tells me she's good and needs to go to tennis camp, even a tennis *school*.' She hinges the last word with cynicism. Carol pauses, takes a long draw on her cigarette. 'I told her we'd see, but it's out of the question. I can't afford it.'

'I can help,' Pierre says.

'It's not your concern, Pierre.'

'Why do you think I've been coming?'

She gives him the bland look again and takes a drag off her cigarette. 'I know why you come, Pierre. I know as well as you do.'

'Then why do you let me?' Pierre asks.

She averts her eyes to the window. Pierre wonders why she is uncomfortable, if she is jealous.

'She likes you,' Carol offers after an awkward pause, her tone softer.

'Do you like me?'

Carol holds back a weary smile, waves him off with the cigarette in her hand. 'You'll do.'

'Is she mine?' Pierre says it. 'Is she Sted's?'

Carol's eyes go to the window and stare off. She cups her chin in her hand and sighs.

'I don't know.' It is almost a whisper. Her face grows sad. 'When Sted left me for Fort Bragg, I did it with anyone who got me stoned.'

She turns to him. 'You want a blood test?' she scoffs. 'What difference does it make? She's my daughter. I've brought her up.'

Pierre starts to speak, but stops. Before Carol's eyes he feels exposed.

'Pierre?' Milly says besides him in the front passenger's seat as they drive back to Carol's house. She pauses. 'You want to go to the tournament with Mom and me Saturday?'

Her eyes hold the question. She glances to Carol in the back seat for approval.

'If he wants to,' Pierre hears Carol after a moment, her tone qualifying.

'Of course,' Pierre answers. He manages a smile. Milly touches his arm and they both grin.

'I'll get a tan this week, buy some O.P. shorts and shirts, Italian sunglasses, prance around in the crowd and act like your manager,' Pierre says.

'Yeah,' Milly laughs. 'My manager. You can code me signals on strategy.'

'Sure.' Pierre hears his gratitude. 'What time?' he asks. 'I need to bring Gatorade or anything?'

'Three o'clock at the city courts,' Milly says. 'And just you.'

Pierre tries to contain his elation, his smile. He utters some inane statement about the weather this spring, almost runs a stop sign, then turns on the radio for Milly, but more to disguise himself. When he chances a glance at Carol in the rearview mirror, her look tells him nothing.

On the way home, Pierre drives by City Hall. In its way, it is like his decaying barn. It, too, has left him. The station has been painted. There is a new fire truck and also a larger EMT van. Soon after he retired, the talk, the work at City Hall became theirs and he was the bystander. He stopped going one morning and time flew. As Pierre brakes at the last stoplight, a black man walks by on the sidewalk before the Texaco Quick Mart. Pierre recognizes the slight swagger, the old suit coat. When the light changes, he drives slowly abreast to the man, pulls over to the curb and rolls down his passenger window.

'Hey, you old bag of bullshit.'

Ned turns, startled. Pierre laughs. Ned makes a slow, distant smile. His close-cropped hair is all white. His eyes are squinted and bloodshot.

'You might wonder,' Ned remarks. He makes a slight stagger, comes forward and leans on the Wagoner door.

Pierre stares him in. 'Hell, man,' he says. He checks his rearview mirror and opens the passenger door. 'Get in,' he says. 'The police'll lock you up.'

Ned obeys, gropes around the door and slumps into the seat. Once in, he seems to have no more energy. Pierre reaches across him, smelling cheap wine on the man's breath as he shuts the door. He looks in his mirrors and drives away. Ned gazes at the windshield.

'Got laid off at the mill,' Ned says simply. 'Work fourteen years and – ,' he waves a finger, 'gone.'

'I'm sorry,' Pierre manages. He doesn't know what else to say. He drives slowly for Ned's sake, fearing the doom evinced by Ned's presence. Pierre tries not to think. He drives over the railroad tracks and turns down a road before the intersection to the highway.

'I seen better days,' Ned says.

Pierre wants to grab him, shake him, but doesn't. He swallows and nods, holds his eyes on the road. When he does look at Ned, a single tear is running down the man's cheek.

Ned sweeps the back of his hand over his eyes and turns his face away. Pierre lets the Wagoner coast off the road to a stop. He places a hand on Ned's bony shoulder, but Ned won't turn. Pierre eventually drives on down the street to the unpainted house with marigolds and a sagging porch. No one seems to be home. He cuts the engine by the mailbox. He and Ned sit in silence.

'Where's Evonna?' Pierre says.

'She work,' Ned says. He turns a stolid face to the windshield.

At least you've got someone, Pierre thinks.

'Ned, don't drink,' Pierre says.

Ned nods, holding his stare.

'You need money?'

Ned shuts his eyes and shakes his head.

'You need work?'

'No,' Ned moans. 'No.' He opens his eyes. 'I ain't cleaning out no dead stalls.'

Pierre parks in the drive and goes into his house. The kitchen sink is full of a week's dishes and fine fuzz floats in the hallway as he goes by Sted's door and to his bedroom. He drops his Stetson on the dresser, kicks off the Florsheims, pulls off the suit and lays it on the rumpled bed. He finds a calico shirt from the closet, a pair of old Liberties and work boots. Dressed, he goes in the kitchen and turns on the receiver atop the counter, which he removed from Sted's room after Laura left. He finds a beer in the fridge and the carton of milk. The NPR commentator's voice follows him through the screened door to the back porch. He pours milk into the cats' bowl, sets the carton on the railing and eases himself into the wicker rocker, twisting open his beer and taking a deep, cold swallow to the beginning of *Eine Kleine Nachtmusik*. Beyond the yard and the field, which he now rents out, is the rotting barn growing shadows, and the cats seem to come running from the shed to the music.

Pierre can still see the barn inside, has dreamed of it; all motionless, in dust: stalls, cobwebs, 'dobber nests and Sted's tack trunk; bridles, halters and saddles hanging dry and stiff. It took six years for the practice ring to fall, eight more for Laura to leave. A year after Sted's death, he and Ned cried as Pierre sold Doc Roy and the mares and padlocked the barn doors. 'It's just going through motions,' Pierre tried to tell him.

'Guilt,' Laura said matter-of-factly, her face set in that resolve as when the three of them used to go to church. 'You loved them more than Sted,' she said. 'He only rode for you.'

Pierre never answered her. A hard, wrinkled contour set into her mouth; a gaunted look. At times, he tried to remember what she once looked like. He thought of how she used to make up her face, to wear new clothes, to care about her hair. Laura stayed, she said, because the minister told her to. But she did not give up her grief. Three months after he had retired, long after their lives had become a mere endurance and City Hall had been the place he could go, she announced at breakfast, while he was thinking about repainting the house, 'Pierre, I can't stand you by yourself.' She quit her job at the dentist's office and her brother came up from Mobile. She rented a U-Haul truck. Pierre stood by as the two of them took what she wanted. She took all that was hers and every picture of Sted, except the one of him in uniform. When Laura said goodbye on the porch, it was with a face made dull by hardness. Pierre wanted to say he was sorry. After all the years, he could only nod. He watched them drive away and she did not look back.

Tuesday night, Pierre washes the dishes in the kitchen sink and thinks about getting out the ironing board to iron shirts. NPR resonates with Italian Opera. Looking at the dingy floor tile, he can't remember when it was mopped. He doesn't know when he'll get to that. Drying his hands on a dish towel while the dishwater drains, he's trying to remember what else needs to be ironed when the wall phone rings. It's Milly.

'Hi, Pierre.'

He feels a sinking in his stomach. 'Milly, what a surprise. What are you doing?'

'Nothing.' She pauses. He steels for the letdown. For some reason, he sees Carol and Milly driving up in Carol's Toyota and walking up to his front door. He hasn't been in the living room for months and he hasn't mowed the grass.

'So, what are you doing?' she says.

'I'm washing dishes, Sweetheart. Getting ready to iron some clothes.'

'Eeu,' Milly says. 'Mom can't go,' she adds. 'She says she has to work.'

'Has to work?' Pierre echoes.

'You still want to go?'

'I wouldn't miss it for anything.'

'Okay,' her voice brightens.

'I won't interfere with your game, will I?' Pierre says.

'No. I don't think of anything when I'm playing. Maybe I'll play extra hard for you.'

'No, no,' Pierre says. 'Don't play for me. Just play for you.'

Pierre is worked up when he phones on Thursday afternoon. It is after Carol's shift. Milly is at tennis practice. 'You old fool,' Carol says. She sounds slow and thick, like awakened from a nap. 'It's going to be all right.'

'You sure?' Pierre says. The phone to his ear, he looks over his kitchen, the cleared counter, the clean, shiny sink and linoleum floor. 'I want to help,' he says. 'If you don't have the time, I will. If you don't have the money, I do …Let's send her to tennis camp. What do you say?'

'Whoa,' Carol says.

'It's going to take a lot of work to get her where she wants to go,' Pierre continues.

'Whoa, Pierre. My daughter's not a show horse.'

'I know,' Pierre tries to moderate his eagerness. 'I just – '

'What if I say no to your partnership, Pierre? To my daughter becoming a Steffi Graf? Another Sted?'

'I'm just saying…I…' Pierre covers the speaker end of the phone, closes his eyes and takes a deep breath. He can feel his heart pounding. 'I'm just saying that I…I *love* Milly,' he blurts into the phone. 'So, stop treating me like a bitch.'

The phone is silent. He wonders if she is overwhelmed, if the line is dead. He imagines Carol's face going deadpan, her voice coming hard.

'You know…' he starts into the phone, afraid she's not there, or will hang up, 'when Sted was alive…' He lets it die, and hears only his breathing. Then a voice beside him, about to crack, begins to gush words.

'– I thought I loved horses. What I loved was Sted. He was my center. When he wanted to go, I let him go. When he died, something in me died, too.'

'Milly is not Sted,' Carol's voice comes.

'I know,' Pierre says. 'I know. But she's alive.'

'Hello?' Pierre says. 'Hello?'

'I'll think about it,' Carol says, and hangs up.

Saturday morning, wearing old painter's overalls, a t-shirt and loafers, Pierre runs his clothes and sheets in the washer and dryer, and sweeps and vacuums the hallway to a turned-up discussion on Braque and Picasso, and then a Vivaldi concerto on NPR. He enters the front living room that he has not seen for months: still furniture and mirrors with Sted's military picture, dark and somehow remote, on the mantle above the fireplace.

He tries not to think as he pulls back the drapes and light enters the room in a myriad of floating fuzz. He begins to dust with Laura's old cleaning rags. He quickly wipes the mantel, lifting and replacing Sted's picture, not looking at the face as he wipes the glass, avoiding his own reflection in the mirror.

81

Vivaldi flows from the kitchen. He tries to whistle to it; he can't. All he ever wanted from NPR was a mellifluous sound. Pierre drags the vacuum cleaner in from the hall and finds a socket for the plug. The sudden, violent roar blocks out everything. He pushes the Hoover, grateful for its drowning out NPR, the washer and dryer, the phone should it ring with Milly or Carol telling him he need not go.

By two fifteen, Pierre has the phone off the hook and his hands tremble. He has dressed and nicked his throat twice while shaving, dabbing the bleeds with small tears of toilet paper. He decided on the same loafers, tan slacks, a white polo shirt and a blue blazer to disguise his waist. The Stetson is a no-no. Leaving the house, Pierre goes back to turn off Sted's receiver. Back out in the sunlight, Pierre realizes the idea of sunglasses is no joke. He finds an old pair in a kitchen drawer. Squinting outside in the sun, Pierre fogs the lenses with his breath, rubs them on his shirt and tries them on. Everything is gray-green. He sees himself in the Wagoner side mirror: an aging man with fallen cheeks. The frames can't fake it.

Pierre falls behind a new Ford pickup onto Chickasaw Street. As he parks at the curb before Carol's house, the pickup turns into Carol's drive and stops behind her Toyota. Pierre stares. Carol is in it with a dark headed man he doesn't know. A swift pang seizes him. He lets it subside with the motor running, and gripping the steering wheel. The man is young with a lean face and a dark shirt. Pierre sees Carol lean over and kiss him before she gets out and runs into the house, wearing old jeans and a silk screened t-shirt.

Pierre waits dumbly and the pickup remains in the drive until Carol comes out of the house, smiling, her purse slung over her shoulder. She glances about the yard and stops. Carol pauses, cocks her hair behind one ear; and then waves at him, motioning away from the house, a broad smile on her face, something forming on her lips. He understands the intent before he understands the word, his relief so immediate, he laughs. *Courts* he reads her lips. He waves and checks his watch. The man in the truck has turned to look at him. Pierre waves to him, too, and speeds away.

Pierre turns into the gravel parking lot before the asphalt courts, across from the baseball field where Sted used to play. There are cars, station wagons, and a van beside a portable concession booth where two women are selling cold drinks and popcorn. He notices parents and children in the aluminum bleachers or about the grounds. Everyone is wearing bright, stylish cotton shirts with shorts or slacks, sunglasses and visors. Pierre parks and slowly gets out of the Wagoner. Through the green mesh on the fence, he sees the forms of players warming up on the courts and hears the rapid, muddled *wop*ping of tennis balls. He goes past the bleachers, buttoning and unbuttoning his blazer, nodding at people he doesn't know and looks for Milly through the mesh-less chain link gate. She's in the same orange warm up suit and new tennis shoes. When she sees him, she smiles, motions to her partner across the net to wait, lays down her racquet and comes sprinting easily behind the baselines, her ponytail bobbing.

'Sorry I'm late,' he mutters as she comes out from the gate.

'You came,' she says. Milly hugs him.

'Sir. *Sir*,' a stern query interrupts. They turn to a thin, brunette woman in a pleated tennis skirt and blouse, her face bent on authority, and posturing with a legal pad in her hands.

'I'm sorry. Only parents are allowed at the gate.' She studies Pierre. 'Are you a parent?'

'Er, no,' Pierre answers, 'I'm not.'

'My uncle,' Milly answers the woman, squeezing his arm.

'Oh,' the woman says. 'Well, you better hurry,' she motions to the bleachers with her pad.

'All right,' Pierre says, and the woman turns away. Milly shoots him a grin and squeezes his arm before she goes through the gate, sprints to her court and picks up her racquet.

Only Pierre can't leave. He stands and waits to see Milly's face become absorbed and intent; her light, orange body with its ponytail to step and move in its own rhythm – run, stop, and swing at oncoming tennis balls – and what to Pierre will be a solitary dance.

The Motherhead

I make the sounds in my head so Mom and Dad won't hear, shooting cars through the rear window of our Buick with the black plastic Luger Dad bought me at the filling station for being good. I pretend I'm Audie Murphy or Vic Morrow. I imagine cars on the highway exploding and drifting off the road in flames. In the front seat, Mother cries as we come into Tuscaloosa. She dabs at her eyes under the black veil with Dad's handkerchief while Dad says nothing behind the wheel, staring ahead, the muscles of his jaw tight, and his hat low over his eyes. I stop shooting and Mother takes her compact from her handbag, peeling the veil up and over her hat. Her blue eyes are bleary and red. The shiner stands out like a large purple plum on her cheek.

Mother lifted her veil this afternoon when they picked me up in the school parking lot, and we were 'going to Tuscaloosa again' – as Dad says during the week in his nagging voice when he and I are alone in the back yard, where he smokes Hav-A-Tampas and makes quiet and serious speeches to the holly bushes as I chase fireflies or shoot Yankees, Mexicans, or maybe Japs with a stick rifle or stick machine gun – 'So I can be with the Motherhead,' he mimics Mother's whine with a sneer. He gripes about taking off from work, about money going to Tuscaloosa; says there's going to be a surprise next time; says these things over and over – things not meant for Mother to hear.

Mother smiled when I climbed into the back seat after

85

school with my books and sweater, and made me kiss her on her good cheek like I did this morning after breakfast. I knew she had packed for us. She looked over her seat and asked about school, the shiner pinching up and down on her cheek as she talked.

'Why are you so quiet, honey?' She studied me with a steady smile, the car already too quiet as Dad started the engine, too heavy with Mother's ruby lips and nails, her hat and veil, and the sweet smell of Chanel Number Five my father gives her every year for her birthday.

I shrugged, not wanting to talk because Dad wouldn't. But Mother got me to by asking more questions: How was lunch? Miss Jones? My Math test? She kept at it until my eyes were on her and I had to answer her with short, single words like Dad would do. Mother smiled at my answers, her eyes said we would be all right, fine, normal; Dad's silly mood would come around, and I was just tired from school, and once we got to Tuscaloosa, we would act better; and she would feel better, too – once we were back with the Motherhead.

The stink of paper mills grows in the air. We go by stores, a cemetery, a dorm, and the football stadium. Dad huffs his breath as Mother turns the rearview mirror to inspect her face, re-line her lipstick, shoot herself a smile. Dad snatches the rearview back into place when she's through.

'Hayden, come here,' Mother says, pulling a comb out of her handbag. She turns and motions me up to the back of her seat, smiling for me to smile back. She begins to part my hair. 'We want to look nice,' she sings. 'Tuck in your shirt.'

I undo my belt, shove my shirt in, remembering the time in church when Dad grabbed Grandmother's arm to stop her from reaching down and pulling up the zipper of my Sunday pants. 'Woman,' he hissed through his teeth, turning people's heads in the pews around us, 'tell him to zip his own zipper.'

Mother finishes my hair, then turns and straightens in her seat. She puts everything into her handbag and carefully lowers the veil over her face as our Buick turns into the narrow alley crowded with houses. But she re-opens her handbag and pulls Dad's handkerchief to dab her eyes.

I reach over the seat and squeeze her shoulder. Mother makes a brave smile through the veil. Dad doesn't say anything. The alley is quiet, empty. No one is about as he turns the Buick before Grandmother's old white house and into the rutted gravel drive, stopping past the porch and before the garage and Grandpa's old red pickup. It's like before, everything is still. Mother stares out at the side of the house as Dad cuts the engine and sets her face serious, like when we are in church, about to pray or sing a hymn.

'All right, now, come on,' she nods to the house, gripping Dad's balled up handkerchief in one hand, the handle of her handbag in the other.

I tuck the Luger under my belt and we get out and shut car doors in the quiet, fading afternoon. Dad unbuttons his collar and tugs his tie loose, and we wait on Mother as she bends over and strokes wrinkles out of her dress. Dad lifts his hat and runs his fingers through his black hair. I catch him staring at Mother's rear end as he replaces his hat on his head. He looks off and around. I smother a laugh in my hand, and look off, too. Dad offers me a stick of Beeman's and I nod. He unwraps it for me, shoving the wrapper into his coat pocket. I take it, nod my thanks and chew, touching the Luger in my belt and keeping a lookout for Germans. 'Where's Grandpa?' I ask Dad.

He shakes his head, staring at Mother. 'I don't know,' Dad sighs and looks tired. Mother straightens and squares her shoulders. Her pumps crunch in the gravel toward the house.

Dad and I follow Mother as she turns on the lights in the high rooms of stained and cracked plaster, varnished furniture and dark, closed drapes. It's just like last week, and the weeks before: our slow parade in floating dust. In the family room, Mother flicks on the lights and her fingers make lines through the thin dust on the closed piano. I can remember Mother standing by the piano with a closed smile and Grandmother sitting large on the piano bench in a house dress, her head tilted back, and her mouth opened wide as she pounded the keys and sang 'When the Saints Go Marching In.'

The Motherhead is smiling in the center of the round dining table, just as we left it, standing on its neck in the cake pan mother gave the mortician when he brought the head back after the funeral. Grandmother's smile is frozen with big shiny teeth, red lips, loud rouge; the way the mortician made her up. Her silver hair is bright and stiff. Her large, wet and black eyes see you wherever you are in the room.

Dad and I stand off and Mom lifts her veil and carefully removes her hat so as not to mess her blonde perm, smiling as if to match the smile on the head. She goes and brushes something off Grandmother's forehead with her fingers.

'There,' she says. She lays her purse and hat in a dining chair and surveys the room, the tall mirror above the cupboard, the matching china cabinet and the armoire.

'There,' she says. She turns to Grandmother's head and steps back, smiling. It's as if the two smiles are drawing from each other.

Dad and I watch. We have done this many times. Dad parts his coat and shoves his hands into his trouser pockets. He forgot to remove his hat when he came in. I draw my Luger and go to the hallway to make sure the place is clear of burglars, sidle up to the opened doorway, peek right, then left, like Peter Gunn on TV. The hall's dark and empty. The phone is in the wall nook by Grandmother's empty easy chair. I fall back into the kitchen. It's empty, too; the counters bare and clean, a plate and a glass in the sink.

In the dining room, my parents' backs are turned to each other. Mother studies her reflection in the mirror, touching her hair; Dad has his hands deep in his pockets, seeming to study the framed pictures of Grandmother's Chihuahuas lined on the opposite wall. His nostrils twitch; he keeps shifting his feet.

'I'm going outside,' Dad finally says with a quick nod to Mother, and he leaves through the living room.

'All right, Tate,' Mom drawls and doesn't turn from the mirror. It's one of those things Dad must do, go outside, be by himself, and smoke a Hav-A-Tampa.

'Hayden?' Mother sings, her eyes finding me in the mirror before I can say Dad's words, too.

'Yes, Ma'am?'

'Haven't I told you not to chew gum in the house?'

'Yes, Ma'am.' I spit it out into my hand.

'Go find where grandfather is,' she says, high and whee-dling. She studies her face from side to side, the shiner flashing in the mirror: now, you see it; now, you don't.

'Tell him I'm here,' she says.

'Okay.'

I back out of the room, my other hand holding my gun, toward the hallway, and watch her back, imagining that if she turns and looks at me, I'm doomed.

I flush the gum down the toilet, and in the hallway, two old-time gangsters like in *The Untouchables* on TV ambush me with machine guns. I shoot them and continue down the hall. Grandpa is in the guest room at the back of the house where he has been every weekend since the funeral: sitting in his rocker, staring out the window, or building bird houses at the work desk next to his bed.

'Y'all here *again*?' he looks up from his desk. The pinups of naked women and calendar girls in swim suits that Mother tore down last week have been mended with scotch tape and are back up on the walls. Wood shavings speck Grandpa's white hair, his glasses; cover his t-shirt and denim overalls.

'Hi, Grandpa.' I tuck my Luger into my belt. Grandpa turns back to nailing roof tile onto a blue bird house with a small hammer. Bird houses of different shapes and colors hang from wires in the ceiling. Unfinished bird houses, tools, and wood shavings litter the floor. Dirty clothes are piled high on the unmade bed, the floor, and the opened dresser. Outside the windows, into the back yard, bird houses hang off every limb of the large pecan tree. They sway or turn in the breeze like mis-matched ornaments.

'Got a Norwegian model here,' Grandpa winks.

Before I can say anything, Grandpa stops hammering and stares out the window over his desk. 'Drat,' he yells, jumping up, dropping the hammer, and opening a desk drawer. He whips out a pistol, heavy and steel, and I stare as he opens the room's door to the back stoop, aims outside and fires. *BOOM.* Bark flies off the pecan tree. A squirrel dashes around the trunk and disappears.

'Damn squirrel!' Grandpa yells as he lowers the pistol. 'Runs my birds off!'

'Hayden! Pop!' Mother shrills from the other end of the house.

Grandpa turns. He and I look at each other. 'I forgot about her,' he says.

Mother's footsteps sound up the hallway. Grandpa tosses the pistol back into the desk drawer and closes it, sending me a nervous grin.

'What are you boys doing?' Mother cries, coming into the room, her face stern and curious. She's wearing Grandmother's large red pinafore apron with pockets. She has taken off the high heels and put on worn moccasins.

'Hey, Mom,' I say, and I smother a laugh in my hand.

'Oh, my god,' Mother takes in the room. Her hands rise slowly and rest on her hips. '*Poppa*,' she scolds. Grandpa's smile turns sheepish. He looks at his feet.

Mother goes and yanks one of the pin ups, letting it fall to the floor. 'And why haven't you kept mother's head covered?' Mom demands.

'I forgot,' Grandpa shrugs. He keeps his eyes on his feet and hooks his thumbs inside his overall straps. 'I don't go out there much.'

'You owe her at least *that*,' Mother's eyes blaze. 'After all she's done for you.'

Grandpa doesn't answer, holds his eyes on his feet and runs his thumbs up and down the inside of his straps.

Mother sighs and shakes her head. 'Here I come all this way to fix dinner, clean house...and this room's a mess,' she says.

Grandpa glances up at her and then looks back to his feet. 'You don't have to clean it,' he says.

'Oh, yes *I* do,' she dismisses him with a wave of her hand. '*Somebody* has to.' She picks up the pillow on Grandpa's bed and begins stuffing it with her fist. 'It won't get cleaned if I don't,' she says, becoming annoyed.

She drops the pillow on the bed and stares at Grandpa, letting a hand rise to her ear, a finger slide over to her shiner. Grandpa doesn't notice and she lets her hand drop.

'I've got to vacuum this floor and wash these clothes,' Mom says, taking in the room. 'Then put down clean bed sheets.'

'Umm, clean sheets,' Grandpa echoes. He looks up at her, then back to his feet. 'Your Momma did that for me,' he says. He turns teary eyed.

Mother sighs, makes a small smile, goes by me and around the bed to Grandpa, slipping her arm through his.

'There, now,' she says, brushing wood shavings from his hair. Grandpa gets choked up. They put their arms around each other.

'You are too good,' Grandpa says. 'You are too good.'

They break. Grandpa wipes his eyes and Mother smiles.

'What happened to your face?' Grandpa says.

Mother blushes, turns shy. 'Oh,' she says, 'it's nothing, a

silly accident.' She gives Grandpa a brave smile, and they hug.

They have forgotten about me. I watch them hug and think that if they leave, I might get the pistol out of the drawer, wave it around, and aim it out of the windows. Then, for some reason, I imagine walking into the kitchen, like Little Joe Cartwright does in *Bonanza* when he goes into a bar, and shooting mother at the stove. Dad would throw away his cigar and come running into the house; Grandpa would come hobbling in as fast as he could from a nap on the sofa. They would brush by me into the kitchen and stand gaping over her limp body with its sweet smile on the linoleum floor. They would kneel, unsure of themselves, and afraid to touch. 'Call somebody,' they would cry out, before they realized that I was holding the gun. They would stare at me, then at her, and begin to gasp, wringing their hands, looking down at her body, and feeling helpless or guilty, or both. Mother would lay there with that sweet smile, in a neat puddle of blood – somehow, I think she would like that. Later, I would have to run and hide from Grandpa, Dad, and the Law all my life; keep running away, looking over my shoulder, just like the Fugitive on TV – do odd jobs and always wear a windbreaker.

Outside is dusk. I hold my Luger at ready and creep around the back yard, stepping out into the drive where Dad is smoking the stub of a Hav-A-Tampa, leaning against the dark front fender, his coat parted and his hat low over his eyes. His look seems to go through me. A squashed cigar butt is at his feet in the gravel. The chrome of the car reflects the last of the evening light.

'Hayden,' Dad says with an edge in his voice, and pushes the brim of his hat up with his thumb as he looks off, 'what is your mother doing?' He draws on the cigar stub and his stomach makes a long, slow growl. I look at him and pretend to smoke, too, with an imaginary cigar in my fingers.

'She's fixing dinner,' I answer. 'And Grandpa's cleaning up.'

'I bet he is,' Dad remarks with a small scowl. It's like in the evenings in our back yard at home. Dad wants to talk to me, more to himself, sneering as he smokes. He will get all worked up.

But he stops himself. He stands up off the car and turns to me.

'Did Grandpa see her face?' he studies me and the cigar stops just short of his mouth.

I nod.

'What did he say?' Dad's eyes grow wide.

'Oh, he's upset,' I say.

'He is?'

'Yeah.' I have Dad watching me. 'He's *real* upset.' I scowl it like Dad would and expect his laugh.

Dad grabs my arm, jerks me to him, making me drop my Luger. His face comes down, twisted, breathing hot and smoky into mine. 'Don't get smart,' he says.

I stare at him and nod fast.

Dad lets go, steps back, straightens, and blinks. He pauses, takes a deep breath and then tries a grin. 'Here, Hayden,' he says, his voice too friendly. He digs into his pocket with his free hand, comes out with a quarter in his palm.

'Go on,' he says.

I shake my head.

'Go on.' He shoves it toward me and waits with a grin. His stomach makes another long growl. I pick the quarter up off his palm.

'Thanks,' I mumble. I drop the quarter into my pocket, pick up my Luger and go running up the drive toward the front porch and shrubbery, keeping my back to him, my cheeks hot, my heart pounding. I blink fast to hold the tears back.

The overhead porch light comes on and Mother comes to the screened door and peers out at the yard and the alley.

'Hey, Mom,' I fake cheer.

She gives me a smile, disappears into the house. I wipe my eyes on my sleeves. Behind me, Dad is walking around the Buick, smoking fast. I can tell he's making a speech to himself by the small motions he makes with his hands. I get my breath and grip my Luger. I make myself search for Germans in the shrubbery. Mother comes to the screened door again and looks out. Her face breaks into a smile. I follow her look to a one-headlight car coming down the alley. I back into the shrubbery with my Luger and hide as Uncle Larry's car turns in and brakes before the porch. In the glow of the porch light, thin smoke rises from under the hood and I can see the green paint brush strokes that cover the car.

Uncle Larry waves to Mom as he cuts the one light and the engine. He's in his yellow sanitation uniform from work, but without his cap, his dirty blonde hair swept behind his ears; and Aunt Louisa is with him this time, looming large in the back seat, her big nose, her flabby arms crossed, and her long and straight dark hair loose about her shoulders. Aunt Louisa's lips are pressed into a line. She stares at Uncle Larry's back as Grandpa and Mother come out onto the porch, Grandpa cleaned up now, in an old brown suit with matching shoes and no tie; Mother smiling and wiping her hands on her apron.

Uncle Larry jumps out of the car in his work boots. He's stick thin with a small nose. He smiles broadly as he opens the back door for Aunt Louisa.

'I knew you wouldn't miss Marlene's meal,' Grandpa says with a laugh. He puts his arms around the column by the porch swing and leans out toward the car, grinning and winking at Uncle Larry. Mother smiles and clasps her hands together. Aunt Louisa sits frozen in the back of the car with her arms crossed and her mouth set.

Uncle Larry smiles. 'C'mon, now, Lou,' Uncle Larry pleads under his breath, holding the car door open. He waves to Dad, who looks on in the almost dark, smoking from our car. 'Hey, Tate,' Uncle Larry says.

'Oh, c'mon Lou,' Mother supports Uncle Larry from the porch in a sweet song voice. 'C'mon inside and eat.'

Uncle Larry makes a laugh and smiles at Mom. 'C'mon, Lou,' he says. He and Mother smile at each other and begin sing-saying the words, '*C'mon Lou, c'mon Lou,*' as Grandpa leans out from the column and grins.

It goes for on about a minute, Mother from the porch and Uncle Larry holding the car door open. Aunt Louisa shuts her eyes. She finally opens them, uncrosses her arms, bows her head and offers a hand out the door to Uncle Larry. Uncle Larry and Mom stop chanting as he takes her hand in both of his, braces in the gravel with his boots and pulls. Aunt Lou's head and leg come out first. She's so big, she barely fits through the door. When she heaves out, the back of the car rises like a sigh of relief.

Mother claps and Uncle Larry and Grandpa smile as Aunt Lou straightens and tosses her hair over her shoulders. Aunt Lou's in a large red sweatshirt, wide tan slacks and sandals. When she turns toward Mother and Grandpa on the porch, she holds her head high, so as not to see them. Uncle Larry sweeps his fallen hair behind his ears, shuts the door and follows Aunt Lou's slow march to the porch. That's when I jump out of the shrubbery with my Luger and my meanest sneer. '*Ka-pow! Ka-pow!*' I shoot them.

Aunt Lou stops and snorts. Uncle Larry jumps in surprise and clutches his chest. 'You got me!' he winks. He play punches my ribs and messes my hair. I grin and push my hair back and I follow them up onto the porch, where Mother and Uncle Larry hug and get teary-eyed and Aunt Louisa stands off to one side with a frown. Uncle Larry sniffs when he and Mother break. 'I miss – ,' he says, but can't finish. Mother's smile understands. Grandpa gives Aunt Lou a smile. He and Uncle Larry hug. Mother wipes her eyes on her apron, goes and puts her arms around Aunt Lou. But Aunt Lou doesn't put her arms around Mother.

'Lou,' Mother says, 'I'm so glad you came.'

'Like hell you are,' says Aunt Lou.

'Now, Lou,' Mother steps back with a smile. She gives me a look. I put my Luger in my belt and go and put my arms around Aunt Lou the best I can. But Aunt Lou doesn't move.

'Well, I'm hungry,' Grandpa announces with a grin.

'We're ready,' Mother beams. She looks to Grandpa, then Uncle Larry. She touches her shiner.

'I noticed that,' Uncle Larry says. 'What happened?'

'Oh,' Mother lowers her hand. 'A silly accident.' She makes that brave smile. 'It doesn't hurt much now.'

Grandpa smiles and Uncle Larry hugs her again. 'You are too sweet,' Uncle Larry says. 'You are just too sweet.'

'Well, *sweetie*,' Aunt Lou announces, and everyone turns to her, 'your mother said I wasn't welcome in her house.' Aunt Lou marches to the wooden bench swing in the corner, and turns and lowers herself into the seat. The swing creaks as it takes her and the chains connecting it to the ceiling hum tight.

'Oh, now, Lou, she did not,' Mother says.

Grandpa and Uncle Larry look on and say nothing. Aunt Lou gives Mother a mean look. She swings her loose hair over her shoulders with a jerk of her head, crosses her arms and stares off.

'Now, Lou,' Mother says.

Aunt Lou doesn't answer. Uncle Larry makes a nervous laugh, looks to Mom, then to Aunt Lou.

'Oh, come on,' Mother's voice fades. She sighs and shakes her head. 'All right, then,' she warns and gives up. She looks at Grandpa, then me.

'You give me that,' Mother says, snatching the Luger out of my hand before I can protest. 'We don't play at dinner.' Mother drops it into her apron pocket, gives Aunt Lou a last look, puts her hands on my shoulders and steers me toward the door.

'C'mon,' Mother says to the men.

Grandpa and Uncle Larry hesitate and follow us inside. Uncle Larry comes in last, catching the screened door and looking back at Aunt Lou.

'Don't worry,' Grandpa says with a knowing wink and a grin. 'They'll get hungry. She and Tate – they'll both get hungry.'

The steady creaking of the porch swing sounds throughout the house while mother finishes setting the food on the dining table and pouring iced tea in all the glasses. The places are all set. Mother has lined the cake pan under Grandmother's head with jonquils from the garden. She has washed her hands and left her apron in the kitchen and Uncle Larry, Grandpa, and I have washed up in the bathroom. We seat ourselves with Mother before Grandmother's head at the table, that is smiling through the steam of her dishes, her bowls, her platters of food. Two chairs are empty: one by me, and one by Mother. We bow our heads with Mother to pray as Dad comes into the dining room from the back of the house. He stands waiting while she says Grace, his coat over one arm, his sleeves rolled up. When Mother says 'Amen,' she looks up with a closed smile.

Dad removes his hat, glances about and nods to everyone. He drops his hat and coat into a corner chair, stands and looks at Mother. His hands won't stay still. He shoves them into his trouser pockets. Grandpa shakes his head at him and grins.

'Go wash up,' Mother says.

Dad nods and leaves down the hallway. We wait before Grandmother's smiling head and the steaming food. Grandpa hums softly to himself while Mother sits with a small, patient smile. Uncle Larry's eyes shift around and Aunt Lou creaks from the porch. Dad comes back, his face damp, his hair wet and combed. 'Sorry,' he mumbles and offers a grin. He takes the chair next to me. I don't look at him as he sits down.

'I'm going to get Lou,' Uncle Larry says.

'No,' Mother's eyes stop him, her voice slow and stern. 'She knows where to find us.'

Uncle Larry makes a nervous grin and stays in his seat. He looks at Dad, then Mother. He runs his fingers over his ears.

Grandpa makes a low chuckle and Uncle Larry gives him an annoyed look. 'What's so funny?' he says.

'Nothing,' Grandpa says, sadly. 'I'm the one with no warm bed.'

In the steady creaking from the porch, we follow Mother's lead and put our napkins into our laps, begin to pass the food, serve ourselves and eat.

'Pass the biscuits,' Dad says to me. I ignore him. Uncle Larry hands him the basket of biscuits.

The food is good and everyone is hungry, except Uncle Larry. The creaking from the porch continues steady as a clock and he begins to squirm in his seat. He only serves himself a piece of chicken and then looks down at his plate.

'I'd better go check on her,' he says quickly, starting to rise from the table.

'You stay right there,' Mother warns, her voice sharp like Grandmom's. She stares Uncle Larry down over Grandmother's head, pausing to serve herself lima beans. Uncle Larry makes a quiet laugh and sits down. He looks at everyone, then Grandmother's head, and hesitates as he takes the mashed potatoes and serves himself. Grandpa watches him with a sad, bemused look as he picks up his iced tea and sips.

'Will you pass the butter?' Dad says to me. I pretend not to hear him and keep looking away.

Dad waits. 'Did you hear me?' he says. I don't move. Grandpa passes him the butter.

We're quiet while we eat. The creaking continues. Uncle Larry stares down at his plate and sighs. 'I'd better go,' he says.

A forkful of black eyed peas stops halfway to Mother's mouth. 'Larry,' she warns.

Uncle Larry doesn't look at her; he rises, drops his napkin on the table and leaves toward the porch.

Mother stares after him, lowering her fork, and Grandpa makes a sad chuckle. Grandpa, Dad, and I keep eating, our eyes down. The front screened door whines and slams shut.

'Go get him,' Mother says.

Dad looks up from his plate to Grandpa, Mother, and then to me. I look away.

He pauses. 'Which one of us?' he says, waiting for Mother to reply.

The Transcendence
of
'Speedy' Joe Kinnard

On a fall night in Fermata Bend, Alabama, on worn turf and under blazing field lights, junior tailback 'Speedy' Joe Kinnard of the Fermata Bend High Raiders took his last and eighteenth handoff over left guard, breaking one tackle, colliding full speed and head down into two Burnsfield High linebackers, and into an oblivion of unconsciousness from which he never returned.

The resounding *crack* of the three helmets and the ensuing stillness of the fallen players stopped everyone. The other players in the play rose and looked on, the cheerleaders forgot their cheer, the home band forgot to play the fight song, and the referees began motioning for assistance even as the trainers were running across the field. The spectators stood and went into a pall and Josiah 'Tee' Reed, play-by-play announcer of local radio WXFBR in the press box, above and behind the pine seedlings and bleachers, was the first to say something for the record.

'Hold up, folks,' he said into the mike. 'Kinnard still down on the play...on the seventeen of Burnsfield...two Eagle tacklers down, too...now being helped up *real* slow.' Tee Reed stalled, reiterated the score and the time: Fermata Bend leading Burnsfield twenty-six to nineteen in Raider Stadium on this Thursday night, with what appeared to be a first down and three fifty-one left to go in the fourth quarter. Tee Reed ran off Speedy's stats: 113 yards in 18 carries, two touchdowns, catching two of three passes for 19 yards; three punt receptions for 23 yards and one lost fumble.

'And *that* was a whale of a hit, ladies and gentlemen,' Tee Reed added. 'This is what you hate to see,' he said, realizing that line had been used countless times as the ambulance went flashing its lights across the field and the people still standing in the bleachers shifted their feet and craned their necks for a better view. Some gasped. And some made utterances like, 'Oh, my God.'

Reverend Paul Stephenson, head pastor of the First Baptist Church, a team booster and a regular sideline guest of the coaching staff, felt compelled to run across the field with head coach Jackie Gibbs after the trainer. The two white, middle-aged men in blue 'Raider' jackets reached the other side as the trainer jumped up, yelling for the ambulance. The minister and coach stopped and stared upon the lanky, supine form of a mahogany football player in royal blue helmet, pants and jersey bearing the bold white numbers '32' and stretched out with hands clapped to his sides as if prepared for the casket. The chin in its strap was jutted up to the night sky and a thin, eerie, beatific smile spread the smooth mahogany face in a catatonic stare of half-closed, unblinking green eyes that seemed to be taking in something beyond the field lights, the night or even the world. Reverend Stephenson couldn't find words. 'Sweet Jesus,' Coach Gibbs whispered.

The paramedics out of the ambulance were too absorbed in their urgent work to take note, kneeling over the limp figure, cutting off the blue jersey, the shoulder pads and the face mask and administering CPR; but the rigid face in the tilted helmet froze everyone else: the on-looking football players, the reverend, the coach, the officials, the trainers, the people nearby in the Visitors' Stands. The upturned and transfixed face of the football player seemed larger than life, radiant and trans-mundane against the thin turf. His face was, as three Burnsfield mothers later observed, so compelling, eerie and serene, so alluring that one could not turn away.

'I thought he became an angel,' said a little girl. 'He was seeing heaven,' said another. 'It was a face like he'd had his first lay,' a referee commented. 'Man, what a way to go,' a teammate shook his head. 'What a way to go.' Coach Gibbs wanted to believe the look was from an ideal team player, elated to have made a first down. He tried to calculate the time remaining, who the backup would be, and what play to run – until the expression on the face so captivated him that he forgot. To Reverend Stephenson, who continued staring on the face of a boy he had not thought of or looked at more than three times among the throng of Fermata Bend High football players, 'It was the look of divinity,' he confessed three days later with slow and careful emphasis to the rapt attention of his congregation, having gone since the incident without sleep, standing pallid and solemn at the pulpit, and after giving a moving and melodious sermon about a particular black boy, a 'Speedy' Joe Kinnard from Fermata Bend, whom he had never known, would never know, but whom he would never forget, nor hope to, 'and,' the reverend paused with a brave smile, 'in whose face God revealed to me the transcendence of the self towards heaven.'

'Speedy' Joe Kinnard was airlifted posthaste by Air Ambulance from the Escatawpa County Hospital to the Emergency Medical Center in Birmingham, but he arrived DOA. The Coroner's Report later stated that the cause of death was a result of 'traumatic impact and hemorrhaging to the front cranial area, possibly over a former injury...and an injury as severe as those found in car crashes.' The report detailed a 'rather bizarre and fixed expression on the victim's face' as could only be explained by the 'severe contortions of locked facial muscles and nerves...the complexion being somewhat lightened from loss of blood upon the exertion and trauma,' and despite everything the medical team attempted to save the boy's life, 'the face had remained fixed and constant.'

In the early hours of Friday morning, the Escatawpha County Hospital Desk Nurse telephoned and awakened Police Chief Edwin Casey at his home, asking him to locate the football player's family with the grim news. The nurse explained that Miss Kinnard had arrived at the hospital after the Air Lift in rubber boots, a warm-up suit, and a threadbare poncho, but then had abruptly left, after revealing that she had no telephone, and leaving an inadequate address. The nurse had called Coach Gibbs, the high school counselor, as well as every black minister in town, but no one knew where the Kinnards stayed.

Chief Casey told the desk nurse he would take care of it. He rose from bed and dressed in his uniform. He called and awakened the Head of Fermata Bend Sanitation, Steve Holland, at his home, who, yes, thought he knew where a Miss Kinnard was on the edge of the Needmore side of town, having seen number '32' jerseys on a clothesline. He recalled an iron washtub in the yard and a mean, three-legged dog. Chief Casey jotted down the directions, thanked him, and then telephoned Coach Jackie Gibbs.

'I was at the hospital,' Coach Gibbs said to the Chief.

'I know, Coach,' the Chief said, 'I know. But I thought you and I should go tell the family in person.'

The line went silent. 'Coach?' Chief Casey said. 'Coach?'

'Oh, God,' Coach Gibbs said.

Chief Casey picked up Coach Gibbs in his coach's cap and blue 'Raider' jacket at the curb in front of his house. The two men rode in a heavy silence through the dark morning in the patrol car to a small, paneled shack on the Needmore side of town. The car's headlights revealed burnt trash in the yard and a barking, three-legged dog tied to a tree. Leaving the headlights on, Chief Casey and Coach Gibbs got out of the car, shut doors, and walked up the front steps. The chief paused and glanced at Coach Gibbs. He knocked on the door for some minutes and called Miss Kinnard's name over the barking of the dog. A single light came on from inside, through the plastic covered windows. 'Yes?' a woman whined.

'Miss Kinnard, ma'am? This is Chief Casey.'

The door opened. The coach and the chief removed their caps. 'Miss Kinnard –' Chief Casey began and stopped before the wide-eyed stare of the older, plump woman in the doorway, in a hair net, cheap cotton sweats and a short bathrobe. 'Miss Kinnard,' the Chief said. 'It's my sad duty to tell you...'

The Chief had to repeat the news three times. 'But they only knocked Joey down,' the woman stared in a daze at the white men, each one kneading a cap in his hands. 'They only knocked Joey down,' her voice grew shrill. Then Miss Kinnard wanted to be certain which son it was.

'Speedy,' both men answered.

'Er, no. Joe,' Coach Gibbs said. 'Joe.'

'Joey?' the woman cried, her mouth remaining open. 'Joey!'

They helped her onto a tattered love seat in the otherwise bare front room of the house that reeked of cooking grease, bleach and marijuana. Under the lone light bulb in the ceiling, the men stood above the woman as she sobbed and covered her face in her hands. Three young women, all in cotton sweats, too; and one of them pregnant, came blinking into the dim room from the back of the house, eyes glazed and pink-shot, kinky hair knotted in conditioner. They blinked in bewilderment at the men and then at the older woman weeping on the sofa. The Chief cleared his throat and told them what had happened. The young women stared at him. One screamed. They began to cry, going to the older woman.

The coach and the chief remained standing. The screaming, weeping women looked up now and then from the sofa with baleful faces at the intruding men. Chief Casey's mouth bent into a sad slant. Coach Gibbs winced and squeezed his eyes. The men could only talk, repeating over and over what had happened, what had been done, and how sorry they were. Chief Casey praised Speedy as being a leader and a model young man, who had never given him any trouble, unlike his friends who were now in reform school. Coach Gibbs nodded and he reminded them he had coached Speedy for three years, had advised that Speedy repeat the Tenth Grade so he could get more growth, and had taken Speedy home with him after football practices so his best running back could get enough to eat – knowing how Speedy had brothers and sisters, Miss Kinnard was on welfare, and that there was no real father to speak of. Chief Casey nodded.

Before the crying women, Coach Gibbs got carried away. Speedy had been destined for greatness, he told them. He had loved Speedy like a son and no one had carried the ball better for Fermata Bend. The women now and then stared up at him as the night turned gray outside and the coach finally exhausted himself with words, repeating how sorry he was, and Chief Casey nodded. Coach Gibbs handed Miss Kinnard his pocket cellular phone, showed her how to use it and told her not to hesitate to contact him. 'Miss Kinnard, don't feel you are alone,' he said. 'Speedy is not just your loss. He's everyone's loss. He's Fermata Bend's loss.' Chief Casey nodded.

'He was Joey,' Miss Kinnard told him. 'He was Joey.'

Friday morning, the story 'Football Death in Fermata Bend' ran on the front page of the *Mobile Register*, with continued coverage and an over-exposed black and white photograph on the Sports Page that, nevertheless, showed the long, thin smile and fixed, beatific stare of 'Speedy' Joe Kinnard through the face mask as he lay rigid and supine upon the ground. In Fermata Bend, those who saw the newspaper photo could not turn their eyes from it, but stared on it, after reading the name of their town, their high school and the tragic story of their star running back – virtually everyone surprising him or herself with a tear or a sigh, captivated by the face and suddenly feeling an identity with it, as if he or she knew him, like he was a lost relative or an unclaimed child, a feeling that hadn't been shared in Fermata Bend since the media projection of the death of Princess Diana.

By mid-morning, every state radio station was carrying the news. By evening, every TV station in the state was broadcasting the story. Before a death certificate and a coroner's report could be filed and a hearse dispatched from Birmingham to Fermata Bend, bearing the football player's body to the Needmore Funeral Home, the death of 'Speedy' Joe Kinnard was already a national fringe item on ESPN, the Fox Network and CNN. In Fermata Bend, people cut out the newspaper photo of 'Speedy' Joe Kinnard and taped it onto their refrigerators, shop windows, bulletin boards, dressing mirrors, and even onto mailboxes and roadside telephone poles with thin, trailing black ribbons; every flag was lowered to half-mast; every school, barber shop and beauty salon was closed for the rest of the day and Monday; Mayor Beau Eddins called for an emergency town hall meeting and the local cable channel began continuous re-runs of 'Speedy's' last game Thursday night, while the Athletic Booster Club placed a black wreath over the entrance to the high school locker room and the Fermata Bend Monday Morning Quarterback Club met at the Co-Op warehouse to begin a Speedy Memorial Fund to help with funeral expenses and a permanent monument in 'Speedy's' honor and to purchase and display bold, blue on white 'Speedy' banners all over the town.

Coach Jackie Gibbs and high school principal, Jonathan Richards, began receiving telephone calls from state media, the *Today*, *Nightline*, and *Dateline* shows, and lawyers for the NAACP; and the mayor, Beau Eddins, was besieged with calls from all over the United States – people wanting facts, wanting to help, wanting to express their condolences to Miss Kinnard – whom they could not reach – and people wanting to give Fermata Bend, Alabama, a piece of their minds. One call to Mayor Eddins came from the governor, himself, who wept over the phone, saying that the face of 'Speedy' Joe Kinnard was the 'noblest young face' he had ever seen. Other calls came from Southern U.S. Senators and Congressmen, scores of state legislators, every college recruiting coach and alumni association in the Southeast, TV sports personalities like Terry Bradshaw, Joe Namath, Bo Jackson, and Peyton Manning; the President of the Christian Athletes Association, The Touchdown Prayer Club, and even the President of the United States, who wanted to know what 'Speedy' Joe Kinnard was really like and where the hell was Fermata Bend, Alabama?

By the time the dead boy's body arrived at the Needmore Funeral Home, the media blitz and rumors had acquired a life of its own. Principally among the rumors was that Auburn University, the University of Alabama and all ten other college football programs in the state each would have given Speedy an athletic scholarship; another was that 'Speedy's' real father was a prominent white man in Fermata Bend who had played for The Bear. Still another and more persistent rumor was that the Burnsfield High football team had plotted to injure Speedy to try and win the football game and save the coach's job, as any team might do. And that evening, Escatawpa County Deputies pulled over and arrested three pickup truck loads of intoxicated and unruly Fermata Bend boys en route to Burnsfield to fight the entire town.

Dozens of Fermata Bend girls claimed Speedy was their boyfriend, unwed mothers insisted he could be the father of their babies, and even proper girls from the east side of town, like Lisa Pinochet, the pharmacist's daughter and the Homecoming Queen, or girls like Jennie Lou Howard, the lawyer's daughter, paled at and quickly dismissed the close association and the dark terror of death. They created fantasies that they could have had relationships with 'Speedy,' nursed feelings of chagrin for having not considered him worthy of their time and for not seeing the football player as perhaps he actually was. Such proper girls cut short their afternoon drive dates with such boyfriends as Bobby Ingram, the banker's son, or Jeff Sesset of old, landed Fermata Bend family, and they went home to mull upon their convoluted feelings, to ponder 'What if?' and similar such questions, later calling up their friends on the telephone in order to talk and feel better.

'But Joey ain't there,' Miss Kinnard cried to the hovering crowd of casually dressed reporters outside the Needmore Funeral Home, standing and sitting among complimentary, sports promotional cords of Osmose-treated lumber that had been delivered to the funeral home because the shipper could not find a permanent Kinnard address. Miss Kinnard's eyes were pink-shot and her face was gaunt with grief. She swayed and glared at the reporters, looking disheveled and uncomfortable in a deep red tunic dress with matching pumps, a black leather string purse and belt, and a high bouffant hairdo held in a crescendo of colorful, butterfly hairpins – all made gratuitously possible by the Fermata Bend Women's Club, along with their boxes of canned foods and Wal-mart Gift Certificates and additional sports promotional, complimentary crates of Coca-cola and Golden Flake Potato Chips and a new pair of Nikes for every member of her family.

'It ain't Joey in the picture,' she tried to tell them. 'It ain't Joey nowhere.'

The reporters smiled and nodded, writing down or recording whatever she said, and knowing not everything she said would make good copy. They would write stories like 'A Mother's Grief,' 'Death on the Gridiron,' or 'A Small Town in Shock' – what people wanted to read – while each of the Mobile nightly news channels would show a well-dressed reporter standing in the dirt yard of the house, summarizing in a solemn face and demeanor what tragedy had happened Thursday night, then a cut away to a close-up of Miss Kinnard weeping in a rusted garden rocker, in drab sweats and a sweater before the Fermata Bend Women's Club got to her, being comforted by her indigent children and neighbors; then a cut away to the co-captains of the football team, Guy Jacobs and Macon Williams, wearing new jeans and blue 'Raider' tee shirts in the parking lot of the Dairy Queen after the private team meeting. Both boys squared their shoulders and placed their hands on their hips, standing akimbo as they were questioned. They cocked their heads, shrugged and sighed. 'We'd give up the win if we could have Speedy back,' each one said, not in unison, but as if remembering what someone else had said, and pressing their lips together with emphatic nods. They described how the coaches and the team had cried and prayed together and voted to wear white crosses on the back of their helmets and to dedicate themselves and the rest of the season to Speedy Joe.

'Don't know how we're going to win without him,' each one said with a shake of his head, one echoing the other. 'But, hey. We gotta try.'

'That boy...was one of ours,' Mayor Beau Eddins stated behind the podium to a packed emergency town hall meeting of mostly white Fermata Bend citizens and town council members seated in rows of folding chairs. The newspaper photo of Speedy was taped to the front of the podium. Reporters and cameramen stood along the back wall. Mayor Eddins was obese, white-haired. He ran the Western Auto Store. His slow, sweeping gaze took in everyone and he stopped and nodded to Miss Kinnard in an honorary front row seat, wearing a shiny black princess dress with a pillbox hat and cheap sunglasses, seated with her children in their mismatched Goodwill Sunday clothes and new Nikes. 'No one,' the mayor said, looking around the room. 'No one,' he emphasized, 'feels the tragic loss of 'Speedy' Joe Kinnard more than his family and this town.

'Speedy Joe,' he struck the podium, 'was born in Fermata Bend...he grew up in Fermata Bend...he carried the ball for Fermata Bend...and, by God,' the mayor swelled, becoming teary-eyed, 'in Fermata Bend...we will honor our own.'

The room erupted in standing applause and spontaneous tears, except for Miss Kinnard and her children who bowed their heads, crying into paper tissues. The cameras whirled and the reporters scribbled in their notepads. Mayor Eddins nodded to everyone, held his hands up for silence and for everyone to be seated.

He called the meeting to order. An instant motion from the back to grant a town funeral procession through Fermata Bend for 'one 'Speedy' Joe Kinnard' was seconded and it carried without opposition, making Speedy the first black football player to be so honored. An immediate second motion that the procession be opened to anyone who 'knew and cared' about Speedy Joe was seconded and it carried, and a third motion to grant an honorary burial plot on town property at the crest of the old cemetery was seconded and it carried as well. With no further motions, the mayor formed a Funeral Procession Committee of those dutiful citizens of Fermata Bend who had experience and time to serve, and business was over in thirty minutes. The cameras whirled, the reporters wrote. Miss Kinnard and her family remained speechless, heads bowed and weeping.

Reverend Stephenson rose and requested permission to speak. He turned, his look sought out everyone in the room, also. '*I* have been changed forever,' he finally said in a soft and assured voice. 'Like you...and you,' he pointed to others, 'everyone,' he paused, spreading his hands out to include them as faces nodded.

'I saw salvation in the face of 'Speedy' Joe Kinnard,' the reverend said, lowering his hands. 'Seeing as Miss Kinnard is not an active member of any church or denomination...that I know of,' he turned and faced Miss Kinnard, 'I would be most willing...indeed honored, if she would let me be the minister for the town procession.'

Miss Kinnard raised her pill-boxed head and tear-stained sunglasses from her tissues to the silence and still, waiting eyes turned on her: waiting and expectant faces as when one is called upon at a revival to be saved – if one wants to be saved. She looked up to the still eyes and small smile of the reverend. She swallowed and managed to nod.

'Feels like being saved,' the mayor described it later, outside to the press, after he had adjourned the meeting and everyone had stood while the Kinnards were escorted out by Chief Casey to the patrol car, and after everyone in the hall had had a good cry and even begun to smile and hug one another. 'We all feel better,' the mayor said with a sigh. 'We've reached out and we're part of it now.'

Saturday morning, in a joint released statement to the press, both the head coaches of Alabama and Auburn expressed their sincere condolences to the Kinnard family, concluding that 'Speedy' Joe Kinnard had been 'a fine football player and prospect,' but they had no doubt, they stressed, 'that he had been an even finer individual.' The *Mobile Register*, the *Birmingham News,* the *Tuscaloosa News*, and other area newspapers, ran editorials on such topics as 'The Promise of 'Speedy' Unfulfilled,' ''Speedy' Joe Kinnard Loved Football more than Life,' and 'Except for the Army, Another Window of Opportunity out of Poverty Closed Forever,' some newspapers and talk shows arguing again that despite the awful tragedy and a national perception of over-emphasis on football in Alabama, the sport was still worth it, a means of state identity and pride, a single emblem of excellence and achievement for Alabama youth to look up to.

Saturday afternoon, Coach Gibbs received a cellular phone call from Miss Kinnard.

'Oh, yes, ma'am,' Coach Gibbs said. 'Yes, ma'am. What can I do for you?'

Miss Kinnard hesitated before asking the coach in a slow whine if her Joey could be buried in a clean football uniform. 'It's the way he would have wanted it,' she said. 'They took the dirty one off of him and he's lying here at the funeral parlor, just staring up at the ceiling as pretty as a mannequin with a jock strap on.' In the coach's sudden silence, Miss Kinnard went on to say that she was beginning to see how it just might, could be her Joey, after all.

Coach Gibbs stammered, but in the end, said yes because he could not say no. He told her he would call back and telephoned Principal Hunt Richards, who was of old, landed Fermata Bend family and had never heard of a Miss Kinnard until Friday. Principal Richards couldn't believe what he was being told, but responded that it was the least they could do, after all, for a boy who had died in a Fermata Bend uniform. 'Yes, of course,' the principal said, and suggested the coach have an assistant deliver a clean uniform, helmet, tube socks, and a new pair of cleats to the funeral home.

Within the hour, Miss Kinnard called the Principal, too, thanking him profusely in her slow whine, and pausing to let the principal fill the voids with 'Yes, ma'ams' until she could pose another favor. 'Yes, ma'am?' Principal Richards said. Could her Joey lie in state in Raider Gym until the procession and burial on Monday?

'It's what he would have wanted,' her voice quickly went shrill and she began to cry. 'And after all, he was *your* football player.'

Principal Richards swallowed several times, but in the end, he could not refuse, either. 'Ma'am,' he said, 'you go right ahead.' The principal called the Superintendent, Edmond Stuart, who was not of old, landed Fermata Bend family, but worse, was married to it, and who also had never heard of Miss Kinnard until Friday. The Superintendent went silent when he was told, but he too could not say no. 'Never, never let it be said,' he told the Principal, 'that in Fermata Bend, a man can refuse the grieving mother of an athlete.'

Sunday morning, students and various citizens of Fermata Bend filed into Raider Gym in their Sunday clothes before and after church, following a rope-cordoned and paper-rolled walkway in mutual silence, under the steel cross beams and humming florescent ceiling lights, and staring on the eerie presence of a clean, uniformed, and dead mahogany football player laid out in an opened casket bordered with white floral arrangements at center basketball court. The corpse's rigid body was sunk into the cushion and a shiny blue, number '32' helmet rested atop the blue-jerseyed chest and shoulder-padded torso, and from within the flowers came the sound of the high school band's rendition of 'Serenade for Winds' played on a reel-to-reel tape recorder. To everyone's surprise, the head was covered with a white silk cloth that blended against the pillow and coffin lining so well that the initial impression was of a headless football player.

The face had been covered at the last moment before the opening of the doors on the frantic insistence of Miss Kinnard as she discovered, after the casket had been wheeled in through the back doors of the basketball court and opened for display among the floral arrangement, that Mr. George Albright, the elderly and nearly blind Needmore undertaker had prepared the body per instructions on the uniform, but having no other instructions, had prepared the face by his accustomed habit, observing nothing at all unique about the face and sewing with unusual difficulty and some two hundred-pound thread, the lips and eyes shut and into the expression of a sad grimace. Miss Kinnard, in a black coat dress, pumps, silver hematite jewelry and the high bouffant hairdo, gasped, stepping back in horror, at first thinking the expression had somehow grotesquely changed by itself, until Mr. Albright told her the truth.

'You – you turned him into a clown,' she said.

Mr. Albright peered through his thick lenses at her and then at the body. He apologized profusely, offering to snip and pull the threading out of the corpse's lips and eyes then and there; although, he warned her, he could not guarantee the result or that embalming fluid would not leak out. Miss Kinnard stared at him even more aghast. 'Well, it was not his face before,' she finally conceded with tears. 'It is not his face now.'

With the help of his assistant, Mr. Albright produced a matching piece of silk cloth from his tool case for Miss Kinnard to inspect and spread over the player's face before the front doors of the gym opened. But Miss Kinnard need not have worried. Everyone who filed by the uniformed corpse of 'Speedy' Joe Kinnard ensconced in silk, nodded or stared on in awe – some in grief – but everyone was, in truth, secretly relieved, assuming the concealment of the face to be a wish for privacy from a grieving mother, and only too glad to remain confident in his or her committed memory of the face from the newspaper photo, and the way he or she wanted to know him.

Throughout the day, traffic jammed the streets and the queue of mourners to the gym was four blocks long. A Key to the City was placed in the casket by the mayor, a bronze plaque proclaiming 'Speedy' Joe Kinnard 'Honorary Alabama High School Athlete of the Year' was inserted into the casket by an Assistant Sports Editor of *The Birmingham News*, a high school diploma was propped next to the helmet by Principal Richards, and the middle-aged and still hippie editor of the *Fermata Bend Bugler* recited at the casket his ballad, 'The Night Speedy Ran,' which was to run in the next issue along with black and white photos of 'Speedy's' last night in action.

The entire football team trooped in with the coaches, weeping in blue coats and ties. The co-captains made tearful speeches on behalf of the team and presented an athletic letter to the corpse. The cheerleaders gave a special, teary-eyed Speedy Cheer under their breaths; and girls like Lisa Pinochet, the pharmacist's daughter and the Homecoming Queen, went through the line three times before she could slip, unnoticed, something like an anemone or an begonia from her mother's greenhouse into the casket, and then turn away, feeling better about herself and what never was and what never would be.

By afternoon, the black football player was covered in mementos: folded letters, photos, poems, trinkets, crosses and even candy bars from the flow of those paying their final respects, the casket's overflowing appearance beginning to look more like the spectacle of a Hindu or pagan rite. Reverend Stephenson had to remind those concerned in the parking lot that this was an outpouring of public grief, the soul had already gone on, and the expressions now taking place were for the needs of the living.

Late afternoon, the governor came, along with scores of state legislators, candidates running for office, athletic suppliers and sales representatives; and the suited men's presence was also accompanied with a sudden and surprising stream of beauty queens from all over the state: smiling, prim and petite young girls in the latest hairdos, tight dresses or suits, each one wanting to be the next Miss Alabama and looking as if she had just stepped off the glossy cover of a magazine. Among these were Miss Gardenia Bloom, Little Miss Peanut, The School Pod Queen, Miss Winston 500, Miss Blue and Gray, The Sorghum Queen, The Bible Belt Queen, Miss Cotton Ball, The Chitling Queen, The Soybean Queen, and Miss Free At Last. The girls filed before the men into the gym and they all cried at the corpse of the football player, dabbing their eyes quickly so as not to streak their makeup. Every beauty made a similar and melodic statement to the press upon leaving that she felt, like the entire state of Alabama, that she had known Speedy all her life.

'Well, it's a tragedy,' the governor drawled to the press when he came out of the gym. 'It's a sad, sad day for the people of Alabama.' Everyone around him nodded, and the cameras whirled and the reporters wrote. 'We all have sons and daughters,' the governor stated. 'When something like this happens in a good town like Fermata Bend – it strikes a nerve in all of us.'

People nodded and the governor paused. 'Say,' he wondered after a moment, 'why did they cover that boy's face?'

The question hung unanswered. No one replied, not the press, the politicians, the athletic suppliers and their representatives; not the mayor, the principal, the coach, nor even the ever-smiling and poised beauty queens. Someone asked about Tort Reform. Someone else asked about The Board of Regents Bill. The press coverage went on.

No one from Fermata Bend knew the answer, either. Or yet, why the next day, as a community, they would follow in a procession, without the beauty queens or the governor and the athletic suppliers, behind the body of 'Speedy' Joe Kinnard in a closed, wreathed casket on the slow bed of the local American Legion horse tram, pulled and flanked by the entire Fermata Bend High football team in their blue coats and ties; followed by Reverend Stephenson, head high and solemn in his minister's robe, and Speedy's mother beside him in another black dress, hat, veil, shoes and full-length gloves, arm-in-arm between Police Chief Casey and Coach Gibbs in dark suits; followed by most of her children and a few neighbors wearing mis-matched Goodwill Sunday clothes and new Nikes, the local American Legion Honor Guard, then the Fermata Bend High School Marching Band playing 'Stairway to Heaven,' the cheerleaders in black shorts and shirts, followed by every person in Escatawpa County who wanted to wear a cap and drive a custom hot rod bearing an Alabama or Auburn sticker, and after that, every person who wanted to wear a hat and ride a horse, followed up by a few stray dogs and the town's only

116

street sweeper – the procession of the people of Fermata Bend, Alabama, that wound past the town square and the ever-waiting press, toward the corroded iron gates, Johnson grass and dull, leaning tombstones of the small town cemetery – each person marching, looking stoically ahead, not behind, and not knowing why they loved him more dead than when he was alive; but carrying an image of 'Speedy' Joe Kinnard as somehow ageless, pure and to be remembered forever and ever.

Grinning in the Dark

There he was: nude, coiled, crouching on the balls of his feet, almost hugging his bare knees under the leafy canopy of a mimosa and a catalpa tree, his gaze intent on something beyond the pond of the neighborhood park. Sam, my yellow lab, barked. The young, naked man looked up, discovering us then, and I laughed. 'Hey,' I called. 'Wait 'til I get my camera.' A look of alarm. He sprang away, thin legs pumping: lean skinned body against the green of spring, the short, limp member between his legs swaying and amassed with hair. He glanced back once, his dark head all but shaved. Sam and I watched his swinging buttocks disappear into the green sheen and the trees. The suddenness of him brought me an instant impression of primitive times, of nude Greek athletes; then of Adam in the Garden of Eden, trying to hide from God. Sam dog-grinned me and wagged his tail. It made no difference to him.

On the other side of the pond, two young women appeared off the foot trail in shorts, blouses and tennis shoes; their gazes intent on plants and trees. One carried a textbook, the other a long insect net. I thought to call to them, but it seemed ridiculous. Was this real? Sam left me to chase a squirrel up a tree. I went up onto the dirt dam, between blooming dogwoods, towards the women. They paused to study high grass. I watched them stroll to the water's edge to peer at water lilies. Then the girl with the net whirled around. She dropped her net and her hands went to her face. The other girl turned from the water, too, and stared. I broke into a run. Sam caught up, loping alongside at my knee while the young woman with the textbook moved forward, keeping the other one behind her. She hugged the textbook to her breasts and yelled something. The other woman retrieved her net and the two of them turned away and walked quickly toward the dam.

'You two okay?' I came to a halt. 'Was it him?'

Their faces were flushed; but on seeing me, they released nervous giggles. Sam circled between us, panting and wagging his tail. I smelled their faint perfume. The one gripping the textbook was red headed, dark eyed; she had a clasp in her hair. The other one holding the net was shorter, plump, and brunette.

'He was talking to us from behind a bush,' the redhead stated. 'He apologized for scaring us; said he only wanted to present himself.' She stressed the word, *present*.

'He said he was swimming in the pond,' the brunette said.

I felt a smirk on my lips and the girls laughed, embarrassed and relieved: young faces with lipstick and mascara. They wore thin jewelry. Their legs were shaved.

'Oh, right,' I said. 'Swimming.' We contained our smiles and shared knowing looks.

'I thought he might be your boyfriend,' I said, bending down to pat Sam's head.

'Nooo,' they both exclaimed with incredulous looks.

I laughed. At that moment the naked youth chose to make a debut. He bounded from hiding in the trees, running away from the dam, and along the edge of the pond: exposed, his eyes ahead, and his face set in a determined indifference, like a child acting unaware of attention.

'Oops,' the redhead commented, watching.

He was thin with nice moving legs. He leaped and snatched a pile of folded clothes on top of the creosote post bearing the NO FISHING sign. We watched him hastily pull on clothes behind a tree, then sit on the ground to pull on shoes. Standing up, he shook his head and went away on the trail.

The girls shot looks at each other and stifled giggles with their hands. They gave me parting, bemused glances as they went on. 'He wasn't white anywhere,' I heard the redhead say. I stole a look at their switching shorts and whistled for Sam, who had followed his nose into the trees again. At that, the brunette girl with the net looked back at me over her shoulder.

At dinner, I am telling my wife about Bob's fishing trip and the homemade video he played on the office VCR/TV we use for showing clients properties. You can tell it's a homemade video, I tell Wendy. We see the camp, the water, the boat, the guide, and then Bob's startled wife in a hair net without her face on, her mouth a surprised snarl. She shields her face from the camera with her hands. Next is Bob: blonde hair, Ray-bans, wearing a cap and vest, gamely holding a rod and smiling too broadly. Next, limp fish hanging on a string. In the office, while we watched, Bob kept wiping his index finger over his brow as if still sweating. 'It was hot,' he kept saying with a grin. We nodded. Then the shot is his wife again. This time she's ready, seated with the fishing guide at the front of the boat with fresh lipstick and a brave smile: a straw hat, sunglasses, shorts and a Jimmy Buffett T-shirt. But, I tell Wendy, the shot doesn't lie. Her expression is tired, maybe bored. And she's overweight. What I don't tell Wendy is men go fishing to be alone or to be among themselves, and that Bob's wife goes with him on every fishing trip now, since he had an affair with a fishing guide's daughter two years ago in Colorado. 'Now, I can't ever get away,' Bob tells us at the office, 'she thinks I won't love her.' I tell Wendy that for a moment, you see Bob's wife smile, then everything goes shaky, a whirl of sky and tree limbs. The film goes dim just before it goes black, but you know it's water because there are darting minnows, a sandy bottom, and an old boot beside a mud-caked Coke bottle.

'"I fell in," Bob said.'

Wendy laughs. She has been listening and nodding as she eats her dinner across the table from me. She has told me about her day with the other nurses at the doctors' office: who got their ears pierced again, who has a new kitten, whose kid has to have braces. And Wendy's partner at the desk, Phyllis, is thinking about getting a Styrofoam boob job because it's safer.

'Oh, and guess what?' I say. I savor my pause and grin. 'Guess what happened this afternoon?'

Wendy looks at me over her spinach salad, placing a forkful of lasagna in her mouth. Her blue eyes widen as she chews and swallows. 'What?' she says. Her vermilion lipstick has washed while eating. Her new, highlighted hair looks good against her blue eyes.

I wipe my mouth on my napkin, grin, and prop my elbows on the table as I tell her: about the girls, the trees, his young naked body, the dog, everything. Wendy's mouth opens, her eyes widen as she watches me. When I'm through, her hand comes up with her napkin and remains at her mouth.

'Tom, that's awful,' she says. She clenches her napkin. 'What's so funny?' she demands.

'Well – ' I catch myself. 'I thought it was funny.'

'Like hell,' her look accuses me. 'Why didn't you do something? Why didn't you call the police?'

'Well, no one was hurt...'

'Oh,' she glares, 'we're supposed to wait until somebody's *hurt*?'

'What is this?' I say. 'It wasn't serious. It didn't bother the girls that much.'

'Because you were there to protect them,' she adds sarcastically.

'No,' I tell her. 'It wasn't like that. He was just being narcissistic. Just showing off.'

'I know what he was showing,' Wendy says. She shakes her head. 'You men,' she scoffs. 'You men can just flaunt it. It's we women...' she says, 'we women have to deal with it.'

121

Wendy drops her balled up napkin onto her plate, starts to take a swallow of iced tea but sets it down. She rises from the table and takes our plates, even though I'm not finished. She hesitates and stares down at our plates. 'Tom, that's terrible,' she mutters. 'That's disgusting.'

She takes the plates to the sink. 'I can't believe you didn't do anything,' she says. 'Somebody should catch his ass with a video camera and play it all over the state.'

'And what could I do?' I ask. 'He was already gone.'

Wendy sets the plates on the counter and turns around. 'You could have stopped smiling about it,' she says.

'Look, I'm sorry,' I say. 'I don't see it that way.'

Wendy shakes her head. 'That's awful,' she says. She comes back to the table, takes up her tea glass, and stares off. 'Now,' she says, 'I'm afraid to go out there.'

The next day when I drive in after work, a police car is parked at the end of the street before the entrance to the park. I change into sweats and running shoes and let Sam out of his pen, and the police car is still there. At the footbridge entrance into the park, two police officers are standing with a teenage girl and boy against a background of white azalea blooms. The teens are in shorts, running shoes and silk screened t-shirts. The boy is talking. He waves his hands. His mouth is fervent. The girl stands beside him with her Walkman headphones on, the CD player attached to her waist. Sam doesn't like it. He whines and veers away from the bridge. The people look at me. The officers appear dark and heavy in their uniforms and burdened belts. Against them, the teens look small. I wave to them and call Sam. The policemen turn back to the boy. 'You say he exposed himself to the girl?' one of them says. The boy is thin, muscular, has a sharp nose and curly blonde hair. Walkman headphones are dropped around his neck. 'Yeah. Yeah,' he says. He searches the policemen's faces and smacks a fist into his palm with bravado. The girl has short brown bands and chews gum. She touches the boy's elbow, but he ignores her.

'This is some shit, man. This is some shit,' he says. He hits his palm with his fist again. 'If I had just caught him. Man, if I had just caught him.'

The policemen make closed smiles. The older officer asks a question. When both teenagers start to talk, he holds his hand up for order.

I lead Sam around to the other entrance and we go into the park where Sam becomes his eager self again, wagging his tail and disappearing into the trees with his nose to the ground. I decide not to jog, and walk in the quiet, in the smell of moist earth and plants. It's Thursday. Wendy will be home soon. She wanted me to pick up some detergent on the way home, but I forgot. She likes for us to be home at the same time, but she doesn't understand why I want to be alone for a time everyday after work. I tell her it's to unwind. 'But why not with me?' she says. I have no answer. Thursday, we usually prepare dinner together, or go out to eat; then go see a movie or maybe watch a video. But on the foot trail now, I am glad to be alone. The trail winds back to the pond and I discover the policemen from the bridge on the bank, standing with impervious faces, hands on their belts, and scanning the water's surface. The younger one looks up and gives a perfunctory nod, the other one gives me a momentary stare. But I'm not a suspect.

'Hey, what happened?' I ask. 'Is something wrong?'

'Exhibitionist,' the older one deadpans without looking at me. 'Scared the boy's girl, and got the boy all riled up.'

The younger officer chuckles and they move along the bank, combing the ground with their eyes. I watch them and don't say anything and continue on the trail, where Sam comes out of the woods to meet me: tail wagging, head bowed, grinning like a thief.

'Hey, chicken,' I say.

Wendy prods me awake under the covers in the night. 'Sam's barking,' she mutters, her voice irritated, brought out of sleep. 'Make him stop.'

I sit up in our bed, and blink at the bedroom window and the moonlit yard. A muffled howl trails from outside. I get out of bed and go raise the window.

'Sam!' I hiss out. 'Shut up!'

Quiet. Moonlight. Then a fierce, trailing howl, louder now through the raised window. I can't see him in his pen. I look to Wendy and softly close the window. In the covers, Wendy turns away. Sam lets loose another barrage. I silently curse, thinking that the neighbors are hearing him, and grope for the chair with my Levis, pulling them on and stumbling down the hallway and through the kitchen to the back door. Outside, the moon is still, the backyard is in white stasis, quiet; until Sam pierces it with a long wail, and then growling. In his chain link pen, I see him at the opposite corner from me. I am about to scold him when I see a figure beyond the fence, at the edge of the yard, lighter than the shadows and the shrubbery. It moves. I freeze and stare. Then I know what it is. Its shade is uniform. I am awake and my alarm subsides into a laugh at this daredevil prank, this lark in the night. I feel myself grinning. 'That would be the way to do it,' I think. 'No one can see you.' Sam comes to the fence and licks my hand through the chain link, then turns away, watching and bristling. It doesn't move. I back step to the back door, reach in and flip the light switch to the TV room. The alien light from the windows shoots across the yard. The figure turns and runs into the shadows.

Mid-morning, as I'm writing up property appraisals at my desk in the office, Steve and Jeff stand around Bob's desk with the front page write up of the exhibitionist in the morning paper. Our coats are off, our sleeves are rolled up. Bob is drinking coffee at his desk while Laura, our only female agent, types at her computer near the front door. The boys give me looks. Steve clears his throat and shakes the newspaper at me.

'Isn't that your neighborhood, Tom? Fennen Park?' They look at me.

'I know it's you,' Bob laughs. The boys grin.

'Yeah,' Jeff says. 'Your backyard. Perfect set up.'

'Imagine,' Bob sighs after a moment, 'approaching any woman you want to.'

'And as you wish,' Jeff adds.

'Says here,' Steve reads the paper, '...young white male, of medium height, lean, dark crew cut, dark eyes...described by several women as having a mole on his left hip.' They laugh.

Bob makes a serious face. 'You got a mole on your hip, now Tom?'

I raise my hands in surrender. 'Sorry,' I say. 'Nor a crew cut.' I motion to my head. Still focused on her computer, Laura makes a closed smile.

'There's something else wrong here, though,' Bob keeps his serious face. He knots his brows and he takes the paper from Steve. 'It says here,' he places his finger on the print, 'a *young male*,' he emphasizes. His face breaks. They laugh again. Laura's smile grows. I look at them and have a flash of them as younger men. Now, they're older with wedding bands on their fingers. I remember me and my fraternity brothers running nude on a dare one spring day across the campus quad, wearing nothing but ski masks. Our spectacle halted traffic at the intersection of the campus circle. My adrenalin pumped and I thrilled at the screams we brought from the girls and the boys who stared at us in disbelief and amusement.

'Laura?' Bob calls with a grin. 'Are you afraid of Tom?' Everyone turns to her.

Laura stops typing and pretends to study me. She's quiet, almost timid, and attractive. She has kept her long black hair. She has two kids and a husband. We like to flirt with her.

She shakes her head. 'No,' she says, smiling.

'Would you be afraid to go to Fennen Park?' Steve takes it up.

'Not if I was with someone,' Laura says.

'Meaning a man who would look after you?'

She nods. 'Yes. Respect me.'

'And how do you mean, respect?' Steve asks.

'Well. Relationship,' Laura says after a moment. 'You do for us. Make us feel secure, important.' She smiles.

'You mean,' Steve says, 'we give what you want to get what we want?'

Laura smiles and nods.

'Yeah,' Bob sighs slowly and folds his hands behind his head. 'That's the old catch.' He makes a sheepish grin. Steve's and Jeff's grins go small, too. The three of them look deflated, chagrined, as if they've been caught at something.

Jeff sighs. 'And after awhile, they don't give it to you when you want it,' he says.

Steve shoots him a knowing look. Their interest killed, Jeff and Steve go back to their desks. Laura goes back to her typing, holding a remnant of her smile.

Saturday morning, I help Wendy fold clothes and towels and match socks from the laundry basket. We lay out the fresh laundry on our stripped bed, place everything in the drawers or on the storage shelf in the bathroom, saving the clean bed sheets for last, spreading and holding each one between us as we make the bed. We're both in denim cutoffs and sweatshirts. A green bandana holds Wendy's hair out of her face. She remains silent and busy, tucking and pulling the sheets. I go around the bed and grab her from behind as she stuffs a pillowcase. She squeals and we fall on the clean sheets. I hold her and kiss her. The bandana falls off; her hair sprays about her face and mouth. I don't let her go. I kiss her again and nibble her ear. The urge comes over me. 'Let's break in the sheets,' I say and move my hands slowly over her, nudging her

126

with my nose and kissing her neck. I kiss her breasts through the sweatshirt.

'Nooo,' she makes a soft, pouting laugh, 'not now.'

I kiss her breasts again.

'Stop it,' she says.

I stop and look up at her face.

'Not now,' she says. She looks away.

'Okay,' I try a laugh. I release her and sit up on the bed. 'What's the matter?'

Wendy sits up, pushing her hair out of her eyes, and cocking it behind her ears. She looks at the wall beyond us. 'I'm sorry,' she says slowly. She pauses. 'I had a dream about you.'

'A dream?'

'Yes.' She frowns. 'I dreamed we were at a cocktail party with our friends, and you took off your clothes in front of everyone and strutted around the house naked.'

'Wendy.'

'Everyone was dressed in fine clothes. They laughed at you. But I assure you – you were ugly.'

'Wendy, you're remaking me with what happened at the park.'

'I know,' Wendy says. 'It doesn't help the way I feel though.'

We go quiet, and she holds her eyes on the wall.

'Well, come on,' I say. I make my voice upbeat and I touch her arm. 'Forget it. It's Saturday. Let's get changed and go grocery shopping, rent a video...wash the car.'

That evening, after dinner, and after we load the dishwasher, we turn off the lights in the TV room and sit on the sofa to watch the video we selected at the video rental. Wendy has been quiet since this morning and she was quiet at dinner. As she watches the TV for the film to begin, I look at the outline of her face, her eyes and closed mouth in the soft light of the TV;

her loose hair, her cotton slacks and blouse. She does not look at me. The video is *Pelle, the Conqueror.* The scenes come on; the story begins slowly and then builds in complexity. The depiction of the Eighteenth century Denmark seacoast is vast, rural, and stark. The characters are real, but the dubbing is bad in places. Wendy holds the remote controller. She stops the tape now and then to replay a scene. We strain to catch the words. Deep in the film, after the Landlady's husband has touched his wife's visiting niece's bare feet on the walking stilts; and the niece, in turn, has given him flirtatious looks in the stable, we see the Landlady's husband come out of the woods, after the Fair, pulling on his large pants by their suspenders. Before him, in the lush, wild grass, the nude niece is kneeling by the stream with blood on her thighs, and trying to scrub the blood out of her white dress. The man stands, looking on, and haughtily drawing on the stub of a cigar.

At this, I am afraid to look at Wendy. I can envision her lips pursing, her eyes narrowing. On that scene, I felt the urge to reach out and touch her, to run my hand over her leg. I like Wendy's long legs. But it would have been a mistake. She will not understand what her body, what the woman's body, does to me. I know we are not going to have sex tonight. There was a chance after the laundry this morning, after she confessed her dream. She could forgive me for being male and forget it. Her mood could change. We could make up. We could cuddle on the sofa as we watch the movie, and later go to bed.

Only now she hates me and all men. We are perpetrators. I cannot touch her now unless she speaks first. I will not take off her gold choker tonight that sometimes catches in my moustache.

On the TV tube, the young niece packs and abruptly leaves the Landlady's house in trepidation and tears. We watch as eventually the sin is revealed. The Landlady castrates her husband in his sleep. We see him screaming, his bare body rolling, his mid-section bloodied in the sheets. His wife is seated on the bed, dressed, and patting his shoulder like a mother to a sick child, as if to say: 'There now. You will get better.'

I steal a glance to Wendy's face: her eyes rapt, intent on the TV. I see a slow sneer of gratified judgment grow from the corner of her mouth – or do I imagine it? I stand up and leave the room. I don't want to know if I saw it – truth is, I don't want her to know that I feel caught. In the kitchen I prance around, look out the window, and don't know where to go. I open the refrigerator out of habit and look in.

'Honey?' Wendy calls after me. 'Bring a glass of wine.'

I look in the back of the refrigerator and find the bottle of white wine, pour two glasses and carry them into the dim TV room: her prints, our bookshelves, her ceramic busts, the sofa; a stilled and static scene of a boy and a girl in a field on the TV tube. Wendy is waiting for me, smiling from her end of the sofa, her sandals on the carpeted floor, her bare feet curled up under her. 'Thank you, honey,' she says, and looks at me as I hand her a glass. The remote control is on the armrest next to her. 'I stopped the movie,' she says. 'Don't you want to watch it?'

'Yeah, okay,' I say.

Wendy looks at the TV, sips her wine and pats the sofa next to her for me to sit down.

I hesitate and remain standing. Eyes on the TV, Wendy calmly flips her hair behind her shoulder and takes up the re-mote controller in her other hand.

'Sit down,' she says, casually.

'I forgot something,' I say.

'What?' she gives me a doubtful look. 'Sit down.'

'Never mind,' I say. 'I don't want to watch. You go ahead.'

Wendy gives me an incredulous look and sighs.

Her call trails after me. I expect to hear a quip about being male. I forget that I am holding a sweating glass of wine until I am out the kitchen and down the hallway. I don't know where I am going. I turn into the hallway bathroom, lock the door, and set the glass on the vanity counter. I think of taking Sam around the pond. Alone with cool, dark tile; a cosmetic mirror set into the vanity mirror, perfumed soap and a shower curtain, I leave the light off. I lower the toilet seat and cover, and sit down. Here, it is confined, quiet. I close my eyes and try to feel that I am hiding. That I cannot be seen.

Lying at the Edge of the World

I know I sing at the edge of silence,
I know I dance around suspension....
> – Sophia De Mello Breyner. 'I Feel the Dead'

He awoke in the dark and didn't know where he was. He sat up, feeling smooth metal bed rails with his hands while loud traffic droned in the night outside a window. 'Where am I?' Louie said. He tried to stare through the dark, feeling a sharp, weakening pang of hunger. A ceiling light came on, blinding and bright. Louie blinked and his eyes adjusted to a white ceiling, white walls, and a green tiled floor. He was in the middle of three hospital beds. An old, frail man in the bed to his right had flipped on the wall light switch. The bed to Louie's left was empty and made-up, a fresh jonquil on its smooth pillow. The old man to his right, in covers and grey pajamas like himself, rubbed his eyes and reached for eyeglasses on a metal night table. He had wispy white hair, no teeth, and sagging bags under dark, hollowed eyes.

'Who are you? What am I doing here?' Louie said. He stared at the old man and around the strange room. The man slipped on his glasses, reached for a black cord clipped onto his bedspread and pressed a button.

'What am I doing here?' Louie demanded. But the old man seemed detached, even bored, and looked to the door of the room as it swung open. A dark-headed woman entered, dressed in starch white, wearing scarlet lipstick. Louie stared at her and realized he had been asleep with his glasses on.

'Yes?' she said.

'Butch is at it again,' the man told her.

Butch? Louie stared at them.

The woman shook her head, came forward. Her large, scarlet lips; dull blue eyes and pinched nose seemed familiar, as if from another time. But it was not his wife.

'Where am I?' Louie said.

'You're home,' Scarlet Lips said, her voice high and false. 'Now, go back to sleep.'

'Home?' He stared at her. He could remember black and white kitchen tile and sunlight in the window of a breakfast nook.

Scarlet Lips placed her hands on his shoulders and pushed him gently down into the bed. 'Go back to sleep.'

'I'm hungry,' he said.

'We eat in the morning,' she answered, her tone not changing.

Louie sat up. 'Answer me,' he demanded. 'Where am I? What am I doing here?'

The woman took a step back, set her lips and crossed her arms.

'Careful, Butch,' the old man made a terse whisper. 'Remember last time.'

Last time? He wasn't sure about last time. He looked at the man, then at the woman. He lay down and pulled the covers up to his chin.

'Much better,' Scarlet Lips said. 'Now go to sleep.'

Louie nodded.

Scarlet Lips gave him a quick smile and left the room, turning out the light.

'Night, Butch,' a sad whisper came in the dark.

'Good night,' Louie echoed, still trying to see through the

132

dark, and listening for familiar sounds in the steady din of traffic outside a window.

Louie awoke and the still room was filled with gray light from the windows. He heard the steady drone of morning street traffic outside and saw his blue bottle of Milk of Magnesia and a glass of water on the metal bedside table. Mac was asleep. Joe's bed was empty, made up, with a fading jonquil on its smooth pillow. Louie realized he had slept with his glasses on and he heard feet shuffling in the hallway on the other side of the door. His legs ached. He was hungry. But he knew to wait until someone came. The door swung open with brighter ceiling light from the hallway and the thin male orderly that all the patients dubbed 'Too Nice' in his white maintenance suit and close, kinky hair, came in with their bedpans. 'Good morning,' he sang out. 'Potty time.'

Too Nice poked Mac awake, holding a broad smile. Louie watched him lift Mac's bed covers and place the bedpan under Mac's body. Too Nice came and lifted Louie's covers, tugged Louie's pajamas down. Louie winced as the cold steel met his bottom. Too Nice watched and smiled while Louie let himself go. He handed them toilet paper and Louie and Mac wiped. He took the bedpans with the wipes into the bathroom, flushed the toilet and left the room without looking back.

Louie watched the door swing closed and Mac drifted back to sleep. The door swung open with 'Orange Hat,' the short, obese dietician in blue overalls and the orange baseball cap, pushing in the food cart.

'Good morning, good morning,' she piped. She had a dimpled face and a lazy eye. She wheeled the cart between Louie and Mac's beds. Mac opened his eyes. Orange Hat grinned and cranked each man's bed into sitting position and slapped clip-on trays across their bed rails.

'Look what we've got for you,' she sang, like she had a surprise. She placed covered plates before them, silverware

133

wrapped in napkins, and plastic, capped glasses of juice. Louie smiled for her. He thought her well intended but not all there. Mac gaped at her with his bare gums, reached for his eyeglasses on the table and slipped them on.

'Why, Mister Smith,' Orange Hat exclaimed, as she removed the lids from their glasses and plates, 'whatever's the matter?'

'Nothing, nothing,' Mac said. He dabbed his eyes under his lenses with the edge of his bed sheet. 'It was just a sudden memory.'

'Now, now,' she patted his leg. 'That does no good.'

'No coffee?' Louie said.

'Afterwards,' Orange Hat trilled, smiling and reprimanding him with a waving finger, as if to a child.

Louie smiled for her until she turned and pushed the cart out of the room. He made a face. He and Mac unwrapped their napkins and began to eat.

'Say, how you feeling, Butch?' Mac skirted his eyes at him, mouthing toast.

'Fine,' Louie said, spooning egg into his mouth.

'You got a little rowdy last night.'

Louie stopped and looked at him. 'Oh, did I?'

'But don't worry,' Mac winked. 'I looked after ya.'

'Thanks,' Louie said, nodding his gratitude. But he could not recall being rowdy or not.

After Orange Hat removed the trays, the younger attendant, 'Blonde Braids,' in small white uniform with freckles and blonde braids and heavy makeup came in. She did not acknowledge him or Mac and began to talk to herself, rehearsing a conversation between herself and her boyfriend about using the condom or the sponge in their love making. She took Louie's glasses and shaved him first, letting him hold the mirror while she talked, intoning a man's husky, demanding voice and then a meeker, wiser and feminine one, stroking lather from Louie's face and wiping the plastic razor on a towel across his chest.

Louie and Mac listened in silent amusement while Blonde Braids shifted her voice and point of view between that of the woman and then that of the man. The woman said she would try to meet his needs and use the sponge, but only on the condition that he teach his eager member to be patient. Blonde Braids finished shaving Louie and wiped his face. She threw off the covers, stripped off his pajamas and gave him a quick and warm sponge bath with her deft fingers, while talking as the man, who said he wanted it when he wanted it. The wet, warm sponge made Louie's skin tingle, but little else. He liked this part. He tried to catch her eye but Blonde Braids didn't meet his look. Her mouth continued to intone like a recording, going on to the weather report or a fashion feature from some television channel she watched. Blonde Braids dried Louie with a towel, handed him his glasses, covered him up, and went to shave Mac.

'Can I shave myself?' Mac asked as she removed his glasses.

'No,' she said. 'You cut yourself, remember?' Mac pouted his lips. In a moment, he wiped tears from his eyes and she ignored him, beginning to lather his face, repeating what some fat man had said about the thrills and dangers of 'bungee jumping' on a Today Show.

Blonde Braids finished Mac's sponge bath and stopped talking long enough to give Mac his glasses and walker, and Louie his cane. She helped them get out of bed and go into the bathroom to brush their gums, put in their dentures, and comb their hair. They came out to her rendition of a Pepsi commercial with a basketball player dribbling in outer space as they sat in the steel chairs by their closets and she helped them dress in frayed underwear, old white shirts, faded suits, and worn shoes. Blonde Braids silently guided them by their elbows out of the room and down the hallway to the lounge where old and shriveled people, most in wheelchairs and in old clothes like themselves, played cards or checkers at tables, stood chatting with or without walkers, or sat gaping on a sofa at the wall TV. Louie recognized the scarecrow thin old woman in the wheelchair with the moth-eaten paisley bathrobe and the frizzled blue hair who gave him a wink.

'I got plans for you, baby,' she chortled.

Louie smiled for her.

'You get sun today,' Blonde Braids announced and led them outside onto the patio, helping Louie and Mac sit at one of the concrete yard tables in the sunlight. She left and an orderly brought them coffee. Mac sipped from his Styrofoam cup, set it down, swelled his chest and looked Louie in the eye. 'It was you and me, Butch,' he declared. 'You and me. We broke the grip at the Battle of the Bulge.'

Louie smiled for Mac, but he could not remember that. He could remember the war. Dead boys and body parts. Hard, grimed faces. The shooting. The ever-constant knot of fear, crumbling buildings, dirt and smoke. Louie watched Mac close his eyes to the sun and felt sad. He shook his head to forget the war. Old people, some with visitors, were seated about the patio and the yard inside the steel linked fence. Some were seated by themselves and stared into space. You could tell the outsiders: younger, louder and over-dressed.

'There is the edge of the world,' Mac interrupted, opening his eyes and nodding to the fence. 'There is the edge of the world.'

Studying the dirt path along the chain link fence, Louie remembered his cue. He rose on his cane and walked to the linked gate before the busy street of the outer world and stopped. He squinted, found his word *walk* scratched onto the post and smiled to himself. He peered about, hung his cane by its handle in a link of the fence and began to swing his arms and take deep, wheezing breaths, hearing the harsh goads of his long dead boxing coach and a scratchy rendition of *Bye, Bye*

Blackbird for some reason. He began his walk, punching the air, unassisted along the fence, feeling the stiffness in his legs; his body tighten then loosen as he lapped the yard, staring out through the links of the fence at the noisy, busy street and people of the other world hurrying by on the sidewalk.

A white limousine went by and Louie remembered a DeSoto. Red and white. Big red steering wheel. Smiling Maude and the kids with him on vacation. He lowered his hands, shook his head and continued walking. Each time Louie lapped the patio, wheezing for breath toward the gate, Mac saluted him from the table. Louie nodded. His breathing began coming fast. His legs ached. But Louie set his dentures and lips and made himself walk two more laps before he stopped and gripped the links, feeling his heart pulse, his hips and legs tremble. He sighed and grinned. He was not a quitter yet. Coach would be proud.

As he took his cane off the gate, Louie turned into the rigid, unseeing stare of a bald, old man in gray pajamas, slumped pale and thin in a wheelchair beneath a tree. Louie met the look that reminded him of a fish. He blinked, dabbing the perspiration on his forehead with his sleeve and quickly turned away.

After lunch in the cafeteria, the nurse, Scarlet Lips, led Louie and Mac to their room for a nap. She took Mac's walker and Louie's cane, helped them remove their glasses, coats and shoes and lie back on their beds. No sooner did she leave than she was back.

'Mail call,' she announced, handing Mac and Louie envelopes.

'My direct deposit slip,' Mac said, slipping on his glasses.

Louie slipped on his glasses, opened a big envelope and pulled out a gold card.

'Happy Birthday, Mr. Burns,' Scarlet Lips informed him. She made a smile. 'Birthday?' Louie said. 'How old am I?'

Scarlet Lips paused. 'Er, well, I'm not sure,' she confessed. 'Eighty-five? Eighty-seven?'

Louie gingerly fingered the card. He opened it to small print he could not read. He looked to the signature. *From the staff*, he could make out, and the last word, *Home*. Louie pondered and blinked. He sighed and looked up into Scarlet Lips' bland gaze.

'May I use your pen?' he asked, seeing a red one in her breast pocket.

'No,' Scarlet Lips said. 'It's time for your nap.'

Louie smiled for her and then he lunged for her pen. Scarlet Lips shrieked and grabbed his arm but Louie clung to her breast pocket. 'No,' she screamed, 'no,' while Mac came off his bed and hugged her from behind. Louie got the pen and the cap off, fell back onto his bed and printed the large, hasty letters *HOME* on the underside of his wrist before other hands came over him, seizing his arms and the pen.

Louie lay in the dark, holding his throbbing hand. *Where am I?* he thought, hearing the steady drone of night traffic outside a window. He tried to peer through the dark, wanting it to become familiar. 'Where am I?'

A ceiling light came on. He blinked and squinted. He had been asleep with his glasses on. A bed on his left was empty and made up with a wilted flower on the smooth pillow. He was in a strange and white room with a green tiled floor. In a bed to his right was an old man in gray pajamas who had flipped on the wall light switch. The man blinked at him. He had mussed, white hair and dark, hollowed eyes.

'Where am I?' Louie said. 'What am I doing here?'

The old man made a sad smile with bare gums and shook his head. He slowly slipped on glasses from a steel side table and raised a cord clipped to his bed cover with a button on the end.

'Don't make me do it, Butch,' he said. 'They've already given you one shot today.'

138

Shot? Butch? Louie stared at him and about the room. He looked down at his bruised, veined hand. Two knuckles were bleeding. He saw the sprawled word *Home* printed in red on the underside of his wrist and then remembered. Louie threw off the covers and climbed over the bed rail onto the floor.

'What are you doing?' Mac said.

'I'm going home.'

Mac stared after him, holding the cord button. Louie went to his closet, opened it and dropped his pajamas. He dressed in the faded suit and an old white shirt, stepped into worn, two toned shoes and pulled on an overcoat.

'Butch,' Mac said. 'Don't do it. They won't let you.'

Louie went toward the door, stopped and turned to the window between his bed and Mac's. He unlatched the window and tried to lift it.

'You can't do it,' Mac said.

Louie closed his eyes and strained against the window. It creaked, lifted. Mac cowered down in his bed. Somewhere an alarm sounded and Louie pushed out the screen.

'Take me with you,' Mac pleaded. 'Take me with you.'

Louie shook his head. Mac's eyes glistened behind his lenses. He dropped the cord and offered his feeble hand. 'Give my best to General Patton, Butch.'

'My name isn't Butch,' Louie told him.

Beyond the window and the shrubbery, shimmering vehicles streamed before him on an ink night street: shining head-lights, brake lights, stop lights flowing among flashing, blinking business lights. Constant noise, motion and blurs. He felt exhilarated with the possibility of adventure, flopped his overcoat like wings past the ice plants and onto the sidewalk, grinning and relieved, thinking of home, realizing he had forgotten his dentures, remembering to look for the North Star like when he hunted raccoons as a boy, and head east to where Fermata Bend, Alabama would be. Louie couldn't find the stars, but a sign flashed *walk,* an arrow sign pointed toward *Eastern Boulevard.* Louie turned east and walked along the curb, hiking up his thumb with a smile at the ever-flowing river of lights, cars and trucks, a scratchy *Waiting for a Train* reverberating in his mind, and remembering this was how his long ago buddy Hal and he once hitchhiked to the Chicago World Fair.

Among cans, broken glass, gravel and weeds, he sat in the warm sunlight before the highway zipping with traffic, wondering where it was going and trying to recall what he had been doing. He tried to take in the sweeping monotony of noise and motion, wanting it to become familiar. Louie rubbed his eyes, rose on stiff hips and legs, feeling a pang of hunger.

Like a slow, growing mirage, a young man came along the side of the road toward him, dragging a heavy wooden cross over his back, sweating in green biblical garb with a cord tied around his waist, long hair and sandals. 'Morning,' the man nodded as he went by. 'Been saved?'

Louie nodded and watched him grow smaller down the highway. He could remember pews and 'Onward Christian soldier, Marching as to war,' but he couldn't remember if he had been saved or not. He tried to recall, turning into a pine thicket to urinate, unzipping and peeing and hearing soft singing that was not in his head but coming from below the bridge on the highway. Louie zipped up his fly and followed the sound down a slope to a sandy bank with a trickle of a creek, discovering a little girl in red overalls playing on the opposite bank with two nude dolls, singing about 'bare necessity'. Louie stopped, stunned by her small face and shrill voice; her dark curls and little fingers. She wore a clean, white tee shirt and small green tennis shoes.

'Hi,' she beamed.

'Hello,' Louie whispered. 'Where,' he managed, 'is your mother?'

The little girl pointed in the direction of nearby houses. But Louie did not dare look away from her. He brushed tears from his eyes.

'Want to play?' she said.

Louie nodded. He stepped over the water and sat beside her in the sand, marveling at her small face and large brown eyes.

'We're digging for worms to go fishing,' she said. 'They can't use their arms,' she explained, 'so they have to use their heads.' She showed him by dragging the dolls' heads through the sand.

'Here, you be one.' She handed him a doll.

Louie smiled and reached for it, noticing rough printed letters in red on his wrist. He dropped the doll and stood up.

'I have to go home now,' he said.

He stumbled across the creek, clambered up the slope to the highway and walked over the bridge as a horn blared; cars and trucks whizzed and blasted by, a scratchy rendition of *Hang on the Belle, Nelle* echoing in his mind, then *Stardust*. He used to drive, too, he remembered. Had a blue Buick and a black Packard. Louie shook his head. Or was it a Blue Packard and a black Buick? Plaid, rayon seats and a wood dash. Maude smiling besides him as he drove, the kids in back. He shook his head to be rid of it. What was gone did no good. But home was a place. He could see the black and white tile of the kitchen and quiet sunlight streaming into the breakfast nook. You could hold your own cup of coffee, listen to Dizzy Dean on the radio, catch the news on TV, or Ernie Ford or Jimmy Durante. You could pee on the floor if you wanted to.

The hill ahead of him began to look familiar. This was the road that went into town and at the foot of the other side was the stone and wood Rabbit Filling Station – no, no, it became a Texaco. And beyond that was Clement's Hardware, the lumber yard he once owned and Julia's Grill, and beyond that were framed houses and the left turn toward his house among the shady oaks. He smiled and walked faster, despite his hard breathing, the rising, stabbing pangs of hunger and his aching legs. A car pulled up even with him, then went ahead of him into the grass and braked.

'Hey,' the driver called from her window. 'Hey.'

Louie stopped, stared. His head spun.

'Need a ride, Old Timer?' She was a smiling girl, blonde ponytail, yellow blouse and gold on her neck.

Louie tapped his chest.

'Yeah, you,' she laughed. 'Get in.'

The back door opened and a giggling brunette girl, clutching a brown beer bottle got out, in shorts, sneakers and a blue blouse. She smiled and led Louie into the back seat, got in beside him and shut the door. Inside, the car was white and cool, a loud and rhythmic noise throbbing from a speaker somewhere, and the faint smell of perfume. Another grinning blonde girl sat in the front passenger's seat. The girls smiled at him: young and bright eyed, in jewelry and in tight tee shirts or blouses.

'So...where to, Grandpa?' the grinning driver said.

'Over the hill,' Louie said.

The brunette beside him lost a swallow of beer onto the floorboard. The girls howled with laughter and Louie tried to smile. The car moved onto the highway with a surge of speed. He watched as they grinned at him and drank from their bottles, the driver grinning at him in the rear view mirror. The girl in front with the driver offered him an opened bottle over the seat.

'Beer, Grandpa?'

'Thank you,' Louie said. He was thirsty. 'Thank you.' He took the bottle and drank.

'Hey, Grandpa likes that stuff,' the girl beside him exclaimed. The girls shrilled and laughed, watching as he finished the bottle and lowered it. 'Thank you,' he gasped.

'Sure,' the girl who gave it to him said, and she winked at everyone.

Louie tried to smile back. 'Am I at the Cross Roads?' he wanted to know. 'Am I at Cross Roads?'

The girls just nodded and grinned. The car went over the hill to no Rabbit Filling Station or hardware store, framed houses, or even trees. Instead, there was a bright, white pavilion and a parking lot, streams of cars, billboards, signs, and fast food stands built of brick and glass. The still-smiling girl in the front seat with the driver offered him another bottle, but Louie shook his head, staring out his window, wanting what was outside to become familiar. His head felt light. Everything began to float into a slow spin in loud and rhythmic noise: the cool, white interior; the sweet, faint smell of perfume; the young faces, their grins and eyes...

Louie awoke. The room was still and full of light, the walls white, and chrome rails were on either side of his bed. He sat up, blinking. There was a bandage on his hand and the steady drone of traffic outside a window. 'Where am I?' he said. He was in the middle of three hospital beds on a green tiled floor. An old, frail man was curled up asleep in the bed to his right and a dried and yellowed stem was curled upon the smooth pillow on the bed to his left.

'Where am I?' Louie called. 'What am I doing here?'

Miming the Lieutenant

The night before Duckie left for boot camp, we stayed up talking and drinking bootleg beer in his car at the ruins of the old Harrison cotton gin. Then, in the early morning hours, and on a whim of Duckie's, we drove to Bryce State Mental Hospital to see the Lieutenant one more time – speeding up Highway 43 from Fermata Bend in Duckie's blue Shelby Cobra Mustang, smoking cigarettes and listening to Ike and Tina Turner, and Bobby Goldsboro on the car's eight-track player, then WLS on the car radio: The Beatles, Joan Baez and Santana. The night air was cool and a crescent moon floated above the whizzing dark treetops. The greenish-yellow glow of the car's instrument panel stood out against the dark steering wheel and seats.

'Whatever you say, man,' I had answered. 'Whatever you say.' Duckie had grinned with the idea, his limp blonde, almost white hair over his ears; his toothy, scimitar-like grin, his keen hazel stare. It was understood. The Lieutenant had been a childhood hero and now Duckie and I were leaving, having enlisted Delayed Entry and been tested before high school graduation which was a little over a week ago. We had been drinking and carousing around town and not checking in with our parents ever since, trying too hard to be loud and boisterous in the hiatus before a coming change. Duckie had to report to Parris Island in two days and I was reporting to Fort Bragg in a week.

When I told my girlfriend, Jimma Nelle, that Duckie and I

144

were going out that night, she got real quiet – and mad. She never liked it when I cut out on my own. 'What did Calera say?' she asked, meaning Duckie's girl. She twisted my class ring that was raised with tape to fit her index finger. Above her breast, she was wearing the gold brooch locket that held a lock of my hair – something that had been done between soldiers and sweethearts in Fermata Bend, Alabama, since the Civil War.

'Why?' she said. 'Where are you going?' I shrugged, there being no particular plans. 'Just something we gotta do,' I answered, it being beyond what I could explain or what she wanted to hear – that men in Fermata Bend had to do things together: hunt, fish, play team sports, or just mill around – and that a man's sense of self-worth was in how he stood physically, actively, or at least as a companion with other men; especially now, with Duckie and myself, when it could be for the last time.

'I know what you're going to do,' Jimma Nelle said, matter-of-factly, sweeping her long red hair back, arching her breasts at me and raising her thin chin and narrow blue eyes. 'Y'all going to drink and brag – and maybe fight.' She bit her lip. 'Well, I hope you die. That's all you boys are good for.' She looked away and got teary eyed. She wouldn't let me kiss her goodnight and there was no use talking.

Speeding toward Tuscaloosa on a late spring night in 1969, wearing Levis with wide belts, Acme Dingo boots, loud patterned shirts and leather watch bands, Duckie and I were as cocky and sure of ourselves as we would ever be, just as we played with utter abandon as linebackers on the Fermata Bend High football team; as we hunted deer and turkey, raced hot rods on the back river roads, and as we would dare one another: water-skiing barefoot on the river to see who could cut closest to water moccasins on floating logs, or going drinking and picking fights with people bigger than we were – that way there

145

was glory if you won, as Duckie would say, grinning, and no disgrace if you lost. We were after glory, wanting some kind of monument to our lives, some kind of feat, having grown up with the likes of *The Gray Ghost*, *The Rifleman*, *Combat!*, and *Twelve O'clock High* on black-and-white TV; having grown up reading the likes of *Sgt. Rock* and *Sgt. Fury* comics, and having grown up in a small, slow and decadent town that was immersed in an aura of past actions and myths – old forests at the river, old fields and Nineteenth or turn-of-the century houses; a dull brass plaque of names on the Confederate statue at the town square and solemn state historical society markers along the sides of the roads stating in emblazoned gold letters that great things had once happened: Desoto fought Chief Catauga, Andrew Jackson fought the Creeks, the Sixth Fermata Bend Confederates held off Canby's Yankees, and Bedford Forrest gave up the Cause at the Surrender Oak.

And there were also blurred legends surrounding the thick-wooded Legger Mound outside of town, where it was said a mansion once stood, where gold, Indians and slaves were buried, where lovers committed suicide and duels were held for honor. That, and the war stories of our fathers and the town veterans: plain farmers now, in boots and overalls, who hung around the Co-Op or the drug store in the late afternoons. We would watch them sigh and shake their heads for emphasis when they reminisced intense and dangerous moments of their lives in World War Two or Korea – and, of course, the Lieutenant, who took us up on our first and only exhilarating flight above the whole world as we knew it – Lieutenant S. Barker – our single and live example from Fermata Bend: a small, taciturn man with dirty blonde hair; loud, pearl-green eyes, and a small, thin grin; who had served in the RAF at Dunkirk and the Battle for Britain, who appeared in Fermata Bend one spring day all by himself from England in a converted Spitfire to crop dust; and all because, he said, he wanted to keep flying dangerous. He owed allegiance to no one; he came and went as he pleased; and he flew the olive green war machine with welded studs where the guns had been, wearing a leather pilot's jacket with goggles, a bright silver ring and a silver aviator's wristwatch that flickered when he moved his wrist.

Duckie and I grew up catching the plane's flashes in the sun during summers and falls, hearing the whines, screams, and drones as the Lieutenant did breathtaking barrel rolls, loops, dives and spirals, and circled in the infinite blue above town and around Legger Mound. He hid in the sun before every screaming dive on the fields, bombing the cotton and the soybeans in soft, settling mists, just clearing the telephone lines and the pine trees. And Duckie and I were there the last morning he flew. The Lieutenant's flying was rusty because of a sudden and surprise marriage to one of the large landowner's daughters and a promise exacted from him, the day she became pregnant, not to fly again.

The morning he broke his promise, Duckie and I were on the school bus in the medley of backed-up traffic and yelling and exclaiming people on the county road. The Lieutenant's new wife and her father – the newborn baby nowhere to be seen – were both standing off to the side of the road on a grassy knoll in their night clothes; the wife screaming with something like cold cream on her face and the aging father firing a shotgun at the plane as it made screaming dive after dive over them, passing low and fast, making everyone drop to the ground and get up again.

Duckie and I stood on our bus seats amid the squealing girls in their curls and dresses and the long-winding screams of the war plane overhead, our breaths misting the window panes while we stared out. 'Oh, wow,' we exclaimed. 'Wow.' We watched the plane drop low and come over the fields in the distance. Its wing took the stilts out from under a water tower; the huge wooden vat fell like a slow, heavy ball and burst. The

147

plane recoiled, rocked, and screamed over us and the road, just clearing a pine thicket, and made a long, dirt-churning crash into a field before the rise of Legger Mound. Dazed and alone, the little Lieutenant limped away from the black, curling smoke and licks of flame while everyone on the road stared after him and his father-in-law began to curse a fierce litany.

The sky over Fermata Bend went quiet after that. We stopped wearing cheap sunglasses, spreading out our arms for wings and playing Fighter Pilot on the playground at school. The women about town would not look twice at the little man as they used to. The men gave him chagrined grins. But the Lieutenant stayed, becoming a silent and virtual recluse. He wore plain clothes and opened a paint store on the square and began to drink, one day urgently warning everyone from atop the Confederate statue of an impending Luftwaffe air raid. His wife had him committed and she quit him after that.

Turning onto I-20 East at Knoxville, it wasn't long before some smart-ass Dodge Marlin tried to race us. Duckie sneered, eased off the gas and let the fool come up even with us before he downshifted and punched the accelerator. The hood of the Cobra Mustang rose in a scream and a squeal of tires, the headers roaring. My head snapped against the seat. I felt my cheeks being pulled back, my heart racing as the lane markers of the interstate blurred into a single line under the headlights and the speedometer climbed toward 140; Duckie's face an intense and demonic grin in the eerie glow of the instrument panel: his eyes wide, eager, glued on the road ahead; his nostrils flared, one fist-grip on the wheel and one on the gear stick. Once Duckie knew he could win, he downshifted and played cat-and-mouse with the Dodge until we heard a *BOOM* and saw blue flame shoot from under the other car's hood as it drifted away and off the road. Duckie and I howled and slapped the dash. 'Smoked his ass!' we said over and over.

Duckie parked the Cobra Mustang on River Road in Tuscaloosa and cut the lights. We got out, shut the doors and crossed the grounds in the gray dawn, walking by the small, drab crosses of the hospital cemetery, under the oak trees and toward the spiked fence. We kept talking and laughing quietly – and, I think, to hear our voices against the pale stillness and the thoughts that came with it. Duckie had to leave. We had not known much other than Fermata Bend, and everything we knew was coming to an end. When I thought of leaving and life without Duckie, Jimma Nelle, our high school, my old man or my mother – a quiver would rise in my stomach.

We sat on a concrete picnic table by the fence with our feet on the bench. Duckie kept grinning, but he was looking off and only answering me in monotones.

'Calera's pissed,' Duckie finally offered with a quick laugh. He looked to me for a reaction, his face flushed and his eyes narrowed from lack of sleep. 'She wants commitment, he said. 'Something *definite*.' He made a scornful grin. 'I told her they weren't in my vocabulary.' He held his grin and looked off. 'I didn't even tell Mom where we were going,' he said.

'Doesn't matter now,' I said, 'you're leav...' I couldn't finish.

'Yeah,' Duckie made a laugh, still looking away. 'It's happening, isn't it? All that talk and dreaming and playing,' he said, 'and now, here's your chance.'

'You ready to go?' I asked.

'Guess so,' Duckie said. 'It's now or never,' he sighed. 'I don't know where else to go if you want to keep going.'

We fell silent. I knew the impatience, the restlessness. There was nothing left in Fermata Bend but monotonous work and neither one of us wanted to go to college in order to become fighter pilots. It was happening. We were going into the service; we were going somewhere. I crossed my arms over my knees, put my head down and closed my eyes.

When Duckie nudged me, the sun was out, soft over the grounds. Squirrels and birds were moving about in the spring green canopy of the oak trees and hospital patients wearing slippers, blue pajamas and bathrobes or worn clothes were coming out of the ruddy-bricked building into the yard, into the sunlight inside the fence; their hair mussed and their stares gaunt. Some were led by nurses or aides, and some meandered alone. Then a barefoot girl, about our age, in faded bell bottoms; a loose, yellow, flower-patterned blouse, wire-rim glasses and long, brown, hippie hair came out strumming a guitar and leading a line of retarded children singing 'We Are Marching To Bryce,' in the tune of 'Marching To Pretoria.' The children sang, clapping hands, following her single file and out of step. They wore children's clothes or hand-me-downs, their hair cropped in bangs, their bland faces and gaping mouths swinging to and fro, some with Downs Syndrome and some staring from thick, horn-rimmed lenses. After them came two elderly women, arm-in-arm, in old-fashioned, white dresses, hats and shoes, smiling and strolling as if going to church decades ago. While they went by, Duckie and I slid off the table and went up to the fence.

'You sure he's here? You sure we'll know him?' I asked, remembering it had been two years since he had last re-committed himself, after escaping from here to Fermata Bend, climbing onto the shoulders of the Confederate statue on the town square at night, among the pigeons, and shouting to everyone below of an impending doom. He wouldn't come down and the fire department had to get him.

We spotted the Lieutenant as he came out into the yard, smaller and more frail-looking than I last remembered him: a shock of white hair but the same glaring, pearl-green eyes. He wore dirty canvas basketball shoes. His clothes hung baggy and limp: a dun sport jacket, an unbuttoned white shirt and wrinkled khaki slacks.

'Lieutenant!' Duckie waved, 'Lieutenant!'

The Lieutenant turned and saw us just as the children were stopped and shushed to silence by the smiling, long-haired girl who then began lining them with their backs to the shrubbery at the opposite end of the yard.

'Lieutenant!' Duckie and I chimed, 'Lieutenant!' The Lieutenant studied us. I waved to an aide that it was all right. As the Lieutenant walked over, the girl cleared her throat, began to play her guitar and sing 'The Whole World in His Hands.' Smiles sprung on the children's faces. They began to clap and repeat her refrains in jangled chorus:

He's got the whooole wooorld . . . in his hands!
He's got the whooole wooorld . . . in his hands!

'Lieutenant,' Duckie raised his voice above the singing. 'Remember us?' he said. 'I'm Duckie Stuart...and this is Steve Morton.' Duckie slapped me on the back and peered at him through the spikes.

'Well, well!' the Lieutenant piped, his voice shriller than the singing. He shoved his hands into his coat pockets and smiled with dull teeth. He tilted his head back to see us better. His skin was sallow from being indoors, there was an old cut on his chin and he had missed a morning's shave. The hippie girl shushed the children to silence, patiently shaking her head. She made the children begin the song over. Duckie grinned. 'You remember?' he said eagerly. You taught us about engines in Steve's uncle's garage. You taught us a lot, man,' Duckie's voice rose with the renewed singing of the children. 'You flew us in your plane when we were kids. Remember?'

The Lieutenant cupped his ear to hear. 'Well, well!' he piped, raising his voice against the singing. He took his hands out of his coat, then re-shoved them into his pockets. We stared at one another and I realized the silver was gone: the aviator's wristwatch and the large ring that had been on his hand. How is...' the Lieutenant pondered, '*Mort?*' he tried his memory, meaning my uncle.

'Oh, fine!' Duckie and I answered together in relief. 'Fine!' We nodded and smiled.

'Still working cars,' Duckie said. 'Gained weight, though,' Duckie added with a grin. 'And his family keeps him tied down.'

The Lieutenant gazed at us. The girl shushed the children to be quiet. Duckie and I grinned back. The Lieutenant made a wan smile, brought a hand out of his coat, pointed to Duckie's breast pocket and mimicked the motion of smoking with his fingers.

'Oh, sure,' Duckie said, reaching for the pack in his pocket while the smiling, long-haired girl began to lead the children now in singing 'Cum-by-ah' without playing her guitar, using sign language. The children stared at her. Their harmony dissipated into bleating-like chants as they aped her hands. The girl patiently shook her head and shushed them to silence. She made them begin again. Duckie offered a cigarette through the spikes to the Lieutenant. The Lieutenant took it, nodding his thanks, and brought the cigarette lengthwise to his nose, closing his eyes and smelling the tobacco. He opened his eyes, smiled, and placed the cigarette into his mouth, and leaned forward to Duckie's Zippo lighter through the spikes. He drew back, nodding and inhaling, and smoking in the old way that we remembered – the way we still imitated whenever we smoked alone – the cigarette held away from the palm between thumb and forefinger, waved gracefully as one talked, like a small wand or a trailing panache.

'*Cum-by-ah,*' the children sang, waving their hands, mimicking the smiling girl. '*Cum-by-ah! Oh, Looord... Cum-by-ah...*'

'They do sing rather poorly,' the Lieutenant commented, giving us a forbearing look. He waved the cigarette in a slow arch and smiled. Americans make good cigarettes,' he added, 'and good razor blades.'

Duckie and I smiled back. I glanced at my watch and tugged Duckie's sleeve. 'We don't have much time, Duckie,' I said. 'You have to get back to catch the bus.'

Duckie nodded, not taking his eyes off the Lieutenant.

'I guess I've come to say goodbye,' Duckie said, raising his voice above the singing. 'I'm becoming a Marine day after tomorrow,' he said. 'And Steve, here, is going into the army.'

'Well, well,' piped the Lieutenant. He nodded and smoked. 'God-speed. Americans make good soldiers, too...especially you Southerners.'

Duckie's face tightened. 'You were real, man,' he gave the Lieutenant an emphatic nod. 'I'm going to be like you.'

But the Lieutenant didn't hear. He made a wan smile and nodded.

'I said, you were *real*, man,' Duckie yelled above the singing. '*I'm going to be like you.*'

The children hushed and stared at us and the girl turned her head. The Lieutenant only smoked and nodded. 'Good,' he said, 'good soldiers.' He waved his cigarette at us. 'I would come out with you, you know, but I wouldn't know where to go.'

The children gaped at us. The girl made a closed smile and shook her head in wonder. But Duckie didn't notice. He offered his hand through the spikes. The Lieutenant studied it. He came forward and put his free hand into Duckie's.

'Goodbye,' said Duckie.

'Goodbye, Lieutenant Barker,' I said, and offered my hand through the spikes, too.

The Lieutenant put the cigarette in his lips and took my hand in his other one. The three of us linked up for a moment through the fence before Duckie I turned away.

Halfway across the grounds toward the car, we heard the children as they began to sing 'Where Have All the Flowers

Gone.' The girl shushed them to be quiet. She made them begin again, but they could not get the harmony right. We stopped to look back and we saluted a small figure of a man who smoked and followed us with steady eyes behind the spikes.

A morning in Tuscaloosa, in 1969. We were eighteen, under the flush spring-green of oak trees, standing and saluting beside the drab crosses of a cemetery, and parked ahead of us, on a curb, a line of chrome and a silvery, coiled cobra emblem on Duckie's blue car glimmered in the sun.

The Procession

Saturday morning, the phone rings. It's Momma. She's in the hospital again. 'Chills and fever, darling,' she says, in her high and aged voice. 'The doctor wants to run tests.' She pauses and I feel her silence, her waiting. I check the old impulse, think of Dad who has been dead seven years now, and of my older sister – but she's in Colorado with a family. Momma breaks the silence with her soft whine, says she's sorry to bother me, knows that I'm busy, but there's no one now at the farm. I sigh and tell her I'll come.

'Are you sure?' she says. 'You sure? Anyway,' she adds, 'I've got bigger news this time.' She pauses. 'Duckie Stuart has been found.'

'Found?'

'Oh, yes,' she says, her voice rising with excitement, 'two and a half months and five days shy of twenty-nine years – can you believe it? The nurses here say poor Lisa Watson Stuart becomes estatic every time someone at Fermata Bend Manor tells her the news. She wants to see his face and begins calling for old Colonel Stuart. Then she begins singing something like *Amazing Grace* – you know, 'he was lost and now he's found' – before she falls back into one of those staring lapses of hers. Bless her senile heart,' Momma adds quietly. 'Lisa Watson used to wait and pray every night to see her little boy again.'

'Momma, Duckie Stuart's been found?'

'Well,' Momma sighs and hesitates. 'All right. In a manner of speaking. A dredging crew turned up his car in a clay bank about oh, six, eight miles down the Tombigbee River...and he was in it,' her voice goes sad. 'You know that fast blue car he used to have when he dated Calera?'

'Yes, Momma.'

'He used to be her boyfriend, you know.'

'You mean...'

'Yes, yes, dear. Oh, poor Duckie,' Momma says, 'packed solidly in that thick river clay all these years. The coroner's report in the paper said the mud forced the water and air out. They found what was left of him clay-colored, wearing his seat belt and still in his prom night formal.'

'Momma...'

'Yes, it's for real,' her voice shrills and trails. 'Let me see, they found him two days before yesterday? I heard it this morning. The coroner has dug his body out and the car is resting on a flatbed off the town square this very minute.'

She pauses and I don't respond; I don't know what to say. Then she tells me that Grady Rhodes, the mayor, and the Fermata Bend Town Council have voted to give Duckie Stuart a town procession – the old traditional funeral march for important town persons, as was done for Old Man Bundt, Dad, Colonel Stuart, and others. Momma tells me the procession is set for Tuesday at ten AM.

'That is, if you come,' she says with an edge in her voice.

I manage something like 'Okay,' or 'Goodbye,' hang up and stare dumbly out my apartment window at the busy Birmingham street below, trying to comprehend, to feel something, but there's nothing, just the dull revelation that I am going to have to go and spend time with my aging mother, alone, now that Darcy is at the university and Calera and I have been divorced for a year. I think of calling Calera with the news, but the idea of her guarded, forbearing tone over the phone disheartens me. She's remarried and the news of Duckie is late. It feels like it's from a time that never was. It won't change things between Calera and me.

The phone rings. I turn and answer.

'Is this Steve Morton?'

'Yes,' I say, half expecting a solicitation.

'Hello, Steve,' the official male voice turns slow and friendly. 'This is Mayor Grady Rhodes. Remember me? Have – have you heard the news?'

'Yes, Grady,' I say. 'I've heard.'

'I'm sorry. I am,' his voice is smooth. 'I know Duckie was an old friend of yours'

'That's nice of you, Grady.'

'Duckie Stuart's body was found in the river, along with his car,' Grady reports, matter-of-fact. 'The coroner has released the body to Bright's Funeral Home and we are planning a procession in his honor for Tuesday at ten in the morning. We felt we should contact everyone who knew him.'

'Yes, I know. It's good you felt something,' I say.

'Well....'

'And you're still a son of a bitch, Grady Rhodes.'

'Well, I...well,' his tone stiffens. 'Well,' he pauses, 'I've done my duty then.'

'And what would you know about *duty* in Fermata Bend?' I ask, feeling an old anger rise. The line goes dead.

I slowly hang up, stare out the window, turn and go into my kitchenette that's cluttered with a week of dirty dishes and glasses with a gnawing feeling that shrewd people like Grady Rhodes get the upper hand in life, and then feeling how disheveled my life has become since the divorce, with only work and this dusty apartment with unopened, taped, cardboard boxes still stacked against the walls, my share of the now mismatched, formal furniture I could fit into the apartment, my meals irregular, my bed unmade for weeks – and I think how I was just a rural, Southern teenager like Duckie, brought up as old Pecan Family, to believe in things like duty and honor, to believe in what my country told me – not like Grady Rhodes, whose only conviction has been himself and his money, who is not old family in Fermata Bend, has always been a small, thin, and smiling equivocator, who wore his hair longer than we did, but always wore nicer clothes, never took sides or hunted much, or played sports, except baseball where he specialized as a bunt hitter while Duckie was the pitcher, who never drank bootleg beer with us or even worked up a sweat doing farm work with the rest of us, while his father rented old houses and shanty shacks. I understand he's now married to an interior decorator from Ohio who refuses to live in Fermata Bend and works and lives in Mobile while they see each other on weekends.

At Fermata Bend High, Duckie was the most popular with the girls, Grady was the most popular with the teachers; Duckie was voted the Most Likely to Succeed, Grady was named president of the Honor Society. After graduation, Duckie volunteered for the Marines, in typical Pecan Family tradition. Grady went to Birmingham-Southern College, got kicked out for drugs or gambling – I don't know which story is true – and fled to Canada to avoid the draft. Years later, after Calera and I had married and moved to Mobile, he quietly came back to Fermata Bend under the President's Pardon, laid low for over a year in his parent's basement, avoiding us Fermata Bend veterans while managing his father's cheap rental houses and trailer parks, keeping his smile and manners and slowly rising back to prominence in real estate and the town council over the years, spearheading such campaigns as bringing industry to Fermata Bend and new rezoning laws, and who now as a mayor no doubt appeals to the 'White Flight' from the cities, younger people, merchants; those with business and short memories, or those who moved to Fermata Bend to work in the new auto parts warehouse outside of town.

I find a dirty glass on the kitchen counter, rinse it out, pour a finger of bourbon from the cabinet and sip it, letting it burn down my throat, not wanting to think about having to go and tend to my mother, or feel the old chagrin again that Duckie and I were young, gullible fools from a small, Southern, rural town that valued patriotism and its military tradition over the anti-war sentiments from the West and the North. But it's no use. I hear my father's voice and see his small, wry smile and weathered face. 'No matter what you do, or where you go,' he once said, 'you are always Fermata Bend.'

I finish my drink, close my eyes, and slowly resign myself to go to Fermata Bend. I will do my duty to my mother. But I will avoid Grady Rhodes. The discovery of Duckie's remains is bizarre, and maybe sad, and I suddenly realize that I was wrong about labeling him a deserter all these years. But that revelation, too – like everything else related to back then – is late, late, and I have little energy for it.

I call my secretary, Mary, at her home and tell her my mother is sick and ask her to move my schedule around. The Robinson interview can go Wednesday. The Tuffit project is ahead of schedule and I can finish it when I get back. I call Jack at his home, my partner of our advertising firm, and tell him my mother's in the hospital. Will he take over things for few days? I hesitate and then add that an old friend of mine died, too. 'Sure, Steve, sure,' he says. Do what you gotta do.' We talk about the Tuffit project, then the RainPure water purifier ad. It's no sweat. Jack can push it for a few days. 'But, Steve, get back when you can,' he says.

I call Susan, a new girlfriend, at her travel agency where she's putting in overtime. She has to put me on hold before I can tell her our dinner date is off. As I tell her my mother is sick, she grows quiet over the phone. But I don't tell her about Duckie. I hear her disappointment. She says she understands. Will I call her when I get there?

'The minute I get there,' I say.

While I pack a suitcase and an overnight bag, I call Darcy in Tuscaloosa to let her know and I get her bright, pragmatic voice on the answering machine. Even though she would deny it's there, I still hear the voice I know from her childhood and our past, and it always tears me up. I try to sound upbeat on my recorded message for her. 'This is Dad,' I say. Grandmomma is not well. I'm in Fermata Bend for the weekend. Call me, okay? Love you. Dad.'

I call Darcy almost every day. I drive down to Tuscaloosa to see her every chance I get, and sometimes feel I see her too much and don't leave her alone. I can't help it. She's all I've got that's me. I want to believe I have not lost everything, that she's still my little girl. Fact is, she's handling the divorce better than I am. She's gotten over her radical, 'hurt' phase and is having fun now in her second year at the university. She's cleaned up her act and joined a sorority, and now goes to the pep rallies, the dances, the football games, the concerts, all of that.

The year before, her freshman year, after Calera divorced me and quickly remarried, Darcy stopped dressing Ivy-League-ish, stopped riding hunt ponies, and stopped being the country club type like her mother. She was an 'X-er', she said, a member of the Thirteenth Generation. 'I am an object of discontinuity,' she told me bluntly. 'There is no identity left but plastic.' She shaved the left side of her head, leaving her long, beautiful black hair on the right. She got a tattoo of an iguana on her shoulder. She wore old military boots, a ring in her nostril, loud lipstick and blush; loud and odd clothes of mixed styles, generations and colors, which she dug up at Goodwill. She renounced all music of the Baby Boomers and began following alternative music like the Smashing Pumpkins or The Jesus Lizards.

Now, though, she's falling back into her old ways. Her hair has evened out now, neat and short. She's buying and wearing more fashionable clothes again and she's letting rich fraternity boys take her out. No rings. No tattoos. She's smiling a lot again and doesn't care to talk about anything serious, the state of the world, the divorce, school or the future. She's enjoying being entertained. More of the old Darcy. More like Calera. I know she's preoccupied with college life and resents my intrusions, but I want to watch my thin, beautiful daughter with my ex-wife's nose and mouth and my hair color and brown eyes. I want to hear her voice, though when I talk to her on the phone, she has little to say, is in a hurry or going somewhere. When I take her out to eat, all she talks about is her latest boyfriend or where Counting Crows or Bonnie Raitt, or whatever group, say, is playing at that very minute in the USA. She loves to travel now and see new places with her sorority sisters. Daytona Beach. Churchill Downs. Gatlingburg. Her eyes widen when she brings up the places she's just been to, what she and her friends did, and she watches the clock. The new 'in' thing is flavored nail polish, making friends and meeting boys on the internet.

I listen, nod, aware of how I am not a participant in her life anymore, feeling like the best thing I can do is be there. The last year and a half has been hard on both of us, since Calera began a turbulent and aberrant menopause, sometimes reverting to youthful behavior, full of sentiment and nostalgia. When we divorced, she found a new man to dote on her within a matter of months, a small, gentle Pakistani in Birmingham who sells handmade rugs from his native country on the international market. Darcy tells me in off-handed ways how he adores Calera, waits on her, buys her presents and even washes her feet every night. 'To have an American woman is a great honor,' Darcy tries to explain it with a slight roll of her eyes.

I'll try to joke. 'Your mother, bless her heart,' I say, 'is worse than just an American woman.'

'She hasn't been the same since...' Darcy will let me know quickly, quietly, and drop the sentence with a small shrug.

I'll nod. 'I know that, Darcy. And I'm sorry. Believe me.'

In my Infiniti, driving South on I-65 to Fermata Bend, I realize I've forgotten to eat again. The traffic is thin. The sun is bright.

The drive will be three hours. I turn the car radio on to 'Oldie Goldie' stations, but then start changing stations whenever there's a Beatle song, a song by The Doors, or any song from the late sixties or early seventies. I snap the radio off when Don Henley's 'The End of the Innocence' comes on and play a Mozart CD instead as the hills fade into flat woodlands, fields and sweeps of pine. I keep calling Darcy on the car cellular phone, but only get her answering machine. 'It's me again. Call me in Fermata Bend. Love you.' I think to call Susan at work, but then decide against it. I'm restless, edgy with having to make a trip alone. The driving, the music, then trying to think of deadlines and projects at work do no good, I find myself thinking of Calera, Darcy, and finally, a young Duckie and myself. Distant, dull memories of Duckie seem like a time that never was: the bond of two youths, a past and a small, Southern town, marked by history, the likes of TV westerns and combat shows, John Wayne and Audie Murphy movies, the impressions of our fathers and the veterans of World War Two or Korea, like The Lieutenant, Josie Brannon and Old Man Bundt; the families' old tradition of manners and serving in the military. Pecan Family boys in Fermata Bend, Alabama, were brought up to know who they were, how to conduct themselves, how to work hard, hunt and play sports. Like our fathers, we were reared to become old-style gentlemen and patriotic soldiers.

I feel the old, creeping chagrin again at how young, resolute and naive Duckie and I were – volunteers, for chrissake, as were a third of the senior class males from Fermata Bend High, and virtually all of us who were Pecan Family. Duckie and I were out of boot camp, and en route to Vietnam: gung ho, invincible Southern males with hard bodies, shaved heads, in loud 70s formals, and back on leave for the high school prom with our girlfriends. I remember Duckie in his powder blue tuxedo, running for his blue Shelby Cobra Mustang, his black patented shoes slipping on the worn chert drive along the cedar trees of the Martin Lake House where we had gone for breakfast after the night of the prom: a shaved blonde head, an eager, curled grin in an instant desertion of our dates and a race for our hotrods to retrieve the French Teacher, Miss Tervin's corsage on her sudden remark that she had left it on top of the upright piano in the ball room of the armory.

We roared off down the drive, spinning up chert and dust, young and fast, reckless in our American hot rods. I came back in my orange SS Camaro, twenty minutes later, taunting our silent and miffed dates, full of myself, the corsage in my fingers – an Army Ranger who had beaten a Marine. Duckie didn't show and I knew it was because he couldn't stand to lose. Much later, taking my girlfriend, Jimma Nelle, and his girlfriend, Calera Brannon, home, his not showing had become odd. After I took the girls home, I drove around Fermata Bend and to all our old haunts along the back roads by the river in the misty wee hours of the morning, but I didn't find him. The next day before I left for Fort Benning, his mother called and I remember grinning to myself on the phone, politely answering her questions, sure that Duckie, proud and defiant, had driven all night back to Parris Island in his powder blue tuxedo, rather than be disgraced. After a week, I was called to my commander's office at Fort Benning and questioned by a Marine official and Sheriff Reed telephoned me from Fermata Bend to ask me questions. Duckie was AWOL. It was a shock. It didn't seem right. Duckie was a winner, our high school athletic hero, Pecan Family and Colonel Stuart's son. But there it was.

I left for Vietnam. Four months into my first tour, I began to receive the scented letters from Calera, who had quit Auburn and gone back to Fermata Bend in order to be 'happy again' as she told it, rather than from Jimma Nelle who was enrolled at South Alabama; letters that wished me well, but mainly poured out her grief, her loss, her confusion. It was as if Duckie had disappeared off the face of the earth. During two tours of

Vietnam and even long after I had come home and married Calera Brannon, I would sometimes dream of Duckie and then myself: Duckie or me grinning in his powder blue formal, his teal blue football uniform, or his Marine Blues – young, blonde and brawny; Duckie or then a version of myself staring me in with those keen hazel eyes that were so sure of themselves. I used to dream of Duckie in a blue fur coat and blue suede shoes, standing beside his blue Shelby Cobra Mustang in the gray sky and snow of Canada, giving me grin-misted breaths.

'That yellow coward,' I would make a point of calling him before Calera in the early years of our marriage. 'A yellow dog,' I would curse. I would swear and berate him in front of her and she learned to give me that resigned and patient expression that knew to wait out my verbal litany on Duckie, her lips formed into a thin line, occasioned with a shake of her head like it was an old, tolerated regret we had risen above together. Her smooth face and large gray eyes, her young body, her long hair then. 'I love *you,*' she'd always let me know quickly, and touch me. 'Duckie *left,*' she would say each time. 'No woman can live with that.'

That was then. I was in my twenties. I was strong and I could still kill a man with my bare hands, with the ruthlessness and the rage from the war to do it. And I was what Calera wanted. Someone she perceived as taking charge, strong and protective, but gentle and kind, and who would treat her as the privilege she was brought up to be. I was Pecan Family from Fermata Bend. I opened the car doors for her, followed after her into the church pew and out again; I knew my manners. She was comfortable. I could wear my wife on my arm, while she smiled.

You're not the man I thought I married, Steve.

From the time we began to date, there were times we repeated what we knew happened the morning after the prom, rehearsing details as if they were new, relevant or something that had somehow been missed, but we would end where we started: the mystery, the wonder, the why. There was no answer. Duckie disappeared. We never saw or heard from him again. The mystery unsolved, we chose each other and got on with our lives. I enrolled at the University of South Alabama and I took Calera away from Fermata Bend. Darcy was born. We moved to Birmingham and I went into advertising, determined after Vietnam not to return or become embedded again in the place and ways of Fermata Bend. Over the years, Duckie became an unspoken and irrelevant subject, until the month Calera began a turbulent menopause not quite two years ago. She went into rash tirades, sobbing spells, and a childlike, sentimental and nostalgic yearning for the time of Duckie. She accused me of letting my conduct and manners deteriorate, said I had lost belief and 'heart' in the way I treated her. She wanted a Duckie again, she said. She wanted a man to 'worship' her. She began smiling and flirting with older, genteel men at dinner parties. She began placing ads in the newspapers for a 'true gentleman,' and despite my personally taking Calera to her gynecologist who prescribed a treatment of hormone pills, and then to counseling, her anger and blame continued to simmer at me until I agreed to dissolve our marriage and she found someone else.

'We should have never left Fermata Bend,' I can still see her wail at me over a year ago in her pink plush bathrobe as we were preparing to go to a dinner party; her outburst loud and sudden, her carefully made-up face beginning to streak with tears. 'You took me away with the promise of a better life and it hasn't been.' Her gray-eyed look held me responsible.

'In Fermata Bend I was somebody,' she said. I was Calera Brannon, Josie and Sarah Brannon's daughter. And now they're dead and so am I – all I have is the memory of what I once was.

'I was *defined*,' she swelled and glared at me. 'I was Pecan Family. Everyone knew who I was...where I belonged and what kind of man I should marry.' She gave me a harrowing look.

I tried to talk. 'Calera, calm down.' 'What is this nonsense you're saying?' 'What do you want?'

Then began a litany of things to be repeated for months, things I still recall off and on:

'Darcy's in Tuscaloosa,' she says with finality. 'You are the dullest man I have ever known... Your manners have become rote... You're old, greedy, all that matters is your career... I find myself waiting on you to wait on me... You treat me like a habit, like I'm some kind of obedient dog on a lease, some burden you've resigned yourself to bear... I'm out on a limb, alone, exposed... I want a man who takes charge... I want a man who appreciates me.' I recall these and in other scenes.

I tried to talk with her. She kept interrupting. We argued. Our words became loud, mean, stupid. She began to sob. 'You're not the man I thought I married, Steve. You're not the man I thought I married.'

She holds up a finger to still me, silence me, taking a deep breath and slowly composing herself, and raising her chin high like my mother or hers would have done.

'I will not be treated like this, Steve Morton,' Calera declared. 'In Fermata Bend, you willingly took me on as a duty, something your father or mine or any decent man in Fermata Bend would do, because they would be grateful. You are not.'

I see her say, 'Duckie Stuart,' like he was the one, the answer.

'Duckie Stuart?' I say.

We argue about Duckie Stuart. I don't remember the exact words. It strikes me as ludicrous. It strikes her as the loss of her life.

'Why bring him up?' I want to know. 'Why bring him up?'

'He *loved* me,' she insists, sobbing, giving me slow, deep nods, her voice whining like a child's, totally oblivious of her messed face. 'You can say what you want, he did,' she says, over and over to my statements of otherwise.

'He left you,' I tell her. 'Why bring him up?' I say. 'That was over a quarter of a century ago.'

Calera just gives me a defiant look and an injured smile. 'He loved me,' she only says. 'And he was a good, *good* boy.'

We were all good Pecan Family boys.

Driving down I-65 South at a safe sixty-nine miles an hour in a Japanese luxury car, repeatedly trying to reach my daughter on the car phone and only getting her answering machine, at middle-age, in a thinning, short styled haircut, Dockers slacks, a Ralph Lauren shirt, and Rockport shoes, and over twenty eight years since the day he disappeared – it suddenly occurs to me I owe Duckie Stuart an apology. He died as he was. My years of blame and contempt toward Duckie were wrong. Duckie was true, Duckie was not a traitor. Duckie was what I was before Vietnam. And now Duckie has been preserved in his 1968 American hot rod, in the red Alabama clay of the Tombigbee River, as a boy of Fermata Bend in a powder blue, 1970s formal with black patented shoes. Innocent. Gung ho. Sure of himself and where he was going. Here I am, divorced, now a shell of something our fathers taught us to be, a lonely partner in an advertising firm, and living in a high-rise apartment that is only a stop-in station while I live to work, my career being all I have. I see Susan when our schedules permit. Sometimes I drive to Sammy's or Hooters for a beer and watch the girls, and sometimes I go to a video game arcade in one the malls where I shoot and kill people or play Mortal Kombat against junior high kids – a video-lit arena of what I once did in Vietnam.

Here I am, driving alone, older, with none of Duckie's attributes, driving toward the fading vestige and the memories of what we were – to Duckie's senile mother and my aging one, divorced from his old girlfriend, who has found someone else to treat her like the lady she was brought up to be; and trying to keep a bond with a daughter who has her own life and interests ahead of her.

I would apologize to Calera, to Duckie, to Darcy, to everyone and everything that we thought we would be, if I could. I would reconcile, absolve my years of feelings and judgment toward my hometown, what was my wife and what was once my best friend. Only there's no energy for it and there seems to be no place to go. In its place are memories of people who are old or dead, and Calera in a white sequined dinner dress,
touching up her lipstick in the vanity mirror of the car, before smiling and telling me again, *You're not the man I thought I married, Steve.*

And there's the distant memory of young, strong, naive boys – me and her boyfriend Duckie – home on leave for the high school prom with notions of how to be men. At the Martin's Lakehouse I got into my orange SS Camaro first. I beat Duckie out the chert drive to the county road and over the bridge in the race for Miss Tervin's corsage. I dimly recall reaching the deserted armory, jumping out of my car in my powder blue formal and black patent-leather shoes and running in, onto the littered, hart pine, ballroom floor, the blur of black and white, framed photographs and daguerreotypes of Fermata Bend soldiers along the walls, past the cloth-draped tables and stone fireplace to the upright piano and Miss Tervin's corsage under the teal blue and white printed banner: FERMATA BEND HIGH PROM 1970. I think back. His blue Shelby Cobra Mustang didn't show. Did he miss the bridge in the chert dust behind me? Did he try a short cut? Did he cross the bridge and turn around? I rack my memory, try for the old details that at one time I rehashed and memorized over and over. It's been almost thirty years. It will always be a mystery, only now it seems as if someone else – not me – was there.

I turn off Interstate 65 onto the long, two-lane county road, driving among old, familiar stretches of pecan groves beginning to flush green on either side for miles. Coming into Fermata Bend, the circular square, the Confederate statue in the median, the World War I artillery pieces, and the tall gray marble obelisk bearing the names of Fermata Bend men who gave their lives as soldiers, I am struck by the smallness and the neglect. Many of the surrounding, two-storey, bricked stores are vacant, boarded up. The businesses have moved out to a new plaza – the work of Grady Rhodes. Driving by the old rock building of City Hall with its adjoining police and fire departments, I imagine Grady Rhodes upstairs in the Mayor's Office, see the office contemporary now, newly furnished, and a stouter Grady at his large desk in something like a Lands End shirt, designer tie and fashion haircut, maybe his coat off, his sleeves rolled up before paperwork and the telephone – and like me – looking and acting busier than he really is. I have an instant wish to park the car, storm upstairs and confront him, embarrass the hell out of him, watch him cringe. But just how to do that, I don't know. I drive on.

At the second light off the square, on the curb before the faded red and white checkered sign of Johnson's Co-Op store, I see the car resting high on the back of a county flatbed truck in a dried wedge of clay, embossed with matted, dead river weeds. The flatbed is lined off with yellow police tape. In the bright sun, the dark, dull top and front grill of the car protrude slightly out from the crude brick of clay like the beginning of some kind of sculpture. I can make out a front, still inflated tire and the mag wheel bearing a Shelby Cobra emblem. I park on the opposite curb from the flatbed before the yard at the old armory building, cut the engine and stare. The yellow police tape sways gently in the breeze. The driver's side has been dug out, the caked door broken off and laid on the flatbed. In the small pit of evacuation are the dirt-caked steering wheel and the bucket seat that I remember as being white. There's no one about. I get out of my car, cross the street to the flatbed and stand there, trying to recognize the car.

'Can I help you...*sir*?' I turn to a young, uniformed police officer crossing the quiet street toward me. He's lean, bareheaded, with a dark crew cut; in dark Ray Bans, a two-way radio clipped onto his shoulder lapel.

'Oh, er, no,' I reply. 'I was just looking.'

'Not much to look at,' he comments with a slight nod of his head toward the truck. 'An old car from long ago....It's off limits, sir,' he informs me in an even, official tone. He gazes calmly at me, his mouth closed and small.

'You live here?' he asks.

I shake my head. 'I'm from the time of the car,' I say and look at him, his Ray Bans, his smug mouth, his thumbs hooked in his gun belt. He's young, sure of himself, and in a uniform – the way Duckie and I were years ago. Maybe it's the thoughts and feelings I've had driving down here; or maybe, it's the car, but an old, dulled anger wells up in me as I am reminded of myself and Duckie before Vietnam. I resent his presence, this pretense from someone young, in uniform, who doesn't know what the edge or the price of ruthlessness is, like the police officer, Ricky Barnes – a would-be boyfriend of Calera's – whom I almost killed one night at Old Man Bundt's vacant home place, the evening after Old Man Bundt's funeral, and three weeks after I had come back from Vietnam. He was loud and from Missouri and said he wanted to see some 'real South.' We were drinking beer. Calera drove us out in her father's Cadillac and we stood in the dark yard before Old Man Bundt's old, dilapidated house with peeling columns, among the great oaks. We went inside the vacant house, found that the lights worked and took a tour of Old Man Bundt's scant and out-dated belongings. Barnes was taunting me, daring me. He said Fermata Bend and our fathers were sorry, Southerners were losers and anyone who had volunteered for Vietnam was a fool.

It was two young men before a girl, and the girl looking on. Barnes was a stupid braggart who pumped iron and took Karate, but he pushed me too close to that edge where he had never been, and where what one wants to think of oneself doesn't make a damn. I put him down on the ground with my Case pocket knife to his throat, ready to kill as I had done before. The only reason I didn't was because he was one of 'us' – not Vietnamese. I scarred him on the neck and he never told anyone for shame. But ever since that night, Calera insisted the power of her presence was what stopped it, a Pecan Family gentleman showing restraint, decency before a Pecan Family lady, something she likened Duckie would have done with some kind of grin, a flair, a handshake, despite, say, a black eye and a bloody lip – after he had beaten the guy into a pulp. It's what I might have done, too – or tried to do – before I went to Nam.

I say nothing more, nod to the officer, turn and cross the street to my car. The night I drank and went with Calera and Rickie Barnes on a dare to Old Man Bundt's vacant farmhouse after his funeral changed everything. Calera saw me go to the edge and thought I would not cross it. What she never understood was that I already had, that I knew how and could and would, if I lost it, and that the time and place of Duckie had died forever, except for those who lived in Fermata Bend. In Calera's eyes, I was Duckie's friend; I was her friend; we were Pecan Family. After that night, Calera began to pursue me. I was supposed to take Duckie's place. The mistake I made twenty-five years ago was that I tried to.

I get into my car, start the engine and back the car out, and I don't look at the flatbed, the officer, or at the still yard or the old armory as I drive away by the framed houses, the churches, and the quiet streets with their old trees; and outside of town on the county highway again, I don't look at Legger Mound either – in the middle of what used to be the Demus Fields, now since covered in billboard signs and a Grady Rhodes trailer park –

where Duckie and I played war as kids and let our imaginations run in the thick rise of ancient oaks and Spanish Moss, inflated from the tales of our fathers and the men in town – a place where, among other stories, the Indians lived, Desoto camped, and the Confederates built breastworks – a centerpiece of Fermata Bend legend – and, more important to us, the place where the Lieutenant, our childhood hero, circled in his converted Spitfire before he bombed rows of cotton with insecticide and rose screaming into the blue sky to hide in the sun before he dove and bombed again.

Eva Jones, the aging head nurse on the floor station of the new, bricked hospital, smiles and recognizes me as I enter. She has large, sagging cheeks now, thick glasses, and flint-colored hair. 'Stevie,' she says. I remember my manners, smile, speak, and ask her about herself and her family. She tells me Momma's room number, tells me the doctor has already seen her. 'Your momma's better and maybe can go home soon,' she says. 'Doctor thinks it's an intestinal virus. But with us old,' Eva gives me a knowing look, 'you never can tell.'

I thank her and go find Momma in a peach hospital gown, propped up in the bed of a semi-private room she's sharing with an elderly black woman who's asleep with a tube in her nose. 'Darling, you came,' Momma beams. She sits up, pallid and smiling; touching her limp hair that is unwashed and more smoke gray than before. I look at her again. She's frail. Her large black eyes seem to protrude at me from her face. She was always a hardy woman. 'Don't touch me,' she scolds when I kiss her. 'I don't want you to catch this.' She puts a finger over her lips and motions to her roommate.

'Okay,' I whisper. I sit in the chair next to her bed, hold her thin hand with varicosed veins and ask how she feels.

'Darling,' she stares me in, her hand trembling in mine, 'you have no idea...you don't know....Did you see Duckie's

172

car?' she interjects. 'Did you see poor Duckie's car?' she whines.

'Yes, Momma, I saw.'

She squeezes her eyes shut, bows her head and presses my hand. 'Oh, that poor, sweet boy,' she cries. 'That good, sweet boy.'

I nod for her. I listen, nod as she retells everything about her sudden illness and how Janis and Gerald, the part-time maid and the yard man, brought her to the doctor's office and then to the hospital, where she heard about the dredging crew and the county coroner finding Duckie's body and Lisa Watson Stuart wailing and singing, 'He's lost and now he's found' at the Fermata Bend Manor Nursing Home, Lisa Watson's crying out again and again for old Colonel Stuart and her boy before lapsing into a catatonic-like silence. I hear it again.

Momma wipes the slow tears from her eyes on the bed sheet. 'It came out of the blue,' she says in a fearful whisper, glancing at the sleeping old woman as if she might intrude on us. 'I woke up feeling cold and achy. I tried to bring the horses in, and then I got nauseous – Oh,' she presses my hand, her face contorts, 'I thought I was going to die...with no one to care for me. She sobs and turns her head away.

'Momma,' is all I can say. I touch her shoulder. 'Momma.'

I hold her hand and wait until she gets herself together, wipes her eyes on the bed sheet and turns back to me, her smile forced, her tone strained and polite. She asks me about Darcy at the university and how I've been, comments on how nice my clothes look. She tells me how the doctor put her in the hospital, her brothers and their wives paying short visits: Uncle Jimmy and Aunt Ruth and Uncle Ron and Aunt Beth. 'I want you to go see them,' she tells me. I nod, hold her hand and listen. She tells me how Reverend Wilcox came, held both her hands, knelt at the bed and said a health prayer for a 'good woman.' And she liked that. She suddenly grips my hand with an urgent stare and tells me she's worried about that there's no one to look after the house and the farm.

'You remember how Old Man Bundt's home place burned down,' she informs me, as if it happened yesterday.

'Don't worry, Momma. I'll stay there.'

'I wish you hadn't divorced Calera,' she whines. 'I wish you had never left.'

I don't answer. It's the old guilt ruse. I was supposed to stay in Fermata Bend, take over Dad's insurance business, manage the pecan orchards and the pulpwood. Instead, I went to college, took a job in Mobile, then Birmingham. And I took Calera with me.

'You can come home now,' she says.

I don't answer. She looks at me, sighs and looks away. I see she's tired. I tell her to rest and that I'll be back in the morning.

'There's food in the refrigerator,' Momma takes over, turning to me, 'but you need to buy milk. And the blankets are in the hall pantry – .'

'I'll be fine, Momma. I'll take care of everything.'

I kiss her on the cheek and rise to go. She reaches out, clasps my hand in both of hers and pulls it down to her cheek. 'I feel better now that you're home,' she whines. I look at her imploring face and feel the absence: Dad's absence, Calera's absence, my youth, Duckie – I feel all absence. Momma and I are older and alone and I am a stranger in a familiar land. I swallow hard, fight the void away. 'Bye, Momma.' I kiss her quickly, turn and leave the room.

Momma's two pointers come barking when I get out of the car in the chert drive before our rock farmhouse. They sniff me for approval and begin wagging their tails. I get my bags out of the trunk, move into my old room in the quiet house and try to call Darcy on the kitchen phone, but only get her answering machine.

'This is Dad,' I say. 'I'm at grandmomma's. Call me, pronto. Love, Dad.'

I hang up and go and stand in the foyer, not knowing what to do. I go to the middle of the family room, feeling the stillness of everything and the empty house. It's similar to after Dad's burial and I think this is what it's going to be like when Momma goes. I look through the double glass doors into the dining room where Dad's body lay during the wake, below the portrait of my great-grandfather Demus in butternut uniform – Momma's grandfather – above the oak mantle of the fireplace. That day, people came dressed in their Sunday best and Reverend Wilcox walked around making sweet smiles, squeezing everyone's shoulder. Calera, my sister and I were too numb to think or talk. But we didn't have to. The people of Fermata Bend brought food, their daughters entertained Darcy. Without saying anything, the people of Fermata Bend went about cleaning the already cleaned house; they stood by smiling, servile, supportive; answering the phone or the door, quietly bringing in the flowers, while old veterans stood guard outside the door.

I look up at the stolid face of my great-grandfather, the dignified portrait of dark eyes that followed me, haunted me everywhere as a child. 'A soldier and a gentleman,' Momma used to say. 'Like your daddy,' she added with pride. It occurs to me that one day it will be a dusty relic in an antique shop. It was here in the family room, I almost killed Momma. I was just back from Nam, couldn't sleep in my bed and was asleep on the floor when she startled me on her way to the kitchen to prepare Dad's breakfast. For one second I had her by the throat. Neither one of us ever spoke about it after that. I feel alone and solemn. I think to go outside and see Momma's horses and pet them like I used to do.

The pointers follow but keep their distance as I go walking in my good shoes past the fallen training ring and along the brook in the old family pasture. The two young chestnut

175

geldings Momma has don't trust me. They walk away when I get close. I finally give up and stand there in the pasture watching them graze, remembering how well my mother could train horses, how well she could sit a horse in her habit, and how she could smile for the judges at horse shows while Dad and I looked on.

It was here, in the level pasture before the first row of pecan trees Dad taught me how to fly a kite and how to ride a bicycle, how to shoot a rifle and how to throw a curve. It was here he taught me how to dance for the Pecan Ball, the annual November event of Fermata Bend Pecan Families held in the old armory building, on the hart pine floorboards before the large stone fireplace, under the black and white, framed photographs and daguerreotypes of soldiers along the walls. At the Pecan Ball, everyone wore formals. Sons had to dance with mothers and every older lady before they could dance with anyone else.

Here in the pasture, in the soft, evening dusks, in jeans and work boots, I smelled my father's sweat through his shirt while we held hands and he taught me to dance. I memorized his splayed, thinning blonde hair, his weathered face; his amused eyes and small, curved smile. Father and son, boots scraping in the dirt, rehearsed the Waltz, the Charleston, and the Two-Step, how to bow and speak, how to place a hand on a woman's waist, how to balance her hand high on one's outside palm and how to keep one's chest a foot from her bosom. 'The measure of a man,' Dad instructed me calmly, over and over, 'is in how he treats a lady.'

As Duckie, as every son of Pecan Family, I wished to be a gentleman and a soldier like my father and my grandfathers. As every son of Pecan Family, I was brought up to work, to play and to hunt with men. As every son of Pecan Family, I danced with my mother at the Pecan Balls, I knew my manners and I went to church.

In the house, I phone Darcy with no luck. I think of calling

176

the office, but call Susan at work. Her secretary answers in a professional voice, 'I will have Ms. Crevar return your call,' she says.

I hang up and look out the front windows at the distant pecan trees and the county road. The intense stillness. In a few minutes, the phone rings.

'Hey, sorry,' Susan excuses herself. 'Clients, even on Saturday. So, when are you coming back?' she says. 'I can get off next weekend.'

'Soon as Mother gets out,' I say. I go over the few details of Momma's illness, not wanting to get too specific with Susan or tell her about Duckie. Typically, Susan doesn't offer much conversation, says 'uh huh' now and then as I mumble along. I hear what I realize is the click of the old metal Zippo lighter she likes to carry and the soft suck and exhale of her breath over the phone as she begins a cigarette. A nervous act of hers. Susan is a go-getter, a tough bird from Philadelphia who divorced her husband over her career and hasn't been in a synagogue in twenty years, she says. She was brought up by a single mother who wasn't always there and she has always lived in townhouses. She wears sharp business clothes, a blue-black, French twist hairdo, has a nice figure, a sharp nose, and a quick, dark look. It's hard for her to sit still or hear everything through, and like I used to be, her career comes first. She wants to be promoted and transferred back North one day and out of this 'Redneck Bonanza' as she calls the South, this 'provincial Bible Belt.'

Our relationship is convenient, sometimes sexual, it evolves around our jobs and the fact that we are lonely. I met her a few months ago while supervising an ad campaign and a film clip for her travel agency. We talked and looked at each other too long. On our first date, Susan watched me with an amused smile – more like a smirk. She let out short, nervous laughs when I opened the car door for her, the restaurant door, or pulled her chair. I indulged her in conversation, lit her cigarettes and made kind talk. I rose whenever she excused herself from the table and I rose when she came back. In the middle of dinner, she abruptly uttered, 'Oh, cut the crap,' leaned forward and lit a cigarette off the candle. 'Stop treating me like I'm a helpless citizen,' she said. Even now, sometimes, she will stare me in with incredulous looks, point out how I avoid being offensive, how I do not say what is on my mind, and how I will be courteous to a fault. 'Who taught you to treat people this way?' she says.

'My mother and father,' I'll say.

She will laugh. 'And I bet you went to the Methodist church every Sunday.'

'Baptist.'

'Bet you don't pretend to shack up, either – listen, Steve, don't treat me like that, okay? I'm not from here,' her hard eyes will level on me. 'Treat me like I'm real, okay?'

When I can think of nothing else to say on the phone, I pause.

'Okay, well, I've got to get back to work,' Susan says, matter-of-fact. 'Call me later, okay?' She hangs up.

'Goodbye, Susan.'

I stand alone in my mother's quiet, dark kitchen. I turn on the lights and walk through the rooms. I go rummaging under the kitchen sink and find an old bottle of Dad's bourbon, about three fingers full, and pour myself a drink in a fruit glass from the cabinet. The best thing to do is not to think too much, about Calera, Duckie, or anything, though I will try and call Darcy later. I sip Dad's bourbon, open the refrigerator and investigate if I will eat.

I awake with a start. I'm in my old bed, the same sagging mattress, a new bedspread, the soft morning light in the room. Darcy used to sleep here when she was little and we visited. Momma has removed some of the furniture, all my paraphernalia of teenhood, and repainted the green walls beige, but she has returned the pictures to the walls: younger, harder-looking faces of something like me in athletic or military uniforms, in hunting clothes with Dad, or in formals with my dates at the Pecan Ball. The framed photos of Duckie and me grinning together I burned when I came back from Vietnam. This morning I wish I hadn't, though I'm not sure a picture of him would change him in my memory.

I get up in my underwear, use the bathroom, walk through the silent house to the kitchen and make coffee. I call the hospital and Eva informs me that Momma is still sleeping, but the doctor will come before lunch. I drink coffee on the back screened porch in the swing to the slow creak of the chains, the sound of birds and the early morning pasture, the orchards and the young horses grazing, daring to imagine what quiet mornings were like with Dad and Momma when I was a boy and before Vietnam. I toy with what life might have been if I had stayed. Maybe I would be some kind of good, hard-working, outdoor-type husband and Calera and I would still be married. I would wear work clothes and she would wear house dresses, except when we went to social events. We might have had more children. I think of sons. They and Darcy would have ridden horses, hunted and fished, gone on hayrides, gone to pep rally bonfires in the middle of a sorghum field, and we would have gone every year to the Pecan Ball. They would know what physical work was. They would have had their Southern drawl and their manners. Darcy would have dated Bubba in his pickup before leaving for college. We would be a part of this close, rural community. We would go to church, feel secure and safe in the routine, the work, and the slow-changing familiarity of Fermata Bend.

I'm fooling myself. I get up from the swing, go into the kitchen, pour more coffee and I dial Darcy.

'Hello? Daddy,' she exclaims. I feel myself smile; almost cry at the sound of her exuberant voice.

'I got your message,' Darcy says. 'Is Grandmomma all right?'

'She'll be okay,' I tell her and I give her the details. *Where have you been?* I want to say. 'How are you, Babe?'

'Great,' she says. 'I've went to Atlanta with my roommate to the Wallflowers concert and got in late. I've got a new boyfriend,' she informs me. 'He's a blues singer and his name is Stan. I've been helping him set up at the Purple Pig Bar.'

'No wonder I couldn't find you,' I try to kid her. I envision her eager face on the phone – her smooth skin, her small mouth, but my brown eyes. I am sorry that her hair is shorter, but I am more sorry that I cannot see her.

'So she's feeling better,' Darcy says. 'When will Grand-mom be home?'

'I hope soon,' I tell her. 'If the doctor says.'

'Okay, give me her room number,' Darcy offers. 'I'll call her and maybe I'll drive down tomorrow.'

'That would be nice.'

'Sure, maybe I will.'

I give her the hospital number from the phone book and give Momma's room number. Then in a gush of words, Darcy tells me about the upcoming gig at the Purple Pig, the latest Tom Cruise movie, and that she's going to an Ozzie Osbourne concert with her roommate next weekend. Her first love is concerts and her second love has become traveling. The Purple Pig has lights, loud noise, smoke and special effects. 'It's fantastic,' she says. 'Divine. Stan is just beside himself.'

Her voice stays eager as she tells me about Stan. He's got a shaved head, a blonde goatee, wears an earring and a yellow bandanna. He's a senior at the university. He's two years older and his band is called Street Feet. He comes from Minnesota; she tells me he says the South is the true home of the blues, though he can't believe she is a Southerner. She doesn't talk or act like it. Darcy says that like it's a compliment.

'He hasn't been down here long, has he?' I say.

'Oh, really Dad? Do you think?' Darcy says. 'The way I talk and all?'

I listen to my daughter, think of Calera and smile to myself. 'You, your mother and your grandmother. You are all Southern ladies.'

'No, Dad, I'm not like them,' she whines. 'I'm *not*.'

Darcy goes on about herself and Stan. It's been all of three weeks. I listen politely and say my 'Okay,' now and then, like a father's supposed to do with his excited daughter. But this is nothing new. Darcy has had lots of boyfriends. This one doesn't sound like he's going to last, either. Running a band and going to school doesn't make much money or leave much free time. And while Darcy, like her mother, would claim she is a new, and 'contemporary' woman, the truth is, Darcy, her mother and my Momma are of the same ilk. They require money and attention. I should know. I was reared by one, I married one, and I helped to rear Darcy.

For all Darcy's pretense of Feminism and independence, she grew up in and likes privilege, as her mother does. Like Calera, Darcy's attractive and knows it. And like her mother, Darcy has been brought up to expect to live in the comfort and protection of men. Darcy may like to dress 'down' and 'rough.' She may pretend to be en vogue, 'grunge,' whatever, but Calera and I bought her the BMW she's driving and she still has clothes hanging in her closet from Neiman Marcus, Saks Fifth Avenue, Laura Ashley, Christian Dior, and others. Just like her mother, all her favorite jewelry comes from private dealers in Birmingham and Darcy likes Chanel No.5 and Italian shoes. Like her mother, she's witty and graceful; but she, too, grew up in the luxury of the country club and social clique where men honored her, paid the way and made the world secure.

'Don't let anything happen to Grandmomma,' Darcy says, her voice childlike and insistent, like I am supposed to fix it. 'What are you going to do?'

'I will take care of things,' I tell her, 'until she is home and well enough for me to leave.'

'And how's your mother?' I offer, making my tone upbeat. 'Oh,' Darcy pauses. 'Oh, she's fine. Er, Daddy?' she says. 'Did someone die?'

I hesitate. 'Yes,' I say. 'The remains of an old friend of your mother's and mine were found in the Tombigbee River. They're going to have a procession for him just like they did for your grandfather. Do you remember?'

'Some of it,' she says. 'So, why didn't you tell me or Momma?'

'Obviously, I didn't have to. Who told you?'

'Momma.' she says. 'Weird,' she adds, pauses. 'Is it true he was Mom's boyfriend? The love of her life?'

'Yes. I guess you could say that's true.'

'And was a star athlete? A Marine? A perfect gentleman from Pecan family? That you and he were the best of friends and racing to retrieve a corsage for a beautiful woman when he disappeared? And that Mom would have married him instead?'

'Darcy, it was a long time ago.'

'Oh, wow,' she says. 'Are you and mom going to this procession?'

'I can't speak for your mother,' I say, 'but I may.'

'That's sad,' Darcy says. 'And sweet.' I imagine her lips turning like a small frown. 'Why would you go to his funeral after all these years?' she wants to know.

I don't have a ready answer and hear myself sigh. 'It's expected, Darcy,' is all I can say. And I think of Momma. 'After all these years...you pay respect. Your grandmother would want the family to...to stand in.'

'Respect for the dead,' Darcy echoes, as if reading it out loud. 'Your best friend. Mother says you called him...a...a traitor.'

I close my eyes, open them. 'That's true, Darce,' I make my voice calm. 'And now,' I say it slowly, 'we know that I was wrong.'

'How was he a traitor?' Darcy wants to know.

'It was a long time ago, Darce. We...we had beliefs. We were young. We were soldiers. We thought that what we were doing – what we were told to do – was right. When he disappeared, I thought he had deserted.'

'Oh,' Darcy says. 'To hear Mom say it, you would think it just happened. She gets a little sniffy and talks about how he was everything she ever wanted...' Darcy stops. I feel her waiting but I don't have a ready comment.

'Well. That's how she wants to remember it, Darcy,' is all I can say, surprised at how quiet my voice sounds.

'She acts like life has passed her by,' Darcy adds.

'It would be good to see you, if you come down,' I change the subject, then ask her how school is, then I ask about Stan's band and Darcy's voice becomes enthusiastic again. She tells me his band has the Purple Pig Bar for three nights and then they may go a BluesFest in Huntsville.

'And you're going to the Purple Pig every night, right?'

'Of course,' she says. 'Huntsville, too.'

I make a laugh. 'Okay,' I say. 'What if I come down next week and take Stan and you out to dinner?'

'But I'm going to the Ozzie Osbourne concert.'

'Oh, that's right.' I feel caught out. 'Sorry. Maybe the next week? Hey, you want me to get you three or four tickets for the next concert in Birmingham?'

'Well,' Darcy hesitates, 'maybe. I'll see.'

'Okay, Babe. I'll let you go. Hey, I love you.'

'I'll call Grandmomma.'

'Wonderful. Let me know if you're coming down.'

When Darcy says, 'Love you, too,' it means everything.

I hang up. I walk around the house, glancing at the family room wall clock. It's still early. I go into my old bedroom, put on some Levis I brought with me, a t-shirt, and my jogging shoes, and I go out on a whim and do chores my father used to do, what Gerald, an old man, now does for mother: shovel out the barn and the furnace, feed the animals, mend a sag in the fence.

I crank up Dad's old International pickup in the barn, drive out and get the mail from the highway, then I turn into the new green haze of the groves like he would do, and pretend to check the irrigation pumps and the automatic squirrel blasters, remembering how Duckie and I used to work in these groves for spending money, how I led Darcy through these groves as a little girl on the Shetland pony Dad had for her, and then remembering how in another time, after I came back from Vietnam, Calera and I would drive out into these groves in this same pickup, strip off our clothes and make love on a horse blanket in the grass under the green leaves and rough gray limbs, among the still trunks. The sunlight warmed our bodies while we dozed. Unlike the quick, cheap whores with cheap smiles in the congested, smoky streets of Saigon, I lost myself in the presence and hope of Calera, suspended my inner rage about Duckie, buddies I had lost in Vietnam and the overall sense of waste and futility of the un-winnable war. Calera was a sweet, naive girl who clung to me with expectations. She gave me purpose.

Back at the house, I'm starving. I make some egg and ham sandwiches and wolf them down with a glass of orange juice. I look at the clock. Before I shower and dress to go see Mother, I call Susan at her office. She's busy at her computer on a stat report. I hear the quick tapping of the keys as she gives me short answers and tells me she doesn't have time for this right now. But I have no one else to tell this to, so I tell her. I tell her that where I come from is an anachronism, a place that has been slow to change because there are few things to change it, a traditional community of old families distinguished by a history of soldiers going back to Andrew Jackson.

'Andrew Jackson?' Susan ponders, still typing.

I tell her it was a community of families distinguished first by cotton and now pecan orchards and pulpwood; that the women – my mother – were brought up as ladies for generations, held up on pedestals all of their lives by the families, the community, then by the husbands.

'She never left?' Susan's tone is incredulous.

'No, not for long.'

'She never cleaned house?'

'No, not much. She had maids.'

'Jesus,' Susan says. The keys stop. 'And never worked?' I hear the slight edge of derision in her voice, then the click of her Zippo lighter.

'No, not really,' I tell her. 'She enjoyed preparing breakfast for us. She inherited pecan groves, a lot of land in pulpwood. My father took care of everything. Now my uncles do.'

'Oh,' Susan says slowly.

'You don't understand,' I tell her. 'That's why I'm telling you. It's the way we were brought up.'

'I see,' Susan says. A long pause. 'Well, go wait on your mother, little boy. I've got work to do.'

Momma sits up and smiles when I enter the hospital room with florist roses in my hand. She has put on make-up and her hair has been permed. She looks more like herself, though still tired. Her roommate is gone and the other bed is made up.

'Darling,' she says.

I hug her. I kiss her on the cheek, sit by her bed and place the roses in her lap.

'Are you doing all right?' she wants to know. 'I feel bad that I'm not home with you.'

'Everything's fine, Momma. Are you better?'

She tells me she thinks so, but the doctor wants her to stay.

'Has Darcy called you?' I say with a smile.

'Why, no,' Momma shakes her head. Her eyes grow wide.

'She will,' I say with a smile. 'She might even come down.'

'Oh, wonderful,' Momma shrills. She touches her hands together like in prayer and smiles.

She wants to know that the dogs and horses have been fed, that the food supply is adequate, that I'm comfortable.

I nod. I say yes, thinking how Momma continues to keep horses even though she can no longer ride.

'I called Janis and Gerald,' Momma tells me, still smiling, 'and told them they need not come in for a few days because my son is home.' She beams at me. 'That's all right, isn't it, dear?'

'You did?' I say and look at her, but don't say anything more as I sit and listen and she tells me how she misses quiet mornings at her house, drinking coffee at the kitchen table, watching the sunlight grow on the dew in the pasture, the horses grazing, the sound of the birds. She tells me the latest about the church, the neighbors and relatives, then what she remembers about sickness, her father's strokes, her grandmother's cancer.

She grows quiet, looks at me and begins to talk about my sister, my sister's two kids, the latest photo my sister sent of the family standing in new Easter clothes. I listen, force a smile and nod, and note again how since Dad's death she has seldom mentioned him. When she has, it has been in some light, offhand way; a memory in which he was along: he was there to bid and hold the halter line when she went to the horse auction in Shelbyville and bought Doc Cee, he was the one paddling and the one that pulled her out the time she went on the church canoe trip and fell in. I listen, smile and nod, remembering how Dad taught us to follow Momma single file down the aisle to the family pew in church and back out again; and I see my father younger, robust and blonde: rolling up his sleeves to bat baseballs so I could field them; the excited, amused squint of his eyes. I see him patiently waiting on Momma. He took orange juice and coffee to her in bed every morning. He took

186

the newspaper and her slippers to her on the recamier arm chair every evening.

'Steve, darling?'

'Sorry, Momma. Just thinking.'

When Momma asks me about Birmingham, they are questions to go around Calera and questions I've answered before. She wants to know what I do when I'm not working.

I shrug. 'Just go out,' I tell her. 'A bar, a movie, a restaurant. Sometimes the mall.'

'Goodness,' she says, 'just go out. Chasing city lights,' she huffs at me. She lays her head back on the pillow. 'We're Pecan Family,' she states. 'You should come back to Fermata Bend, settle down. We're somebody, you know. We're Demuses...and Mortons.'

'How about Dad,' I say. 'Did he count?'

Momma blinks, her eyes widen. 'But of course – '

'He paid a hell of a price to be married to you,' I blurt out. 'He loved you more than anything. He did nothing but cater to you.'

'Yes,' Momma hesitates, blinks. 'He did love me,' her voice grows kind. 'He was a gentleman,' she says. 'A perfect gentleman.'

Momma gazes at me. I bite my lip, look away, say nothing more. It does no good. After a while, Momma begins to talk about needing to feed the blue hydrangeas under her bedroom window, Myrtle Sue's charity shoe sale to be on the town square, and the upcoming church breakfast which she is going to try and get Janis to cook something for.

Later, I find the doctor in the hallway. He's new in town, young, thin and bald. He says it's a stomach virus and Momma is getting stronger, but because of her age, he wants to be careful, would like to keep her one more night. If she's stronger in the morning, she can leave. I thank him and remember to thank Eva at the nurse's station.

Back at the farm, each of the women farm neighbors come to the house in their dusty cars, in simple dresses and plain shoes, their faces older. They ring the doorbell: Mrs. Knox, Mrs. Jones, then Old Widow Swartz. Each one presents herself on the front porch, smiling and bringing food. They have already been to see Momma. 'Welcome home,' they say. 'Why, Steve Morton,' each exclaims, 'you've grown so tall and handsome. I can remember when...'

'Yes Ma'am,' I feel a sheepish grin. 'I remember.'

Respectively, the women bring fried chicken, fried okra and cornbread, buttermilk and cookies. Each politely refuses to come in, asks if she can do more. I say no, thank her, 'Yes Ma'am her, remember to ask her to come in again. After they are gone, I eat the chicken, cornbread and cookies, throw out the okra, and give the buttermilk to the dogs. I can't stay still; I can't stay in the house. I get in my car and drive up and down the highway by the groves and fields, the woods and poor blacks' shacks, listening to the Dave Matthew's Band, Blue Traveler, and the Counting Crows on my car CD player, wishing to God there was a bar where no one would recognize me, or video game room where I can pretend to kill people, as I do at the malls in Birmingham. I don't want to see anyone, I don't want to remember, I don't want to hear another polite voice.

Driving back into town, I take the shortcut by our church and see Reverend Wilcox, older, ash-haired, and pot-bellied now; his coat off, his sleeves rolled up while he directs young boys digging in the shrubbery of the church grounds. He looks up, raises an automatic hand, makes an instant smile but doesn't recognize me. I look ahead and drive on, remembering how he married Calera and me, and how at the funeral Reverend Wilcox made a sweet, sentimental sermon on Dad as an example for us all, as a 'good man.' Everyone cried. He gave that same smile, hugged my momma and patted her hand.

I keep driving, go around the square and then out by the old high school which has been remodeled, listening to FM Rock KZX on the radio. The old Texaco filling station has been boarded up and beside it is a new Sunny South Supermart. Teenagers mill out in front of the Dari Creem, by pick-up trucks and old cars, watching the traffic go by. I stare at them as I drive back around from the high school again, wondering if I grew up here, thinking they must be the children of kids I went through high school with. I hear my father's voice: 'What our town has is little distraction.' I see his small, rueful grin. 'And a common set of values,' he'd add. I see my father who always smiled and spoke to people; was large, blonde and kind; who was a decorated veteran, a hunter and an athlete; and who, above all else, loved my Momma, was always there for the woman who made him choose between Atlanta and her: her land, her home, and her name; between being a Regional Manager or a local insurance salesman. I think of how late and hard he worked as an insurance agent and in the pecan groves. I wonder if it shortened his life. I turn the volume up on the radio, and remember how he told me, solemn and alone in the truck at the bus station before I was to leave for boot camp – that duty was the 'sublimest word in the English language.' A man could not hope to do more, a man should not wish to do less. Then he hugged me tight with tears in his eyes and told me he could not tell me what was about to happen, but that whatever happened, he expected me to do my duty.

That evening, I try to play fetch with the dogs but they won't return the sticks. I devour three Stouffer's Casseroles from the Sunny South Supermart and listen to Paul Harvey on Momma's radio. Momma has no VCR, no cable – and she wouldn't use it if she did. I flip through the three clear channels on Momma's TV, then lie on the sofa, alone in the empty house, my muscles sore from doing chores again. I find silt under my nails. I will myself not to call Darcy and wonder if she has called Momma, like she said she would, wonder if she's going to drive down. There's no movie in town, no video game arcade where I can play Mortal Kombat. The only things to read are the Bible, *Reader's Digest*, and the *Mobile Register*.

'This is a mess,' I call Susan at her townhouse. 'You don't know what boredom is 'til you've come back to the sticks.'

'What did you do before?'

'We didn't know any better.'

'Why, no,' Susan's voice rises, 'I can't come stay in your mother's house. In a small Southern town? What would people think?'

It was a wild thought of mine. I know Susan's not coming. Besides, she has to work. I keep her on the phone anyway, thinking of things to say, talking about nothing in particular, until she tells me she has to go. I hang up, thinking how this thing with Susan isn't going to work – never was – but that I hold on because I'm lonely. I pace the empty house of my childhood, peering out the windows at the night, feeling the absence of Calera and then Darcy. I try not to think, but find myself remembering the morning I awoke with a start and almost killed my mother, and the night I fought Ricky Barnes, years ago at Old Man Bundt's, and how it changed everything.

Calera was right. We took each other on to save ourselves, falling back on the old Fermata Bend ways. We wanted to love each other, but the marriage was an act. For my part, I couldn't keep the act up. Calera wanted a permanent 'Duckie' and I wanted the belief that was mine before Duckie was lost. I lied to myself with Calera and with Susan I am lying to myself now. But, damn it, like Duckie, like every good Fermata Bend son, I wanted to believe in my father.

I think to drive into town, buy two six packs at the Sunny South SuperMart and get drunk at the old railroad tracks under the stars and moon and the smell of honeysuckle like Duckie and I used to do when we were young, full of ourselves and sure. Maybe that young, smartass cop will try to take me in. I'd like for him to try. More likely though, I'll end up drinking the beer and searching for an address in the phone book and driving by Grady Rhodes' residence just to see what kind of car he has, what kind of house he lives in, expecting a light in a big upstairs window. And even later, under an old and waning moon, I'll find myself making a tearful speech at the fence to my Momma's horses.

In the morning, I enter Momma's hospital room and she looks up, greets me with an anxious look, seated on the end of the made-up bed, her face heavy with make-up, thick red lipstick and pearls. She's in a red and white print dress and white, high heeled shoes, her thin, veined hands folded in her lap. Her purse, cosmetic bag and overnight suitcase are packed and beside her on the bed. She makes a smile.

'I'm sorry I'm late, Mother. How do you feel?' I talk fast, my head throbbing from the beer last night and the blaring phone call from Eva a little over thirty minutes ago. I note Momma looks stronger and her perm from yesterday is still good.

'Better,' she makes another smile. 'Where have you been?'

I tell her I didn't sleep well.

'And you don't look so good,' she says.

'Has Darcy called?' I think to ask.

'No,' Momma says quietly.

I stop at that. 'I'm sorry, Momma,' is all I can say. 'I've done the paperwork,' I offer after a moment. 'We can go as soon as they bring a wheelchair.'

'Have you been to see Uncle Jimmy or Uncle Ron?' She studies me with a closed smile. I can tell by her look that she already knows the answer. I tell her no.

'I've saved you once again,' her smile turns sad. 'I didn't tell them you were here.'

Mother stares quietly, with a resigned expression, and I don't say anything. When a young nurse enters the room pushing a wheelchair, my mother sighs and raises her hand to me like she would do with Dad. The nurse and I help her up and into the wheelchair. I follow with mother's purse, her cosmetic bag and suitcase while the nurse pushes her out and down the hall toward the hospital exit. Eva Jones comes around the front desk, hugs Momma and says goodbye. Mother squeezes her hand. 'Thank you, Eva,' she says.

'Now, Miz Morton,' Eva says, 'don't you plan to come back anytime soon. You hear?'

In the car, before we drive away from the hospital, Momma reaches out and touches my arm from the front passenger's seat. She gives me a quiet, solemn look. 'Take me to the funeral home,' she says.

'Funeral home?' I look at her. 'Bright's Funeral Home?'

'Very good,' she says. 'Yes, Bright's Funeral Home. Where else?' she answers my stare. 'There is no other funeral home for whites in town.

'Duckie is lying in wait,' Momma explains, 'and Lisa Watson Stuart is there. I just heard it in the hospital.'

'In wait?' I echo.

Momma looks at me, calm and serious. She raises her chin and doesn't say anything. I look to the road and turn the car from the hospital toward the town square. We ride in silence, even by the old armory and by the dried clay slab of Duckie's car atop the flatbed at the curb before Johnson's Co-Op. I turn from the square over the railroad tracks to the circular asphalt drive of Bright's Funeral Home: a white bricked building with white Ionic columns and wide white double doors with brass knobs, brass footplates and brass jamb lanterns. In the parking lot are perhaps a half dozen cars and a van from the Fermata Bend Manor Nursing Home. I recognize Uncle Jimmy's pickup and Uncle Ron's Oldsmobile. I park beside the van while Momma inspects herself, pursing her lips and smiling into the rearview mirror. She takes a deep breath of resolve and looks at me.

There's nothing to do but cut the engine, get out of the car, go around and open her door, as Dad would. I help her out of the car, shut her door and hold Momma's arm as we go up the bricked walk. My head still hurts and my heart begins to pound and a knot rises in my throat at the sudden thought that the casket will not be closed and we are going see something skeletal, wasted and grotesque that Duckie's crazy and senile mother, and indeed, the old-timers and the veterans of Fermata Bend are quite capable of making happen. When I open one of the large double doors and we enter the lobby, Mr. Joe Bright comes around the reception desk to greet us with an eerie, slanted smile of shiny dentures, his thin, salt and pepper mustache. He's in a dark gray suit and bright yellow tie, and is wearing his blue legion cap. He gives me a wink, hugs Momma. 'Joanne,' he says. He shakes my hand, holds on to it. 'Steve.' He shakes his head sadly, looking down,

'I know how close you two were. I know how much Duckie meant to you.' His voice is kind. 'If only the old Colonel and your Dad could be here now.'

I can only nod. I sign for Momma and myself in the Visitors' Book and Mr. Bright leads us personally to the Main Viewing Room on our immediate left, through double doors to thick green carpet, high white walls and white ceiling with a centered medallion and chandelier, too; a semi-circle of metal chairs, a handful of people and a simple, closed metal casket covered in an American flag on a steel roller with wreaths of red roses on stands beside it. Old veterans in dark suits and blue caps stand guard at either end. Beyond the semi-circle of chairs, parked before the casket in a wheelchair, is Lisa Watson Stuart, her pallid, shriveled face with thick lenses and close-cropped, snow white hair. Her small body is slumped in the wheelchair, in an old fashioned, green cocktail dress.

Uncle Jimmy comes forward to meet us and Uncle Ron, too, both of them older, thinner, in their suits and legion caps. They smile, hug Momma and shake my hand. They do not know that I've been here for two days. Three other senior Fermata Bend veterans, dressed like my uncles, whose faces I can vaguely recognize, stand quietly to the side of the semi-circle of chairs as if on duty.

Momma pats her brothers' arms, nods for them, sets her face and goes toward Lisa Watson Stuart. Mr. White stands with us as we watch her go. Uncle Jimmy slaps my arm and Uncle Ron smiles.

'How long you been here, boy?' Uncle Jimmy says.

'Oh. Not long, Uncle Jim,' I say and smile. I see none of my cousins. Most of the girls, all married now, have moved away. My uncles' sons, after serving in the armed forces, either help my uncles keep the pecan groves and pulpwood, or have moved away, too.

'You want a cap?' Uncle Ron says.

'Steve's never officially joined us,' Mr. Bright comments with a wry grin. 'Can you believe it?'

'I'm never in town long enough,' I smile.

Uncle Jimmy shakes his head. 'The young don't join us anymore,' he says. 'Not even the Desert Storm ones.'

'You missed Grady Rhodes,' Mr. Bright tells me. 'He stood out in the lobby, spruced-up and smiling, handing out business cards to everyone and shaking hands….He wouldn't come in here with us and the casket, though.'

'After about fifteen minutes, he left,' Uncle Jim comments.

'Nervous and sweating,' Uncle Ron says.

'A pity,' I say.

'Yes,' Mr. Bright says, slow and sarcastic. 'A pity.'

'We took care of everything,' Mr. Bright leans forward and whispers to me while my uncles look on. He places a hand on my shoulder, gives me a sympathetic squeeze. 'I took care of the body myself,' he says with a nod. 'Though,' Mr. Bright shrugs, 'there wasn't much that could be done.'

'Good,' I say. My uncles look at me. I smile and look to find Momma on her knees at Lisa Watson Stuart's wheelchair before the casket, her purse beside her on the carpet as she holds the gaping woman's limp and bony hand. I see Momma's red lips moving fervently beside the still woman's ear.

'We called the Marines,' Mr. Bright continues. 'And your Uncle Jimmy and I have filed the paperwork with the coroner's report. The AWOL will be removed,' he says solemnly. He squeezes my shoulder. 'His name is restored, his military insurance will pay.' My uncles and Mr. Bright watch me.

'Good,' I nod. 'That's good.'

'His name will be added to the memorial on the square,' Mr. Bright says to me with an emphatic nod.

'I always knew he was a good boy,' Uncle Ron states. Uncle Jimmy sniffs, makes an emphatic nod, too.

'Hell, yes, he was a good boy,' Mr. Bright says. 'He was the best...and Colonel Stuart's son,' he adds. I see tears coming to Mr. Bright's eyes.

'Well, excuse me,' I say, making a polite nod and walking away, feeling their eyes on me as I go toward the casket. The wreaths of roses in front have long sky blue sashes and gold lettering. One is from the Fermata Bend High School Athletic Club – Coach Haynes who coached us in both football and baseball is now the principal. The other is from the Fermata Bend Veteran's Lodge with *HONOR* printed in a bold gold font on an adjoining sleeve.

'Steve,' Momma looks up by the wheelchair and shoots me a knowing wink, 'speak to Lisa Watson.' She turns back to the old woman. 'Lisa?' she says loudly into her ear. 'Stevie's here. You remember Stevie?'

Lisa Watson grips Momma's hand and seems to know she's being talked to. Momma rises and releases her grip. Mr. Bright and my uncles are looking on. I oblige, move into Momma's place, kneel by the wheelchair and take the old woman's hand, who gapes at me.

'Mrs. Watson?' I tell her. 'This is Steve, Stevie Morton. Remember me?'

She ponders. 'Stevie!' the feeble old woman shrills, gaping with clouded eyes behind the lenses. 'Stevie!'

'Yes, ma'am,' I say. 'It's me.'

'Stevie!' She shrills. 'Hug me!'

Everyone is watching. I hug her as best I can over the armrest of the wheelchair, a small frail body in an outdated dress. 'I'm sorry,' is all I can think to say. I release her and she gapes up at me.

'Stevie! Hug me!'

So I hug her for a longer time, her dry, flaccid cheek against mine; the smell of her dead skin and her stale, shallow breath. I release her and stand up, remembering how she was a dominant, loud woman with red hair; chain-smoked cigarettes and had camp stew for Duckie and me when we would come inside at sundown from hunting in Old Man Bundt's woods.

'I'm sorry,' is all I can say.

Momma and I walk to the car from Bright's Funeral Home, blinking in the bright sunlight, and saying nothing as I hold her elbow. I help her into the front passenger side and fasten her seatbelt for her. I go around and get into the driver's side.

'Take me to the cemetery.' She says quietly and insistent, staring ahead as I shut the door. I look at her small, closed, mouth and I don't argue. I start the car and drive out of the parking lot, across the town square and turn down the back road along the old oak trees in their new spring green and toward the WPA rock wall bordering the rise of Johnson grass and tombstones. 'Now, please stop,' Momma says.

I turn the car off onto the border of the road and brake beside the pillar of the rocked arch with the centered dark marble keystone and the worn, scissored letters that read, *FERMATA BEND CEMETARY 1832*, half expecting Momma to tell me to drive on in over the new black-topped entranceway to where Duckie's grave will be, or to Dad's grave, or to her father and mother's graves, or even her grandparent's, knowing how Momma comes here for silent vigils to resuscitate her 'inner strength,' as she calls it. I have imagined her out here alone, walking slowly among the tombstones of Fermata Bend, pulling a few weeds, and conversing with the dead.

But Momma doesn't tell me to drive in. In the front passenger's seat, she gazes beyond the car and the old WPA wall at the shaded and cluttered hill of tombstones, a few rusted iron gates and obelisks, the stained angel of the Stevenson's family plot, and the weathered statue of Confederate General Cantrell with its missing nose.

'We bury poor Duckie here tomorrow,' Momma sighs. 'With his kind,' she nods, 'after all these years.'

'Momma,' I say, 'Duckie died a long time ago.'

Momma doesn't answer, her gaze remains over the WPA wall. I put the transmission into park, cut the ignition and we sit saying nothing by the quiet road and in the stillness that a cemetery can bring. I remember Calera's parents' funerals and Dad's funeral. My grandparents, Old Man Bundt, the Lieutenant – almost every adult I looked up to in my youth is buried here, and I remember as a child, how in April the old women of the UDC took us out of kindergarten or elementary school and we placed flags on the veterans' graves. We had a picnic and heard speeches on how people were significant and should not be forgotten. As teenagers, Duckie and I used to come out here on Halloween nights to see who was the bravest. How ironic time is. Classmates of mine killed in Vietnam are buried here. Now we are burying Duckie here tomorrow.

'You're wrong,' Momma whispers. She turns her aged face and large eyes on me. 'He died when we found him,' she says. 'And as we remember him.'

'All right,' I say and don't challenge it. I look away over the steering wheel.

'And here I am,' Momma continues, 'an old woman, alone and one step in this cemetery myself – but I will follow Duckie

197

tomorrow and see him to his grave.' She pauses. 'Do you know why?'

'No, Momma,' I turn to her. 'Why?'

'He was one of us,' she says, 'and he was a *good* boy. You remember that,' she says, arching her neck and holding her eyes on me. 'You remember our stopping here when the time comes to put me in the ground.' Momma sniffs and touches her hair.

'We have heritage,' she begins. 'After the Cantwells and the Stuarts, the Demuses, and the Mortons are the oldest names in Fermata Bend.'

'All the way back to the Fermata Bend of Andrew Jackson,' I say from rote.

Momma's eyes go hard.

'You left out Old Man Bundt,' I say.

'Yes, that's right. Charles,' Momma says with a nod. 'Your father's good friend. He was from even older family.'

'But he's dead,' I add.

'With no one to carry his name,' Momma's voice rises. 'You remember that,' she nods. 'You carry your father's name – a *good* man. He did his duty. He served his country. He brought you up a Morton and a gentleman. And you remember that I did my duty to you, too – like the time...' she pauses, 'the time you almost...'

'Momma...'

'You *remember,*' she insists, glaring, her eyes filling. 'You were back from Vietnam,' she tells me. I watch her solemn face, her red lips and old teeth move. 'Sleeping on the den floor while I was crossing to the kitchen to make breakfast...and you sprang on me like an animal...grabbed me by the throat,' she stares at me, her hand goes slowly toward her throat, 'before that *look* went out of your eyes – '

'Momma, it wasn't – '

'Hush,' she says. 'I did my duty,' she tells me. 'What a lady in this town does.' Momma raises her chin at me. 'I hid the bruises on my neck with a scarf, I lied to your father, and I told no one – no one! Because we are better than that...the same reason I have paid your tithings to the church since you stopped going, the same reason I continue to write Calera and Darcy. We,' she states, 'are better than that.'

'Momma, I – '

'We are better than that,' she insists.

I lift my hand towards her and let it drop. 'Yes, ma'am,' I say.

'I expect you to conduct my funeral with the same dignity and respect.'

'Yes, ma'am,' I say, wanting to get it over.

'Yes, ma'am,' Momma mimics me. 'Why don't you say anything?'

'Because I don't believe it,' I say.

'Don't believe what?'

'I don't believe any of it,' I shout and hit the steering wheel. I look away, up at the cemetery wall, the ever-still tombstones, and eventually back to her. 'Dad,' I try to say it, 'they,' I say, 'we...were all naive.' I look at her and grip the steering wheel in both my hands. 'Fermata Bend painted a world for us that is not true.'

'It did not,' Momma whines. She blinks at me as if I am speaking a foreign language.

I give a hard laugh and shake my head. It does no good.

'Why don't you take me home,' she says.

I hear myself laugh again. I shake my head, take a long, deep breath and start the car.

On the way home, I glance now and then at Momma sitting silent, her thin shoulders squared, staring straight ahead, but her look apprehensive. I can't think of anything to say. Then, as if nothing has happened, she abruptly comments on Jessica Lindey's shower next week to be held at the church parish hall. She asks if there is enough dog food, enough food for dinner, if I have clean clothes, would I like toasted cheese sandwiches for lunch? – she fires one quick question after another, each time briefly pausing, her large eyes waiting for an answer, a verbal commitment from me. I find myself nodding and saying yes, just like Dad used to do, until she seems satisfied.

At the farm house, I help Momma out of the car and she hugs her dogs. I help her inside and she goes to the phone to call her friends. I go outside for the luggage and come in to find her on her recamier arm chair, stretched out with her shoes off before the old TV. She smiles.

'Feeling better, Momma?'

She nods. 'Home,' she says. 'But tired.'

I tell her to rest. I take the luggage into her bedroom, go to the kitchen, make some toasted cheese sandwiches, heat some soup and take it to her on the TV tray like Dad used to do. Momma smiles her thanks. I get another tray for myself, sit on the sofa and we eat and watch the news and a soap.

'Thank you, darling,' Momma says with a smile. She rises slowly, waving me away and goes to her bedroom. I watch her leave, reflecting on how old she is now. It bothers me that Darcy hasn't even called.

'This is Dad,' I say on the kitchen phone to Darcy's machine, realizing again that Momma has no portable phone or answering machine. The only other phone is in her bedroom. 'Momma is home. All is well. We hope to talk to you soon.' I try not to hedge my voice. I hang up and think to call Susan, but I wouldn't know what else to say to her and I don't like her silences over the phone.

I go to my room, put on my Levis, running shoes and a t-shirt, go downstairs, shovel out and stoke the furnace. I go outside, feed the animals and re-stack some loose bales in the barn loft. I walk to the road for the mail, recollecting my thoughts and studying the fences. I come back and crank up Momma's Buick in the garage to keep the battery good.

When I come inside, Momma is on the recamier arm chair in a white wrap dress, barefoot, her perm tied up in a net and her make-up off.

'I'm sorry,' she says, 'I'm being slothful.'

'It's all right, Momma,' I make a smile and hand her the mail. While she opens the newspaper, I go into the kitchen, wash my hands and make coffee. I take her a cup, go into her bedroom and bring her slippers to her.

'Oh, thank you, dear,' she smiles as I put them on her feet. 'Just like your daddy.'

I nod in affirmation.

I go get myself a cup of coffee and sit to drink with Momma. The phone rings. I almost rise to answer it. 'I think that's for you,' I tell her with a grin, wanting it to be Darcy and wanting Darcy to talk to her first.

'Oh?' Momma says. She puts her cup down on the side table, rises and slowly goes into the kitchen. I hear her answer, then say 'Darcy' with surprise and begin to chatter, her shrill voice rising. I sip coffee and feel a quiet relief.

'Oh, yes,' I hear Momma say. They chat. 'He's taking good care of me...' she says. I hear her talking about her stay at the hospital. 'And I told Janis and Gerald to take the week off because my Stevie was home,' Momma says. She asks Darcy questions when she doesn't have anything else to say. How is Tuscaloosa? How is Calera?

'Oh, yes,' she says. 'You want to talk to him?'

Momma calls me. I put my cup down on her side table, go into the kitchen and she hands me the phone, smiling.

'Hey, Babe,' I say.

'Hey,' Darcy says brightly.

'Are you two talking about me?'

'Sure,' Darcy laughs, 'the man, don't you know? Hey, I tried to call yesterday – got no answer.'

'That's funny,' I say. 'Momma didn't get a call at the hospital and I didn't hear the phone last night.'

'I'm sorry, Dad,' Darcy admits. 'I was at the Purple Pig with Stan...and, well, I forgot to.'

'It worked out,' I try to let it go. 'Momma didn't come home until today. So, how was the Purple Pig?'

'Oh, it's swell, Daddy,' Darcy says. 'Big success. And we had *sooo* much fun.'

It's pretty obvious Darcy's not coming. I don't bring it up. I nod and listen to her gush about her roommate's new car, how a KA has asked her to go to the 'A' Day spring football scrimmage, trying to remember how I was once young, too, and how it was hard to see beyond myself and to think beyond the moment I was in. We're on the telephone. I know she's on her own. I try to let my feelings go.

For dinner I prepare more soup and baked potatoes and instead of the dining room table as Momma would normally have it, I serve both of us on trays again before the TV. While we eat, I tell Momma what I did on the farm today and Momma nods. We watch some TV and then Momma says she wants to turn in early. I go help her up from the recamier arm chair. She smiles, hugs me, kisses me goodnight.

'You're taking good care of me,' she says.

I smile.

After Momma goes to her bedroom, I turn off the TV, clean up and wash the dishes and then I stand around, awake and restless, repressing an urge to call my thoughtless daughter in the too quiet house. I stare at my great-grandfather's portrait and peer out the windows at the dark, and realize tomorrow we are going to bury Duckie.

I go peek into Momma's room to be sure she's asleep, and I slip out of the house and into my car, letting it roll in neutral down the drive a ways before starting the engine and keeping the headlights off until I reach the county highway – an old trick Duckie and I used to do when we sneaked out. I go drive, in a light drizzle this time, along the narrow paved country roads near the river, though not taking the now muddy river roads to our old haunts, to the beat of the wipers, the headlights like dual prods against the night mists, and with no music this time, like we used to do, no other noise but the sweep of the road in the dark: the still, wet silence of fields and trees. It has come to this. My car is the only place I belong now: transient, temporary, where I go somewhere, everywhere, nowhere.

I drive in the night over the old land that Duckie and I grew up in, playing with make-believe weapons, dreaming of history, glory and manhood as inspired by our fathers, the veterans' talk of American honor and the likes of flying stunts from our childhood hero, the Lieutenant, in his crop dusting Spitfire; or men like Old Man Bundt, who led us on the deer drives. Driving after the orbs of my headlights, I envision my Momma and Daddy's generation as a penumbra over us that is dissolving and the boy souls of Duckie and myself and others are somehow still under it in the woods beyond, where we grew to fish, hunt, water ski and ride horseback; where on dirt river roads, we bragged and dared other boys, drank bootleg beer and raced our American hotrods after playing baseball or football, and where we listened to the likes of the Beatles, Iron Butterfly, Blood, Sweat and Tears, Bob Dylan, and others on our car stereo systems.

I drive, feeling irrevocably disconnected, feeling age in my joints. My hair is thinning and beginning to gray and there is no mystery or wonder to any one person, this place or that music anymore. I am not young, hard, resolute, and sure of myself. I wish it was that simple again, in black and white, like the combat and western TV movies Duckie and I grew up with.

I remember five days before my last tour was up, dropping a young Vietnamese boy running across a rice paddy in black pajamas with a single, quick shot from my M-16 at about eighty yards. I felt no remorse, did not think anything of it, did not even recall it until I was en route by train toward Mobile, two weeks later, out of service, looking out my window into the bayous of Louisiana, suddenly seeing again the thick, vivid green, rice stalks and the boy running again in brown water and in slow motion, as in a film.

I came home and the war was irrevocably lost and forever unclear. Duckie was irretrievably gone, the Lieutenant was dead, classmates of mine were maimed or dead; Old Man Bundt was dying and my father had suddenly become middle-aged. There was no parade. My first week home, Momma and Dad hugged me again and again, they smiled and wanted me to wear my uniform. At church, Reverend Wilcox loudly praised the Lord for my return and Lisa Watson Stuart cried silently in her family pew. No one talked about Grady Rhodes or Duckie Stuart, or those from Fermata Bend who had been killed or were Missing In Action – it was as if those subjects were to be ignored and they would go away.

My first week back, Dad and I did not talk much, either, though he gave me long looks, slapped me on the back often, and gave me a lot of farm chores to do. He told me he was proud of me, knew I had seen horror, and but that I would come around, as we all had to. I remember nodding. My first week back, I badly wanted the peace but could not embrace it. I could not sleep in my bed, and instead, made a pallet on the floor of the family room. I dreamed of my platoon, the heavy 'chopping' sound of Hueys, C rations, the blanched heat, and rice paddies. I saw myself shoot the young boy over and over. And I dreamed of Duckie, seeing a vision of my former self grinning at me from inside his blue Shelby Cobra Mustang, in a teal blue football uniform, in a powder blue tuxedo, or in Marine blues. I woke up sweating, still seeing the grin. And one morning, I almost killed Momma.

And the night I almost killed Ricky Barnes at Old Man Bundt's house after his funeral, right before Calera's eyes, changed everything. She began to look at me differently and pursue me. In her auburn metallic Corvette, with the 'T' tops off. She somehow would find me whenever I was in town. She found me when I couldn't sleep nights and was running up and down the highway in my old high school sweats and tennis shoes. She drove her Corvette into the field of our farm and wherever I was working. I was invited to tea at the Brannon's. Then I was invited to dinner. Calera was waiting to dance with me after I danced with Momma and all the older ladies at the Pecan Ball. She was pretty. She was Duckie's old girlfriend. I was flattered and wanted to believe it.

I gave in, eventually marrying the Fermata Bend in Calera Brannon, wanting to believe I could find myself, find a peace in accepting the old duty she wanted from me, that I could bury myself in something soft, dependent, female, and full of belief, too. Our act lasted twenty-four years. We married. We moved. We had Darcy. I made money. And now, over a quarter of a century later, on the eve of Duckie Stuart's late, late funeral, I drive, following pressing prods of headlights into a night, reflecting on how enthusiasm, routine and ritual, as well as one's family and family name, will go a long way.

In the morning, I take orange juice and coffee to Momma in bed. I go and prepare eggs and toast and we have a quick, quiet breakfast at the kitchen table in our bathrobes, with small talk, each of us aware that we are going to Duckie's procession. Momma thanks me, waves me away as she rises and goes to her room to get ready. I go shower and shave in the bathroom my sister and I used to share. I go dress in my old room, in a dark suit, dress shirt and tie that I brought with me from Birmingham. I am about to put on my black socks and shoes when the phone rings in the kitchen. It rings two or three times before I get to it in my bare feet.

'Dad? Hey,' Darcy says. 'I tried to call you, just now. There's no answering machine.'

I take a deep breath. 'Is that right?' I say. 'You know Grandmomma doesn't have an answering machine.' I bite my lip, suppressing the urge to tell her what a young, thoughtless and selfish shit she is – how unaware she is of what a simple phone call means to a sick, aging person, or to a father.

'Dad, I...I just didn't want you to think I was coming.'

'I didn't think you were coming, Darcy.'

'It's just that – well, Grandmomma's better now and everything. And – you know – this funeral's important to you and Momma, but not me.'

Let the dead bury the dead, I think.

I sigh. 'That's all right, Darcy,' I make myself say. 'No one said you had to come. But speak to your Grandmomma, won't you? She's the one that's been in the hospital, remember?'

'Right. Sure, Dad.'

'Hold on.'

I lay the phone on the kitchen counter, go down the hall to Momma's room and knock softly on her door. 'Momma?' I call. 'Darcy's on the phone and she wants to talk to you.'

'Oh,' Momma's voice rises in her room.

I go back to the kitchen, put the phone to my ear until I hear Momma pick up in her bedroom. 'Darcy,' she says shrilly. I hang up the phone and go my room and put on my socks and shoes. It's no use. I have to let my daughter go.

Momma is waiting in the living room when I come out, in a black princess dress, cartwheel hat and pumps. She has on ruby lipstick and has powdered her face pale. She reaches up to straighten my coat lapel. 'There,' she says brightly, as if she is the one taking me to this. 'Ready, darling?'

'I'm sorry about Darcy,' I tell her. 'You know, tied up, busy,' I say. 'She's – she's young.'

Momma nods and gives me a sad smile that knows. I suddenly feel what she has probably been through with me.

'Momma. I'm sorry,' I hug her. 'I'm sorry I can't be Dad again.'

She hugs me tight. We part. She sniffs and makes a brave smile.

'Are you ready?' she says.

I nod, take her elbow. We go slowly outside and down the macadam walk to my car in the bright and cool sunlight. I open the car door for her.

'Did you get enough to eat?' she looks at me when we are both in the front seat.

'Yes, Momma.'

'I don't want you to be hungry.'

'I'm fine.'

She pats my hand and sighs. 'A beautiful day...to be buried,' she offers. I nod, and for a second, wonder where Calera is, what she is doing and what she might think if she knew what I was doing now.

I put on my sunglasses and start the car. I drive down the chert drive to the highway and toward town while Momma holds a calm, closed smile and looks out the window.

We drive past the old, wooden armory building to the square and cars, trucks and people are everywhere. The dried slab of Duckie's car still sits off the square on the flatbed in front of Johnson's Co-Op, like some kind of curious, roped-off exhibit. The Fermata Bend police and a few deputy sheriffs are standing in front of the stores and shops along the sidewalks with most of the bystanders, looking on at the Fermata Bend High School Band gathered on the grassy median before the Confederate statue in their blue and white uniforms and hats, warming up their instruments around the flag poles and among the World War I artillery pieces. I slowly circle the square in the thick traffic, looking for a parking space. The band director, a balding and round-faced man in khakis and polo shirt, about my age and who looks vaguely familiar, steps up above the band on the base of the statue and begins directing the warm-up with one hand.

Among the vehicles parked along the curb of the median are two TV news vans from Mobile. Two well-dressed female reporters are doing smiling takes into their hand mikes in the street in front of their cameramen. The same policeman I met the other day steps out into the street and motions me into a parking space in front of the NAPA Auto Parts store. I wave my thanks, park, get out and help Momma out from her side of the car just as the band strikes up louder scales. I grip Momma's elbow and we look on at the commotion, like everyone standing behind us on the sidewalk, people I don't know. Most of the faces appear younger, a few faces appear my age or older. A man in denim overalls with no shirt and a red baseball cap nods to me and I smile, not sure if I recognize him.

Grady Rhodes is giving an interview to the female TV reporters on the curb across the median from us while the cameramen shoot. He looks forty pounds heavier than I last remember him. He has a crisp haircut and is in a blue-striped designer shirt with a loud yellow tie and a dark business suit, his coat unbuttoned; his hands thrust deep into his pants pockets. He acts thoughtful and serious, pausing now and then as he speaks into the extended hand mikes. He smiles into cameras. I look away, glad to have sunglasses on. The spirit of Duckie does not deserve this. A large man is crossing the street from the band and median towards us. I look and then recognize his black face and smile. The same front gold tooth.

'Zach,' I say. 'Hey, Zachary.'

He's in a light, opened, green overcoat, dark slacks, a spread-collared shirt and a loose brown tie. Zachary comes smiling, bigger, his hair grayer.

'Look, Momma. Zachary,' I tell her. She nods. I let go of her arm.

'Stevie,' Zachary says softly. We grin and shake hands.

'Never thought it would end like this,' Zachary says, smiling, shaking his head. 'You, me and Duckie. We've come to an end.'

'I know,' I say. 'You, me, Duckie...our Dads...' I can't finish.

Zachary nods. He nods to Momma. 'Mrs. Morton,' he says.
'Hello, Zachary,' Momma shrills.
'You're a preacher, now, right?' I say.
Zach nods. 'And build houses on the side.'

Before I can ask about his family, Zach gives me a look and
nods down the street. I look and Bob Lyles, who lost both legs
to a claymore in Nam, is wheeling toward us in his motor
wheelchair, a small American flag and a small black MIA-
POW flag stuck in either side of his bush hat band. Medals,
pins and ribbons cover his flak jacket. He doffs his hat to
Momma as he wheels up and brakes. His white head looks too
large for his body. His hair is long, prematurely white. He's in
old Vietnam fatigues, his pants folded under each stump.

'Is this it, boys?' Bob quips in a quavering voice, slapping
the bush hat back on his head. 'Is this it? Are we the only ones
here?'

Zach and I each shake his hand.

'Where's the rest of 'em?' Bob insists. 'Where's John
Barrow? Mickey Jones? 'Where are the boys who went with
us?'

'Don't see them, Bob,' Zachary answers.

'But this is important,' Bob says. 'We're vets. We're
Fermata Bend vets. And Duckie was one of us.'

Zachary and I can only nod.

'I wouldn't miss this for the world,' Bob declares loudly.
'No sir. Duckie was the best of us,' he says. 'Hell, Duckie's the
reason I'm where I am today.' He slaps his leg stumps. 'Sorry,
ma'am,' he mumbles to Momma.

'Duckie was a winner, now,' Zachary admits. 'He sure was.
Back then, he was a good one.'

'I'll never forget him,' Bob declares. 'A solid kid like
Duckie. I can see him grinning at me now – that's how I want
to remember him.'

Zach and I make closed smiles, nod. The band suddenly
hushes. We look to the median. 'Ladies and Gentlemen,'

209

Grady's voice blares on a megaphone from somewhere. He walks out onto the street ahead of us, lowering a megaphone. The band and the band director turn to him, the reporters and their cameramen stand on the median curb, and everyone looks to him from the sidewalks. Grady stops, makes a deep nod to everyone, spreads his legs and raises the megaphone to his mouth.

'Ladies and gentlemen,' Grady's drawl reverberates, 'as mayor...and on behalf of the town of Fermata Bend,' he pauses, 'I welcome you to this solemn and dutiful tradition of Fermata Bend in honor of a United States Marine...a citizen of Fermata Bend...a standout student of Fermata Bend High School...and an exceptional individual... Duckie Stuart was one of us...' the *us* reverberates. 'And we are here to give him his proper due and respect in the time-honored tradition of a town procession...'

'You son of a bitch,' Bob mutters softly.

I look at Bob, then at Momma. If she heard it, she doesn't let on.

'...the procession will begin as soon as the hearse arrives... I ask those of you who wish to participate in the procession, please file behind the hearse...immediate family and friends leading the way... We ask that everyone be quiet and respectful...thank you...the band will file behind you...' the *you* reverberates...'and play until the procession reaches the cemetery... Thank you, thank you,' Grady says through the megaphone. His *thank yous* reverberate.

'Anybody drink with him?' I comment.

Zach makes a wry smile.

'Hell, I don't,' Bob says.

'Who does?' I say.

'New people. People who don't remember. People who don't know,' Bob says. 'People who don't care. Most of them are newcomers, young and don't care,' Bob says morosely.

'Boys,' Zach says, 'boys. The war's over.'

'Not for me it ain't,' Bob says. He slaps a leg stump and turns his bottom lip up at Zach in a childish pout. 'For me, it ain't never over.'

'Hush,' Momma whispers. 'You boys hush.'

We look at Momma and nod. Grady has lowered the megaphone and is glancing expectantly in the direction of the railroad tracks and Bright's Funeral Home.

'So that's it? That's all there's to say? Jesus,' Bob mutters. 'Oh, I'm sorry,' he says to Zach. 'Sorry,' he says to Momma.

I take Momma's elbow. 'Let's get in the car and I'll drive you behind the hearse,' I suggest.

'No,' Momma shakes her head, her face sets and her lips press together. 'I'm walking.'

'Momma – ' But it's no use. Her frail body goes rigid. She grips my arm and stares ahead.

'I'm walking,' she says.

I look to Zachary and Bob, then to the railroad tracks. The high school band flag bearers and flanking saber guards come first: serious faces, white boots slowly stomping over the rise and the railroad tracks, the U.S. flag high, the state flag tilted slightly down. The long grey hearse comes slowly up and over the railroad tracks behind them and with four veteran guards flanked on either side – old men from my father's era. They march solemnly, stiffly in-step, eyes straight ahead, in pressed blue suits, blue garrison caps, their shined black shoes and right-shouldered Springfields. In same step behind them come the six veteran pall bearer guards, two abreast, in same suits, white gloves and without rifles. Mr. Bright and my uncles are among these. Behind the pall bearer guards comes the white van from Fermata Bend Manor.

The TV cameramen shoot. Everyone on the square watches the procession as it approaches the Southern end of the square and stops. You can see the U.S. flag-draped casket through the glass panes of the hearse. A male nursing home attendant in a white uniform gets out from the driver's side of the Manor van,

211

opens the side sliding door and steps inside. The TV crews rush forward.

'Wait! Stop!' one of the female reporter's cries breaks the silence. 'We want to get this!'

The reporters reach the van. Their cameramen run after, shooting from their shoulder cameras. Reverend Wilcox steps out from the side door of the van in his robe and vestments, slow, solemn and dignified. He waits before the reporters and cameras while the attendant rolls Lisa Watson Stuart in her wheelchair onto the electric platform and lowers her to the street. She is in an old-fashioned black coat dress and blue shoes with a gold pin on her dress lapel, her face startlingly wrinkled and pale, her glasses glinting in the sun, and her thin, veined hand clutching a white carnation in her lap.

A female nurse, also in white uniform, steps out from the side door of the van and helps down an elderly woman with stringy, sparse, splayed grey hair and large age spots on her face, dressed in a grey print wrap dress and old-fashioned brown pumps.

'Joanna Wills,' Momma informs me in whisper. 'Lisa Watson's roommate.

'Oh,' I say. 'Look, Momma – '

'No,' she shakes her head. 'I'm walking.'

I nod to Zachary and Bob. Momma leans on my arm and we walk out into the street and toward the hearse. Zachary and Bob come behind us. A half dozen or so people come off the sidewalks or curbs around the square. Two or three of them look familiar, from high school days. We converge after Lisa Watson Stuart and Joanna Wills behind the veteran pall bearers while the women reporters look on and the cameramen continue to shoot. The male attendant pushes Lisa Watson Stuart in her wheelchair with Reverend Wilcox walking alongside her. The cameramen make particular effort in shooting Joanna Wills as the nurse holds her arm and leads her slowly to the other side of the Lisa Watson Stuart's wheelchair. They shoot Reverend Wilcox and Joanna Wills leaning over and squeezing Lisa Watson Stuart's free hand. Lisa Watson Stuart stares up at them, her mouth gaping open and quiet.

The cameramen turn and shoot the rest of us. One of the young female reporters in a blonde pompadour and a lime green business suit, motions to her cameraman to follow and goes toward Momma and me. She's wearing a thick gold choker. Her makeup and smile are as smooth as a beauty contestant's.

'Ma'am,' she comes up, her voice flat and even, peering at Momma as she speaks into her large hand mike, 'after thirty years, why have you come to bury this Marine?' She thrusts the mike at Momma, her smile bright, expectant. The cameraman shoots us from behind her.

'Well,' Momma blinks, ponders. 'He was a fine, fine boy,' she shrills, '...and we loved him.'

'I see,' the young woman says. 'And you, sir?' she turns the mike into my face, smiling the same and the camera turns on me. 'After thirty years, why did you come to bury this Marine?'

I stare at her. 'He was a friend,' I say, surprised at my voice that is almost in a whisper.

'Friend?' she nods as if she knows, turning the mike to herself to speak. 'What kind of friend?' She thrushes the mike back at me.

'A good one,' I say and offer nothing else.

'Oh?' she dismisses me. 'And what about you, sir,' she moves quickly behind me. 'After thirty years, why have you come to bury this Marine?'

'Same reason,' I hear Zachary say.

'Memories?' she suggests. 'Any memories?'

'My memories,' Zachary says calmly. 'Not yours.'

'Oh?' the reporter says, nonplussed. 'Doesn't anyone have more to say than that?'

'It was a long time ago,' I hear Bob offer in his quavering voice. 'He was one of us. He was a kid. He was an American soldier. He didn't know we were gonna lose.'

'Sooo,' the reporter tries in her professional voice, 'the emotions and old pains of Vietnam resurface once again in a duty to bury an old friend.'

Bob squeals in a high and bitter laugh. 'No, honey,' he says, 'it's worse than that. 'We were not what we thought we were.'

'So,' the reporter keeps trying, 'you're burying your past, your childhood...your memories?'

'Hey, save yourself, honey.' Bob's voice is hard. 'It's too deep for a thirty second spot.'

But she is already turning away, asking questions to those behind him. In a few minutes, she steps aside and begins a story line in the street to her cameraman, a fast summary with her professional face and pose.

Grady Rhodes walks smartly by us to the front of the procession without his megaphone. He stops before the young, stern-faced flag bearers and saber guards, turns, and eyes everyone as if inspecting us for a review. Then with a solemn nod, he turns, motions the procession forward and begins the slow march.

'Forwaaard march!' one of the saber guards orders. The flag bearers and saber guards stomp the pavement several times in step and then lead off on their left feet. The hearse and the veteran guards move forward. Momma grips my arm and we fall in a slow walk behind the attendant pushing Lisa Watson Stuart's wheelchair, Reverend Wilcox, and the nurse with her arm around Joanna Wills. On the median, the high school band's bass drummer begins a heavy beat and the band begins to play a slow, soft *Auld Lang Sang* and filing off the town square median by fours behind us.

I can remember when a procession was the entire town, people who knew each other, knew the history and cared: Colonel Stuart's funeral when Duckie and I were just children,

Joab Stevenson's, Cynthia Wilcox's, Calera's father. Others. About fifty people were in my Dad's procession seven years ago. Those of us walking now are a smaller assembly than the band or the people looking on about the square.

The cameramen follow and shoot us as our slow procession goes around the bend of the square and down the street toward the turn to the town cemetery. As the cameramen stop shooting and turn for their vans, Grady Rhodes veers off the street, steps off onto the curb at the turn off the square and lets the procession go by him, waving and scanning us with a large, bland smile, as though he has done his job and is letting us go.

I will not look in his direction. I slide my hand down Momma's elbow into her hand, grip it and stare ahead beyond the hearse and the flag bearers to the flashing lights of the police car blocking off the incoming traffic at the turn and I find Calera, standing behind a white Cadillac Seville at the curb before the rock building of city hall. She's in black fashion sunglasses. Her mahogany hair has been cut into a short, tight bob. Her lipstick is a dark burgundy and she's in a loose, two-piece black dress and black shoes. I watch her search the procession, see us, bite her lower lip and look away, gripping the small black purse at her hip that hangs by string-straps from her shoulder. But I know her too well. The memory of Duckie is important.

Calera brings her head up, squares her shoulders, steps off the curb and joins Momma and me as we go by.

'Hello, Momma,' Calera says softly, shifting her purse strap and sliding her hand into Momma's other one. 'Let me walk with you.'

'Oh, Calera,' Momma says. They hug and make brave smiles. I can't see Calera's eyes for her sunglasses.

'Talked to Darcy?' I ask.

Calera makes a thin smile. 'She's young,' she dismisses our daughter. 'Would like to – but can't...you know.' She faces me, then turns her head away as the three of us walk.

215

'Oh, Calera,' Momma sighs, clamping her eyes shut and clenching our hands in either one of hers. 'Oh, Calera,' she sobs.

'Momma,' Calera says. We walk after the flag bearers, the hearse, the veterans and Lisa Watson Stuart's wheelchair; Zachery, Bob and the others behind us, the high school band continuing a slow *Auld Lang Sang*. Joined by Momma's hands, Calera and I turn with her and the procession at the stop sign onto the cemetery road and the policemen saluting at the flashing car. We begin the old walk in a semblance of memory along the WPA rock wall and below the shaded and cluttered hill of tombstones.

Turning to me as we begin, Calera lifts off her sunglasses with her free hand and stares me in across from Momma.

'He was not a traitor,' she says, watching me quietly. Momma looks at us. I look at Calera, see the fine wrinkles about her eyes, her heavy eye-liner; her waiting, expectant expression.

'No,' I admit and nod for her. 'He was not.'

She holds her look on me as we walk. I get her point.

I give her a small, closed smile, look ahead toward the hearse and say nothing. It would do no good to try. Later, when I leave Fermata Bend, there will be time to think about where I am going; but right now, I am trying to recall who Duckie was and where we once were, anticipating Reverend Wilcox's soft and sentimental words, anticipating what the reports of the twenty-one gun salute are going to do to me among the unbearable silence of tombstones, sky, trees, and my father's grave; and realizing how, walking slowly, linked together towards this final burial of Duckie Stuart, the three of us will never walk together again.

Theron Montgomery teaches English and creative writing at Troy University in Alabama and he is fiction editor for the international ezine, *The Blue Moon Review*.

Credits

'The Transcendence of 'Speedy' Joe Kinnard' appeared in *The Blue Moon Review* (e-zine, www.thebluemoon.com); Spring, 2000. 'Emma Saw' appeared in the *Texas Review*; vol.13 no. 1&2, Spring/Summer 1992. 'I Hear You' appeared in the *Tampa Review* #6: Spring 1993. 'The Motherhead' appeared in *CrossConnect* #7; May 1997 (e-zine, <u>www.ccat.sas.upenn.edu</u> /~xconnect). 'Grinning in the Dark' appeared in the *South Carolina Review*; vol. 29, no.3, Summer 1997. 'Pierre's New Game,' appeared in *Habersham Review*; vol 1:3, 1992. 'Miming the Lieutenant' appeared in *Echoes Magazine, Memorial Day Issue,* 1995: vol. 2:3. 'Lying at the Edge of the World' appeared in *Alabama Literary Review*, #14, Spring, 2000. 'The Lieutenant: A Faulknerian Tale' appeared in *Alabama Literary Review*, Fall 2004. An earlier version of 'The Procession' was awarded 'Top Cut' in the James Jones Novel Writing Contest, 1998.

Printed in the United Kingdom
by Lightning Source UK Ltd.
102938UKS00001B/176